Bender

Chet Stevens

Copyright © 2017 Chet Stevens

All rights reserved.

ISBN: 154117156X
ISBN-13: 978-1541171565

DEDICATION

For my wife Linda,
the soulmate I never thought was possible.

There, but for the Grace of God, go I.

Alcoholics Anonymous Slogan

PART ONE

A Crack in Paradise

CHAPTER 1

The wind blew hard across the beach, sending cyclones of sand high into the air. I watched as the evening thunderstorm progressed southward along the shore. Dark clouds heavy with rain would soon dampen the cyclonic magic. Such is life on the west coast of Florida in the summertime, and I wouldn't trade it for anything.

But lately, a crack has appeared in paradise.

Most of the time, the dark covers all manner of scary things, but flip on the light, and the vermin go scurrying for cover. Laughing, I remembered when I first moved to Florida ten years earlier.

I met a woman in a bar, and when the lights came on for last call - sorry, only kidding. The woman was a fox. A long, cool drink of water as they say: tall and thin, blonde and sexy, a real surfer girl. We went to her place after the bar closed. She turned on the lights. What must have been twenty giant roaches scurried for cover. I didn't spend the night.

Now I realize how naive I'd been about this world. The creatures are there, right under your nose, where you can't readily see them. My thoughts did a one-eighty as I spied another kind of strange creature walking across the beach parking lot, oblivious to the approaching thunderstorm. The man's shabby, graying, white dress shirt, unbuttoned except for the very top button, blew backward in the wind from his shoulders, making him look like a down-on-his-luck, caped crusader. His arms were not in the sleeves. Instead, he kept them behind his back like an ice skater. A big straw hat, khaki shorts, and flip-flops completed his ensemble. He looked harmless, maybe a bit daft, hair long and graying like his beard and his shirt. The intense expression never varied. He seemed determined to get somewhere. I wondered where he was headed.

I laughed. Obviously, some of the creatures remained out in the open, daring the universe to take offense. The Florida sunshine had an uncanny ability to attract all kinds of disreputable denizens like pirates, smugglers, and of course, me.

My name is Mason Prophet Long, and before I go any further, let me shed a little light on the origination of my name; it might explain a few things. My parents were into country rock, and bales of marijuana, so they named me after a band called Mason Proffit. Note the misspelling between the band's name and my name, a by-product of smoking joint after joint. My older brother's name is Poco Long, another sixties band.

I drive a taxicab for a living, so I get around. I don't

particularly like driving a cab; the hours are too long. But it's something to do, and besides, some of the most interesting people get in your cab.

"Cab twenty-four, are you out there?" The dispatcher's voice dripped with frustration. "Mason, are you hearing me?"

I reluctantly snatched the microphone from its cradle; I really didn't want to be bothered with a fare in the rain. "Yes, Arthur. I hear you."

"What the heck are you doing? I've been trying to raise you for the last fifteen minutes. Don't forget to pick up Carmen at eight o'clock. Are you going?"

I had forgotten all about Carmen. I glanced at my watch, which said 7:47. I had plenty of time to make it down to her house on Isla del Luna, a small island off the southern tip of Sunset Beach. "I guess I'll go get her," I droned.

"Don't do me any favors, Mason. Next time we go fishing, I'll use you as the anchor."

Arthur Clement and I both worked for the Tropical Cab Company of Sunset Beach. We played high school football together back in Colorado, and when I followed my father to Florida ten years back, I guess Arthur must have missed my charming personality. He joined us within six months. Now we both had dead end jobs in a small Florida beach town. I always thought I would do better.

By the time I reached down and put the microphone back in its cradle, Arthur had moved on to the next cabbie, who was probably not as reluctant as I was to work in the rain. No doubt that as soon as I pulled up in front of Carmen's house, the clouds would open up.

Carmen Lopez was one of my regulars. I vaguely remembered her calling me a few days ago about needing a ride to Tampa International Airport. Apparently, she must have also called the cab company and told them, so I figured I better do my job. And what the hell, the fare would be good for me on a couple of levels. One, the fare to the airport was at least forty dollars and Carmen tipped well. Two, Carmen was a beautiful and funny friend, who I had gotten to know pretty well over the years.

When I finally looked up again, the parking lot was deserted. Apparently, the caped crusader had moved on. I put the cab in gear and turned right out of the driveway, heading south down Sunset Boulevard. I glanced at my watch again and guessed that I would be at Carmen's house a few minutes before eight.

My hangover had returned with a vengeance, and the small amount of Valium that I took earlier had worn off. Self-medication seemed to be the only way to get through the day without pain. My hands were beginning to shake again, and that damn crack in paradise grew more pronounced. I decided that after I dropped off Carmen at the airport, I would do a couple of shooters from the bottle of vodka I had stashed in the trunk. My fares didn't seem to notice or care as long as I drank medicinally, just enough to keep the demons at bay.

* * *

The city of Sunset Beach actually consists of two islands: the main island of Sunset Beach and a smaller island named Isla Del Luna, where all the rich folks lived. As I was crossing the bridge over to Isla del Luna, I could see the Sunset Pass Marina, which occupied the southern tip of the main island. As always, I quickly checked to see if the old fishing boat my daddy left me was still tied up safely in its slip. All was normal. The boat bobbed silently in concert with the other power and sailboats. The neon beer signs of the marina's bar, The Reef, beckoned to me.

Isla del Luna is a pretty expensive place to live. One side of Island Drive is lined with outrageously priced condominiums; the other side is populated with mansions. Carmen's place was of the mansion variety, and three houses past Dolphin Lane, I turned right into the driveway. I put the cab into park and tapped the horn a couple of times. Carmen was usually waiting, eager to go. She was always eager about something. After a minute with no response, I laid on the horn long and hard.

Still no response.

Annoyed, I climbed out of the cab, slamming the door behind me. Maybe, she was in the bathroom and couldn't hear me. After all, the house was big enough to get lost in. The two story edifice seemed to be all glass. Large, blue-tinted windows reflected the lightning of the approaching storm. The deep blue tile roof stood in stark contrast to the rest of the houses on her side of the canal, which were mostly white stucco with bright orange tiled roofs.

I walked casually up the three steps to the front door and rang the bell. No response. A minute later, I tried it again.

Still nothing, so I tried the door. It was locked. I backed out from under the canopy and looked up towards the second floor windows of Carmen's bedroom. The room was dark.

For no discernible reason, I suddenly felt a knot in my stomach, probably nothing more than my increasingly nervous reaction to anything out of the ordinary. Fear seemed a constant companion these days. But still, something didn't seem right. Carmen was always on time. Not knowing what else to do, I walked around back to see if she was out by the pool. As soon as I opened the gate to the pool area, I noticed the door. The bottom right pane had been broken in. My first thought was to run like hell, but what if Carmen was hurt? I needed to find out.

A hard gust of wind tipped a plastic folding chair on its side, sliding it part way across the deck. I felt a drop of rain on my face. Another one hit my arm. Big drops started pelting the pavement around me with increasing intensity. The crack and sizzle of a nearby lightning strike was followed immediately by the accompanying loud thunderclap. The noise shook me to my core. Sometimes the bolts seemed to come out of nowhere.

The rain hastened my decision, and I quickly ran up the steps. Stopping momentarily to find my courage at the door, I turned the knob and quietly entered the kitchen. Despite the abundance of windows, the kitchen was dark. I stopped to listen. Whoever broke the window might still be inside the house somewhere. I strained to hear, but I heard nothing, not even the sound of a clock. The digital world has silenced the clocks. Very odd, the things I think about when I'm scared.

I knew I couldn't leave without finding out if Carmen was okay, so I steeled myself and walked through the kitchen and into the great room. More of the same darkness and gloom surrounded me, but instead of silence, I was greeted by a loud thunderclap. I quickened my search, and within a few minutes, I had covered the ground floor. Nothing seemed amiss downstairs, and I had heard nothing from above.

Back in the great room, I stood looking at the stairway to the second floor trying to catch my breath. I had been in this room many times before, but I had never stopped and noticed the elegance. I always had other things on my mind, as Carmen and I hurried upstairs to satisfy our appetites. We had a short affair a couple of years back, nothing serious. I wouldn't even call it a love affair, but we found out that we really liked each other and decided to remain friends "with benefits". The benefits were wonderful.

This time, I knew I would have to make the journey upstairs alone, and the foreboding hit the pit of my stomach hard. I was deathly afraid of what I might find. As I slowly climbed the stairs, I wiped away an errant drip of rainwater that had fallen from my hair into my right eye. I knew the way, and when I reached the top of the stairs, I turned right and stopped.

Carmen's bedroom sat at the end of the hall in the dark. The door stood open and I could see through the doorway and beyond the windows to the canal. The masts of several sailboats rocked in the wind and rain. In my mind, I could hear the clank of the metal hooks on the metal masts. I fought to put one foot in front of the other as my mind flashed back to my youth.

"C'mon, Mason. You can do it," Arthur said.

I was standing on a cliff overlooking the South Platte river in Colorado. Adrenaline and 100 proof rum coursed through my veins. The frigid water rushed down stream towards the small town of Deckers. From my vantage point, I could see my old jeep parked at the gas station a half mile away. The bright sun highlighted the foaming rapids. All my friends had already made the leap into the raging water, and now all eyes were on me. I closed my eyes and jumped.

Once again, I closed my eyes and found my resolve. I walked slowly down the hall until I reached the doorway of Carmen's room. I stopped and looked inside.

"Oh, God." I moaned as the sight on the bed turned my stomach sour.

I hurried to Carmen's side, leaned over and grabbed her gently by the hand. She was cold to the touch and quite stiff. I knew immediately that she was dead. I stroked her forearm lightly. "Oh, God, Carmen. What happened?" The lifeless form did not respond.

The body lay face up on the bed, a white satin sheet draped across the torso and legs, bare shoulders and head visible above the sheet. Her magnificent dark, raven hair fanned out across the white pillow. She stared wide-eyed at the ceiling. My feet had turned to concrete, merging with the rest of the building, inanimate objects that wouldn't move. I stood transfixed, mind racing, reliving memories of Carmen in the pool, at the beach, in a restaurant, in bed. I wondered if she was naked under the sheet.

"Aw, Carmen. What kind of evil mother fucker could do something like this?"

Carmen had been murdered. That much was obvious. Horrid, blue-purple-black-yellow bruises ringed her throat. I didn't need to be a coroner to know that someone had strangled Carmen to death. As I stood staring down at the corpse, it suddenly dawned on me that I was standing alone in a room over a dead body. Not a place I particularly wanted to be, no matter whose body lay on the bed.

Immediately, fear and guilt swept over me. What if they think I killed Carmen? After all, she was a girlfriend, lover, whatever you wanted to call her. Don't the police always look to people who knew the victim? The fact that I hadn't done anything didn't seem to matter to my psyche, nor to my stomach for that matter. I could understand the fear, but guilt is a very strange emotion, at times invading the mind and body without good reason.

I forced myself to calm down while I backed out of the bedroom and into the hall, trying to think of what I should do next. Looking around, I spied the phone on a small table near the end of the hall. Simple, call the police and report the crime. I walked to the phone and took the receiver from the cradle, but when I put the phone to my ear, I couldn't hear a dial tone. Still simple, use the radio in the cab. It was good to know that I was still thinking pretty quickly. I put the receiver gently back in the cradle and headed down the stairs to the great room.

At the bottom, I turned and walked into the kitchen, but before I had gotten half way across the room, I noticed the refrigerator. I quickly veered in that direction, thinking that there should be four beers left. I didn't think she'd mind if I drank the beers; she couldn't drink them now. I found the four cans of beer in the vegetable bin. I wanted to pop one open and swallow it in one gulp, but I had to call the police first. So instead, I raised the four pack of beer by the plastic rings and said, "Here's to you, Carmen."

* * *

The wind-whipped rain pelted me as I climbed into the driver's seat of my cab, wiping the water from my face with my hands. I reached under the seat and ripped a few sheets from the roll of paper towels that I had stashed. I dried my face and hands completely before grabbing the microphone from its cradle.

I pressed the talk button on the microphone and said, "Mayday. Mayday."

The dispatcher had not heard me; Arthur kept talking to another cab driver downtown.

"Mayday. Mayday." The radio went silent.

"Everybody quiet down. We have a mayday," the dispatcher ordered. "Who's the cab with the mayday?" Arthur had taken control of the air.

"Arthur, it's me, Mason. There's been a murder."

"Repeat, Mason."

"There's been a murder, Arthur. Carmen's dead. Her body

is in the upstairs bedroom. Call the paramedics, police, whatever. I'm still here parked in the driveway." I ran out of breath, so I released my grip on the talk button.

"Do you need an ambulance?"

"No, she's dead."

"Are you sure?"

"Yes, I'm sure."

"Okay. Okay. Let me find the address." Murder was not the kind of thing Arthur would talk about over open air, and the other drivers couldn't hear me. They'd all be wondering what was happening. I'd be the talk of the town.

The radio went silent once again, allowing me to marvel at the lack of white noise within the cab. After driving a cab for a while, I learned to ignore all the radio chatter that didn't pertain to me. In fact, it had gotten to the point that I didn't hear the radio at all unless a dispatcher called my number.

"Twenty-four? Mason, you hearing me, sir?"

"I hear you, Arthur. Are the cops on the way?"

"Yes, sir. They should be there any minute. I told them that you had called me. They know you are there and that it isn't a crime in progress. You should be okay. Do you need me to do anything else, Mason?"

"No thanks, Arthur. I'll catch up with you later."

"Okay, everybody. We're back in business." Arthur the dispatcher called, "Anybody near Madeira Beach?"

Life moved on. Business is business. Time is money in the cab business, and several more clichés ran through my mind. I switched off the radio. No sense in keeping it on at this point. Noticing the four pack of beer on the front seat, I climbed out of the cab and stashed them in the trunk. The rain had finally stopped while I was calling in the mayday, so I brushed away whatever rain drops I could, leaned my butt on the back of the trunk, and quietly waited for the police to arrive.

CHAPTER 2

Usually when a woman pays any attention at all to the family jewels, it brings a smile to my face, but when the bitch detective tapped my testicles with the police baton as she ran it up my leg, it ticked me off. "What the hell is the matter with you?" I felt helpless, locked in the basic search position, body forward, hands on top of my orange taxi, feet backward, legs spread. My protest fell on deaf ears.

She ignored me entirely. "He's clean," she said to her partner. To me she said, "Okay. You can turn around."

"I haven't done anything." I continued to protest, becoming angrier by the second, but grateful that I could stand up straight and face my tormentor. Her name tag read HALL.

"That remains to be seen," she replied coldly.

"You can't treat me like that." I said as low as I could. I looked to her male partner for confirmation. He simply shrugged his shoulders. I got the feeling that he didn't fare much better than me on a daily basis.

"I'll treat scum like you anyway I want." She waved to a pair of uniformed police officers from another police cruiser, who quickly came over and joined us. "You'll answer my questions, or we'll take you downtown and you can answer them there. Your choice."

I usually have mixed emotions when facing the police. On the one hand, I hate being ordered around. On the other hand, I didn't particularly want to go to jail, so I nodded obediently.

"What is your name?"

"Mason Prophet Long," I answered curtly.

"Mason Prophet, as in P-R-O-P-H-E-T?" She asked with a quizzical expression.

"Yes. Long story."

"Let me see some ID."

I reached behind me and pulled my wallet out of the back pocket of my shorts. "Here's my license," I said as I took the license out of the wallet and handed it to her.

She took the license from my hand and examined it for a minute before she said, "Is this your correct address? You live here on First Street in Sunset Beach?"

"That's correct."

She shrugged her shoulders and handed the license back to me. To the uniformed officers she ordered, "Keep Mr. Long company until we call for you all." The uniforms nodded obediently.

"Mark, let's take a closer look at what we have before we continue our conversation with Mr. Long," she turned and headed up the driveway toward the house.

When Detective Kendyll Hall had first arrived on the scene, I never would have thought she was an evil bitch. She exited the unmarked police car all grace and class. Although I had never met her personally, she looked vaguely familiar. The woman was definitely beautiful, long light brown hair with blonde highlights, trim figure, looking great in black slacks and light blue blouse. She was like a beautiful Afghan hound that looks so cute, you want to pet her, hug her, but as soon as you get close, the pit bull inside wants to bite your damn hand off.

"She's a piece of work," I said to my police guards.

"You ain't seen nothing yet," the one on the left said. They both laughed heartily at the comment.

* * *

Twenty minutes later, Detective Hall stepped through the front door of the house and out on to the porch. She waved in a come here motion to me and my guards. The cops had set up a perimeter around the crime scene, determined to keep the press and the curious public at arm's length. The driveway was littered with police vehicles. Murder never happened in Sunset Beach.

As we threaded our way through the maze and up the driveway, I kept wondering why Kendyll Hall had taken such an immediate dislike to me. The only answer I could come up with centered on the fact that Sunset Beach was a small town, a total of two and half miles long, and maybe half a mile wide. If you hung around long enough, sooner or later most people in town looked familiar. She must have seen me around town, driving my taxi, hanging out at the bars and restaurants, and apparently she hadn't liked what she'd seen. I did tend to get in a bit of trouble, but nothing that would make the headlines of a newspaper, even a small town newspaper. All I seemed to do these days was work, drink, and fish, not necessarily in that order.

Once inside the front door, I reminded myself that I had done nothing wrong, had nothing to hide. I was scared, but I wasn't going to let Hall know that. All I had to do was be reasonable and tell the truth, and try my hardest not to further antagonize the dear detective. As we entered the great room, Kendyll Hall was standing with half a dozen other officers in the middle of the room. When she saw us, she motioned for me to follow and led the way into Carmen's office, which had an entrance off the foyer. I immediately sat down in Carmen's dark brown, soft leather desk chair, then leaned back and put my feet on the edge of the desk.

"Get your feet off the desk. We don't want you contaminating the crime scene any more than necessary."

I obliged and removed my feet from the desk, but I didn't get up. My resolution to not antagonize Detective Hall had dropped by the wayside, for I was really enjoying her reaction. I couldn't help myself.

"You've been here before, I take it?"

Kendyll Hall had sensed my familiarity with the surroundings. I had to admit that she was very sharp, but I wasn't about to let her know that, so instead I asked, "What was your first clue, Sherlock?"

Daggers from the eyes, but this time she appealed to my sense of reason. "Look, Mr. Long. Can I call you, Mason?"

"Sure."

"Mason, can we have a truce? You've got nothing to hide right?"

Her voice had softened, but I didn't trust her for a second. "Right, can I call you Kendyll?"

"No. The name is Detective Hall."

I displayed a deeply disappointed face, letting my sarcasm get the best of me. I watched her partner for any change of expression. I had hoped for a sign of sympathy, but there was none. He remained silent.

"Let's get on with this, and we'll get you out of here."

Now that was the first thing she had said that made sense to me. I was dying for a drink, so I said, "Okay, truce."

"Let's start again. You've been here before?"

"Many times. Carmen was one of my regulars."

"You've known her a long time?"

"A few years. Anytime she needed a cab, she'd call me first."

"You were friends?"

"I guess you could say that." For some strange reason, I found myself not wanting to tell her that Carmen and I had been more than friends. It was none of her business.

"So tell me what happened when you got here."

During the next few minutes, I told the detectives about the eight o'clock pick up, the broken pane of glass in the back door, the trip upstairs to find Carmen lying dead on her bed, and finally the call on the radio for help.

"What exactly did you do when you found the body?" The male detective asked, finally breaking his silence.

"Who are you?" I asked in return.

"Detective Mark Makowiak, SBPD." He answered and waited for a reply.

I shrugged and answered his question. "Well, I could tell immediately that Carmen was dead, but I grabbed her by the hand anyway to make sure. She was cold and stiff."

"What else did you touch?" Makowiak asked.

"I tried the phone in the hall, but I didn't get a dial tone. Then I went out through the back door." I left out the part about raiding Carmen's refrigerator for the beer. I didn't think that would make me look too good. The truth was that I really did feel bad about Carmen, but I never have been able to demonstrate much emotion.

The woman lay flat on her back on a Denver sidewalk bleeding profusely from her forehead. The heap of an Oldsmobile spewed hot steam from the radiator. A good Samaritan with a damp hanky kept dabbing up the blood. Three deep cuts were clearly evident from one side of the forehead to the other. She looked about to go into shock. I watched and looked around. About a dozen people had circled the fallen women. I couldn't help but laugh as I remembered an old newspaper cartoon. I was a part of the "Uh-Oh" squad.

People came away thinking that I didn't give a damn about anything, that I was callous and had no feelings. But the truth of matter was that joking helped me to keep the fear and the bad feelings in check. "Look my prints will be all over this house. I've been here many times before. Carmen traveled at least once a month."

"How good a friend were you?" Kendyll Hall asked nonchalantly.

"We went out once in a while for lunch or dinner, or a few drinks."

"Out, as in dating?"

"No, as in friends." I lied. Actually, I didn't really lie. We were friends. I simply left out the benefits part of my relationship with Carmen. "What are you implying?"

"Nothing."

I didn't believe her.

"Do you know any of her other friends? Do you know of anyone who would want to do this to her?"

"That's a good question." I answered sincerely. "I didn't know her whole life story or anything, but Carmen was a nice woman. I can't imagine anyone hating her enough to want to murder her."

"Did you kill Carmen?"

The question took me by surprise. "No. Come on give me a break. She's been dead since last night probably."

"How do you know that?" Makowiak asked.

"I watch television like everyone else. I'm a forensics expert." Once again, my sarcasm got the best of me, but I didn't like the idea that they might think I could possibly kill Carmen.

"That begs the next question," Hall began. "Where were you last night?"

"I was at the Coconut Hut getting drunk. I'm sure you know where it is."

"I know the place."

I would have been surprised had Hall not known about the Coconut Hut. After all, there were only a few bars in town. I didn't remember ever seeing her have a drink in the place. She probably drank at one of the nicer places on Sunset Boulevard.

"Then what did you do?" She asked.

"Then I went home and passed out." I didn't see any sense in lying. I was sure she would ask around.

"How drunk were you?"

"I'll admit I was pretty drunk, but I wasn't driving or anything. I always ride my bicycle to the Hut from my apartment." I figured if I was as honest as I could be, then I would be able to put an end to this whole line of questioning. It was really beginning to annoy the hell out of me.

"Is there anyone to verify that you were at home all night?"

"My girlfriend Marci."

Hall looked to her partner. "We can turn him loose. He isn't going anywhere." Then she turned her attention to me. "You're not planning on going anywhere, are you Mr. Long?"

"I live right here. Where am I going to go?" Most times, I have a problem masking my true feelings. This was one of those times. I was sure that both of the detectives knew exactly what I thought of them without my having to verbalize it.

"Get him out of here. I'm tired of him." Hall said in

response to my expression. "Walk him out, Mark. Make sure he doesn't touch anything else."

I followed Makowiak into the foyer without saying another word, but interrogation was the word that kept popping into my mind. Why do police have to beat up on innocent people? All I did was find the body. I didn't murder Carmen. They made me feel as though I was guilty of the crime. I would need more than that four-pack to wash the taste away.

* * *

As I sat behind the wheel of my cab, trying to make good on my escape from the scene of the crime, I suddenly stopped. The strange man, I had seen earlier in the parking lot at the beach, stood in the crowd across the street. Apparently he got around pretty good, because there he was again, staring straight at me from behind the yellow and black crime scene tape. The dirty white shirt flapped behind him like a cape in the wind. I couldn't help but stare back, and when I did, he gave me a strange smile and a wink. I winked back. Before I could do anything else, a hand reached in through the open window and grabbed me by the shoulder. Please, let it be a male hand, I thought. No luck. When I glanced back to my left, I could see the blood-red, painted fingernails.

"One more question, Mr. Long."

I shifted the cab back into park, silently cursing my luck. If it had not been for the caped crusader, I would have been long gone. I turned and faced Detective Hall. "Uh, sure." I mumbled.

"Did you see anyone that looked out of place around the house earlier?"

"You mean when I first got here?"

"Yes, Sherlock, when you first got here."

I supposed I deserved the comment, so I let it pass. "No, I didn't see anyone at all."

"Did you see anyone suspicious hanging around here during any of your past pick-ups?"

Very good questions, and they weren't focused on me. I tried to think back to the last few times I had come by to pick up Carmen. Nothing. I also scanned my memory banks of the last few times Carmen and I had gone out, but I didn't remember any weird guys lurking around anywhere. I answered honestly. "I don't remember seeing anyone strange around the house during any of the calls, unless you count that guy over there." I pointed towards the caped crusader as a joke.

Hall's eyes briefly followed my finger into the crowd, before she turned and shrugged her shoulders in a question.

My eyes focused once again on the people behind the crime scene tape, but the man had disappeared into the crowd. "Never mind. He's gone."

"Who's gone?"

"Oh, nothing. Just a guy who dresses pretty weird. Probably harmless."

"You never know," she said. "Did Carmen mention having any problems with anyone lately?"

"She never mentioned anything."

"Okay. Thank you, Mason. You can go."

I simply nodded and put the cab into gear.

"One more thing," she said, holding up a finger for me to wait. She dug her hand into the right front pocket of her black slacks and retrieved a card. Handing me the card, she said, "If you remember anything at all, please call me."

I stashed the card in my shirt pocket and said, "Okay." Detective Hall backed away from the cab, and a uniformed police officer opened the way for me to pull out of the driveway. I scanned the crowd once more for the strange man in the dress-shirt cape. Not finding him, I sped off.

CHAPTER 3

I sped on, until I reached the nearly deserted parking lot of the cab company. Whipping through the chain link gate, I quickly found a spot near the back. I had wanted to go straight to the Coconut Hut for a few quick beers, but I figured I'd better pay my cab's weekly lease first. There was always the danger of blowing my lease money if I went to the bar first. I'd have a hard time making any money without my taxi. Besides, I wanted to talk to my best friend and dispatcher Arthur Clement, and I was sure he wanted to talk to me.

The Tropical Cab Company of Sunset Beach occupied about half a city block, right down the street from City Hall and the SBPD police station. Painted in bright orange and yellow pastels, the new façade, added three, maybe four years ago, gave the outside of the building a nice tropical appearance. The inside was a different story. Nothing had changed in the ten years that I'd been there, and probably hadn't changed significantly during the thirty years of the cab company's existence.

Mechanics toiled with their charges in extremely greasy, shabby conditions all day and half the night, keeping as many cabs on the street as possible. As I walked through the garage interior toward the business office, I thought how there wasn't enough money in the world to get me to do their job, cooped up inside like that all the time. I liked the freedom part of driving a cab. I only wished it paid better.

The business office and break room shared the far wall of the garage, roughly fifty percent each. The front walls of both rooms contained windowed doors and large picture windows that allowed views of everything and everyone within. Bad news, I could see Chemo standing in front of the pay window. I had nicknamed him Chemo several years ago because of his big mouth, slovenly appearance, and lousy personal hygiene. Most sane people that got too close to Chemo had the same reaction: they wanted to puke. I couldn't imagine how anyone would want to actually get in a cab with the man. I opened the door to the business office and steeled myself for the assault to my senses.

Chemo heard the door open and turned to face me. As soon as he recognized me, he asked, "Hey, Mason. Find any dead bodies lately?" He let out a roar that shook the giant potbelly and sent waves of body odor in my direction.

Not knowing how to reply, I said, "As always, Chemo. You're so quick." The statement did have a shred of truth. Apparently, news had traveled rather quickly around Sunset Beach, which I actually thought was just as well. I wouldn't have to explain all the gory details to people like Chemo.

"Give me the skinny, Mason."

Judging from Chemo's comments, I guessed that the word going around the streets is that I had found a dead body. The details must not have been made public. "Read the newspaper, asshole." That seemed to quiet him for the moment. He shrugged his shoulders and turned back to Arthur who stood behind the protective glass pay window.

Chemo retrieved a few bills from the counter and stashed them in his shirt. He turned to leave, but couldn't stand not having the last word. "You're the asshole, Mason."

"Takes one to know one." I responded juvenilely.

Chemo gave me a scowl and stomped his way out of the business office. Unfortunately, he left behind the aroma that had prompted his nickname.

"Hey, Arthur." I reached through the window to shake his hand.

"You okay, Mason?"

"I've been better. You're off soon, right?"

"Five minutes."

Tropical Cab Company dispatchers attended the pay window when they weren't on the air. They worked around the clock in eight-hour shifts. Arthur worked from two in the afternoon until ten in the evening, hours that allowed him to party after work without having to get up too early. "Let me settle up my lease. Then I'll tell you all about it. Maybe, somewhere where there aren't so many ears." I handed him a check for the weekly lease.

Arthur grabbed the check and wrote something down in his log book. Computers were still a part of the future as far as the Tropical Cab Company was concerned. He handed me a hand written receipt for the lease. "Meet me in the break room."

I nodded and walked out the door of the business office and then in through the door of the room next door. The separation of break room from main office offered a bit of privacy for drivers who wanted to escape the ever watchful eyes of dispatchers and supervisors. The room was as shabby as the rest of the place, but vending machines offered caffeine and high caloric sugar treats. A nice buzz could be had by all. I put a dollar's worth of change into one of the machines and pressed the button for a package of cookies. Lately, my dietary habits had become more dismal than usual. I drank more than I ate. I heard the door to the break room open behind me at about the same time the cookies dropped into the metal bin with a clang.

"What the hell happened, Mason?" Arthur got right to the point.

We both sat down at the long table in the center of the room and made ourselves comfortable. I took the seat facing the door. "Carmen was dead when I got there, lying on the bed, stone cold dead. It freaked me out, man."

"What do you mean dead? You said murdered when you called."

"Yes, like in murdered dead."

"How?"

"Looked like she was strangled last night some time."

"Oh, man. That's terrible."

"Tell me about it," I sighed. We both sat there silently

nodding to each other for a few moments, like best friends do, trying to digest the significance of the situation.

"Did you talk to the cops?" Arthur asked.

"Yeah, a bitch of a detective."

"Don't tell me. Kendyll Hall."

"How'd you know that?"

"The word bitch was a dead give away. Pardon the pun."

"She seemed to want to think that I had something to do with Carmen's' murder."

"Oh, boy. I hate to be the bearer of bad news, good buddy, but do you remember Tommy Bell?"

I vaguely remembered a cabbie by that name from a few years back. "Yes. Nice guy. Got into some kind of trouble, didn't he?"

"Yes. It wasn't his fault, though. And that's the relevant point of my Kendyll Hall story. You can add judgmental and vindictive to the word bitch."

"Great. That's just what I need."

"You want to hear it?"

"No, but I guess I better." I figured that the more I knew about Kendyll Hall the better. She took an immediate disliking to me, and I should probably try to understand where that was coming from.

"Tommy worked here about four or five years back, if I remember right. The dude was married to a crazy woman. She got pissed one day because Tommy was out with us getting drunk. She called the cops later that night. You remember?"

"Yeah, yeah, yeah. I remember. She told the cops that

Tommy had beat her up. But she was fucking some other dude, and he was the one who beat her up, right?"

"Yes. Eventually it turned out all right, but in the meantime poor Tommy went through all kinds of hell, mostly due to your friend Kendyll Hall. For whatever reason, she decided that Tommy was a woman beater and wanted to make sure he paid dearly. For Christ's sake, she had his cab license suspended. The dude couldn't make any money. He had to go out with one of the fishing boats." Arthur paused in the story and reached into his pocket for a dollar bill. He walked over to the soda machine. "You want a soda?"

Arthur's story had me going, and it took me a moment to realize what he was asking. "No thanks, man. I'm going to go over to the Hut and get drunk."

"Something different, eh?"

"What would you do, wise ass?"

"I'd probably get drunk too." While Arthur beat on the machine for his root beer, I thought about how good a friend he had been over the years. He was loyal almost to a fault, standing by me in good times and bad. He returned to his seat and continued the story. "Now don't get me wrong. I think wife beaters deserve what they get, but she had Tommy tried and convicted without a single shred of evidence. That's not good police work, if you ask me."

"I don't understand how a man could beat or rape a woman," I said.

"Or murder," Arthur added.

"Yeah, or murder. I can't imagine who would want to kill Carmen." Dark urges reside in everyone, but the majority of us never act on them. I took some comfort in that thought until the cold truth slapped me in the face: someone had acted in the darkness last night. A shiver ran through me.

"Were you and Carmen still friends with benefits?" Arthur asked, breaking me out of my reverie.

"Yes."

"What about Marci?"

Marci Glass was my current girlfriend. The relationship had been dead for some time, but neither one of us had been willing to officially lay it to rest. She was a nice woman, but woefully addicted to both drugs and alcohol. Worse than me, even. We kind of captured each other a while back, living and getting high together. "What about Marci? I don't think she had any idea about Carmen."

"That's not what I mean."

I knew what he meant, and in fact, my benefits with Carmen had overlapped several other girlfriends. Arthur shook his head in disbelief over my lack of faithfulness, so I added, "I may like to chase women, but I'm no murderer. Besides, Marci and I won't be together much longer."

Arthur was one of those guys that never seemed to have a long term relationship with a woman. It wasn't that he was ugly or something. He was a big good-looking guy, at least six-foot-two with short-cropped blonde hair, and buff. He couldn't relate to women, and over the years, he had simply given up trying. Now, he didn't date much, happy living alone and not worrying about them. I didn't understand his viewpoint at all, but to each his own as they say.

"I know you're not a murderer, Mason. What makes you

think Hall likes you as the killer?"

"Well, she asked me for an alibi and made it very clear that she didn't like me."

"Hell, the police ask everyone for an alibi. I wouldn't take that personal."

"No, but Tommy Bell's story might explain a few things."

"Like?" Arthur gave me a questioning look.

"Like a woman was strangled, murdered. More than likely by a guy. It seems that Detective Hall really gets hot over crimes against women."

"Good point."

"Speaking of my alibi. What time did *you* leave the bar last night, Arthur?"

"Around one or one fifteen."

"Was I still there?"

"You don't remember?"

"No, man. I must have blacked out. The last thing I remember – you and I were shooting pool. The next thing I remember is waking up in the hammock at home." I had a long history of blackouts when I drank too much, and apparently I'd lost much of the memory of the night before, and if the truth be told, from several nights past. "I told Hall that I had gotten drunk at the Hut and then went home and passed out."

"That's probably what you did. When I left you were sitting with Marci at the bar with a beer in your hand. She looked to be as drunk and miserable as you."

"I have to know for sure, Arthur, so my next stop is the Coconut Hut to do some research." I smiled broadly at the thought. "Are you coming?"

"I'll be right behind you."

A few blackouts would not stop me from drinking my fill.

CHAPTER 4

Most of us need a place to hang out where we feel safe. For me, the Coconut Hut was that place. The Hut wasn't the nicest place to drink in Sunset Beach. Hell, the Hut wasn't even the nicest place to drink on the block. Designed for the Florida beach scene, a dreary, nondescript inside bar gave way to an outside grass hut next to the canal, thatched roof and all, where both tourists and locals could get fancy fruit cocktails and play volleyball in the sand.

"Nice shot, Lenny," I shouted over the music from my perch on a barstool.

Lenny DeCarlo had cleanly banked the nine ball two rails and into the corner pocket, but he still had two balls left. Obviously feeling confident, he asked, "Want to raise the stakes?"

"What did you have in mind?" I asked, watching as he circled the pool table, chalking the tip of cue as he walked.

"You want to make it double or nothing, Mason?"

Gambling was never one of my addictions, but I liked to

spice up a game of Eight Ball on occasion, especially when I played DeCarlo. Besides, his only play was a long fourteen ball in the corner, and I didn't think he could make that shot. "Okay, let's make it twenty."

"You're on." DeCarlo leaned over and took aim at the dark-green-striped fourteen ball. "Fourteen in the corner pocket," he said and cleanly dropped the ball into the pocket.

I pounded the base of my pool cue multiple times on the barroom floor in recognition of his shot, already wishing that we hadn't raised the bet from ten to twenty dollars. Sometimes my mouth was faster than my brain. I couldn't sit still, so I walked over to the side of the table and grabbed a piece of chalk. I stood chalking the tip of my stick, but couldn't resist trying to throw him off his game by interrupting him and saying, "Tough shot, Lenny."

DeCarlo shot me a dirty look, and said, "Ten ball in the side pocket." Lenny DeCarlo owned the Coconut Hut, and if you can imagine an older, mafia movie type from New Jersey, then you have a picture of DeCarlo. The once black shiny hair had grayed and thinned considerably, leaving him more salt than pepper, but the dark brown eyes had kept their intensity. He slammed the ten ball home. All he had left was the eight ball to win.

Fingers tapped me on the shoulder from behind. "What's happening, bro?" My good friend Arthur Clement had arrived. He held out his hand to me.

I shook his hand. "Not much, Arthur. Lenny's kicking my ass in pool."

Arthur turned to DeCarlo and said, "Hey, Lenny. How's it

going."

"Watch me beat this punk, Arthur." DeCarlo grinned and added, "Eight ball in the corner, Mason."

"Yeah, yeah, yeah. I hear you, Lenny." I started to dig in my pocket for a twenty. It wouldn't be the first time I had donated money to DeCarlo's wallet. Being the classic choke artist, I had a habit of losing any time I had money on a game. You would think I'd have learned my lesson by now.

"Get him, Lenny."

"Thanks, Arthur."

"No problem, man."

DeCarlo stroked the eight ball softly. It rolled straight and true, falling easily into the corner pocket. "Who's next?"

"I'll take you on, Lenny." Arthur moved over to the wall and grabbed the ball rack.

I put the cue back in the rack, and slipped DeCarlo the twenty. "Here, Lenny. Good game. I'm going to get a shooter."

"Thanks, Mason." He turned towards the bar and yelled to Annie Jones, the closest of the two bartenders, "Annie, get Mason a shooter on me."

I slapped him on the back and said, "Thanks, Lenny. You're a good man." I turned and headed back to my bar stool. Even though I had lost the game, I was feeling better than I had all evening. Finding Carmen's body, and worse yet, having to deal with the police had depressed the hell out of me. I figured another couple of whiskey shooters and the fear and depression would be long gone.

Annie placed a shot glass on the bar in front of me and

reached down for the bottle of whiskey in the well. She poured the shot and asked, "Are you okay, Mason? I heard about Carmen." Annie Jones was another transplant to the Florida beaches. She hailed from somewhere like Long Island or Boston, judging from the way she pronounced words with an 'r' in them. I liked her anyway.

"I've been better, but thanks for asking." I smiled broadly before downing the shooter in a quick gulp. Although Annie and I had always been friendly, the next thought surprised me. As soon as Marci and I parted ways, perhaps Annie and I could make a go of it. Her short, petite figure, brown eyes and long blonde hair, tied back into a ponytail, worked for me. And sometimes I sensed that she felt the same way.

"You want to talk?" She asked, motioning toward one of the booths in back.

"Sure, I think I'd like that." I grabbed my beer from the bar and followed her to a booth. She let me slide in first, then slid in next to me, not stopping until we were thigh to thigh.

"I'm so sorry about Carmen," she said, resting her left hand lightly on my knee. "You and Carmen were pretty good friends, weren't you?"

"Yes, we were friends. I thought she was pretty special."

"You have other friends, you know?" She shifted slightly in her seat and took both my hands in hers. "We'll all help you get through this. It must have been hard on you finding her body like that."

"It was a shock. I've been wracking my brain all night, and I still can't imagine who would want to kill her."

"Makes me shudder. Do they know what really happened

to her?"

"No one knows for sure. Only that she was strangled some time last night."

"God, that's scary. I don't like to walk home alone after we close up. I make somebody take me home, usually Lenny. You never know who might be out there."

"Speaking of closing time, were Marci and I still here when you closed up last night?"

"You don't remember?"

I tried not to react to her question, but I was sure tired of people asking me whether I remembered or not. It was down right embarrassing. Why would I ask the question, if I could fucking remember. I calmed myself and said, "I guess I was pretty drunk because I'm not sure what time it was when we left. You got any idea what time we left?"

"I think you guys left around a quarter to two, because I don't remember you sitting there after I turned the lights on for last call."

"We left together?"

"As far as I know. How are you and Marci getting along?"

I read her face for underlying motives. She appeared sincerely concerned, and dare I say, interested? I hoped I wasn't making up that last part. "We won't be together much longer. She parties too much."

Annie laughed. "Isn't that like the dog calling the cat black?"

"What?" I laughed and squeezed her hand.

"Never mind. You know what I mean. You're one to talk about partying too much."

"True. But she is way out of control. We never do anything together." The last statement wasn't exactly the truth. Marci and I were still very good in bed together. She was always horny. "Looking back on it, we probably should never have tried it as a couple in the first place."

"Well, you know what they say? Hindsight is fifty-fifty."

"You mean twenty-twenty?" I laughed again, finding her rewriting of old sayings quite amusing.

"Whatever," she giggled as she said it, taking no offense at all to my correction.

"You're all right, Annie."

"You are too, Mason." Annie rose from the booth, then leaned back in and kissed me lightly on the cheek. "Call me if you need anything." When she turned to go, she ran directly into Arthur Clement, who had come up behind her as she kissed me.

"Whoa, am I interrupting something?" Arthur asked, smiling with his right eyebrow raised in an arc.

"Didn't see you, Arthur," Annie said, smiling shyly, her eyes downcast.

"I guess not." He let her squirm.

"Excuse me," she said, highly accenting the first word. "I have to go back to work."

I watched as Annie walked away. She made me smile. I needed to put an end to my relationship with Marci real soon. "Sit, Arthur. What's happening?"

"Did you hear about any storm damage at the marina?" Arthur asked as he slid into the seat across from me.

"No, what happened?" Although my boat was fine when I

drove across the bridge earlier, I immediately assumed the worst. My father bought the *Tramp* when we moved down here ten years ago. He left the thirty-six foot cruiser and fishing boat to me when he died. The *Tramp* was my pride and joy, and the thought that it might have been damaged had me worried. In my mind, I could see a hole in the side of the hull, and she was taking on water, slowly sinking.

> *The water snake dropped into the canoe from an oak branch overhanging the Hillsborough River, landing in the open space between the seats. Without thinking, without being the operative word, Arthur grabbed the hatchet from behind him, and swinging mightily, he cleanly cut the snake in two as he drove the hatchet through the bottom of the canoe. The canoe filled completely with water in a very short time. We swam the damaged canoe to the bank. We were pretty stupid when we were younger.*

"But the storm didn't last very long," I complained.

"No, but it was pretty intense. I was told that some of the wind gusts got up near eighty miles an hour."

"Shit, that is pretty intense. Was there a lot of damage? I hope my boat's okay."

"I was talking with Moore and he didn't mention too much damage to boats. But the wind did blow down one of the marina signs. Some of the pieces went flying around like shrapnel."

Joe Moore owned the fuel dock at the marina. He usually had a good handle on what was going down. "Man, Arthur, it's always something. I guess I better go down and check on the boat later. I'd hate to find out too late about something."

"What's up with you and Annie?"

"I think she likes me."

"Why in the world would any woman like you?" Arthur grinned and added. "The only big thing on your body is your nose."

"You wish. After I piss, I have to fold it twice to put it back in." The bantering between Arthur and I sounded every bit like similar exchanges that took place in elementary and high school. Good friends always make each other feel better, no matter the circumstances. "Did you beat, Lenny?" I asked him.

"No," he said in disgust.

"Maybe, you need a bigger cue stick too."

"Very funny. How are you doing otherwise?"

"What do you mean otherwise?" I said, knowing full well what Arthur meant, but willing to let him squirm a bit like he did with Annie.

"You know what I'm talking about. You okay?"

"I'm okay. I keep trying to remember last night, but I'm not having much luck. Annie said that I left the Hut with Marci just before closing."

"You probably went home and passed out."

"Probably, but I don't even remember leaving here."

"Man, Mason, you have to cut down on your drinking. It is not natural to have blackouts like that."

"Everyone has blackouts. Don't they?" I knew deep down in my heart that Arthur was right. He didn't have anything but my best interest in mind. I needed to slow down, at least to the point where I could remember my nights out. My greatest fear was that I would one day simply lose my mind. I saw a movie once where the dude was diagnosed as having a wet brain from drinking too much alcohol. I'd rather be dead.

"You know damn well that not everybody has blackouts. One of these days you're going to find yourself in real trouble. The jails are loaded with people who can't remember how they got there." Arthur kept talking, but the mind is cruel. One minute I sat listening to him, the next minute I could see his lips move, but I couldn't hear the words. Heat rushed to my face, fear cramped my belly. Arthur must have noticed, for he said, "What's the matter, Mason? You look like you're going to be sick, man. Don't throw up on me."

I leaned forward, and Arthur responded by pressing back into the booth cushion as hard as he could. I guessed he thought I was going to hurl on him. I ignored his response and looked around the room quickly before I motioned for him to also lean forward. Once he got close enough, I said in a very low voice, "I knew the beers were there."

"What?"

"I knew the beers were there." I could hardly find a voice for my racing thoughts.

"What the hell are you talking about, Mason. You're starting to scare me."

My mind started to slow down. "At Carmen's house. I knew there were four beers in the refrigerator before I opened the door."

"Slow down and give me some damn context."

"Just before I called you on the radio from Carmen's

driveway, I stopped at the refrigerator in the kitchen. I grabbed four beers from the vegetable bin."

"Yeah, so?"

"I knew the beers were there. I knew there were four beers stashed in the bin."

"I'm not following you."

"How would I know that?" I held up both hands in a questioning gesture.

Arthur's face took on the same ashen expression that mine had a few minutes earlier. "You were there."

"Apparently."

"When was the last time you remember being at her house?"

The last time I remembered being at Carmen's house was a week earlier. I had spent a couple of hours Wednesday evening in her bed, part of the benefits we shared. I didn't remember any beers in the refrigerator on that visit, so I said, "A week ago, but I didn't leave any beer in the refrigerator. Besides, they wouldn't last that long with Carmen around anyway."

"It doesn't mean you were there last night."

"That's true." I calmed down. Arthur was right. I must have paid Carmen a visit within the past week, but not necessarily last night. I'd been blacking out a lot of evenings lately. "I have to know for sure."

"Then you need to talk to Marci."

"Obviously," I snapped. The look on Arthur's face told me that I had hurt his feelings. "I'm sorry, man. This whole thing has got me rattled. And I hate the idea of talking to

Marci about last night, or anything else for that matter." Arthur shrugged his shoulders. "What if she tells me that we had an argument and I walked out? I've been doing a lot of that lately."

"What if she tells you that the two of you went to bed and did the dirty deed. You said earlier that you woke up at home in the hammock."

"That's true." Arthur was right again. Even though the relationship had seen better days, Marci and I still did the dirty deed as Arthur called it. My mind always seemed to jump to conclusions before having any real evidence to the contrary. The thought made me think of Detective Kendyll Hall and the way she jumped to the conclusion that our old friend Tommie Bell had been guilty of beating his wife. Guilty until proven innocent. "Do you think Hall has already talked to Marci?"

"Who?"

"Detective Hall, mother fucker. The bitch detective we talked about earlier."

"I doubt it. It's late. But I bet she'll talk to everybody tomorrow. So if I was you, I wouldn't put off talking to Marci."

"Shit."

"In fact, maybe you ought to talk to your brother."

"Poco? Why would I talk to Poco. He's an ass."

"He is a lawyer, and he is your brother."

My brother Poco practiced law in downtown Sunset Beach. In fact, he was one hell of defense attorney. How convenient for a slug like me, except that I didn't like him and he didn't like me. The gulf between us seemed to grow as the years went by, and I'd bet that a big part of the distance was caused when Daddy left the *Tramp* to me and not to Poco. But Arthur was right. Poco was family. He would stand up for his little brother. Daddy had taught us both that years ago. "I'm no killer, Arthur."

"I know you're not, but remember what happens when Hall takes a dislike to someone."

CHAPTER 5

Home is not always what it is cracked up to be. The old wooden hovel where Marci and I lived sat amidst several very expensive houses on the canal side of the main island. In dire need of some paint, the graying structure stood in stark contrast to the beautiful glass and steel edifice next door. Sunset Beach was a rare combination of the old and the new, existing in a somewhat shaky balance. However, if you asked my millionaire neighbor about this harmonic coexistence, you would get a different answer. He'd love to see all of these older beach houses torn down.

"Speak of the devil." My son of a bitch neighbor was on the move, coming down the steps of his front porch wagging his finger at me as I rode my bicycle into our driveway. A jumbled confusion of words streamed from his mouth. I couldn't understand what he was saying yet, but I was sure that it wasn't nice. As he got within range I could hear, "Son of bitch. Can't you people keep your cars on your own damn driveway and out of my fucking yard." I didn't know what he was talking about until I noticed that the passenger side tires of Marci's light-green VW bug were not resting on the driveway, but instead were firmly planted into his yard. "Take it easy, man." I said, leaning my bicycle against the house. I used my bike when I drank heavily, and as always my cab was parked on the left hand side of the driveway, leaving plenty of room for Marci to park, but she had missed by several feet.

"Xerascape costs money. You going to pay for the damage?"

Now I could understand the concept of xerascape, landscaping that required very little water for survival, and I would certainly agree that we needed to conserve water; however, most of the plants that grew wild in his xerascape landscape looked like weeds. A few run-ins with Marci's VW tires would not have much of an impact.

"I should call the police."

"Give me a break, man." He had edged perilously close into my personal space, and I was doing my best to remain calm. "She didn't hurt anything."

"Bullshit, look at the damage," he said, waving his arms wildly in the direction of his yard.

I went over and inspected the area where the VW had gone over the edge of the driveway. It didn't seem to me that her car had done any damage, but he was definitely one to carry out his threats. He had called the police on us a couple of weeks ago. We had several people over partying. I didn't think we got that loud, but he called the police anyway, and we had to grovel to the cops so they'd let us alone. "I'll move the car. Stop being an asshole." As I watched the man, I realized that he could never fulfill my request that he stop being an asshole. I quickly decided that although I would love to, I couldn't kick his ass right now for two reasons: one, I had promised Marci that I wouldn't, and two, it seemed prudent to skip any confrontations with the police at the present time.

"You're the asshole. You both think that you can do anything you want with little or no regard to someone else's private property." He started coming closer and closer as he spoke.

I held up both hands in an, *I don't want any trouble posture*, while simultaneously giving him a murderous look. Instead of punching him in the face, I said in a threatening voice, "Look man, I told you I'd move the fucking car." That did it. He decided not to pursue the matter any further. He backed off and gave me a smirk. Once again, I wanted to smash him in the face, but thought that I could come up with some other kind of revenge. The thought made me smile, an evil kind of smile. My smile must have scared him.

"You see to it that your cars stay on the driveway." He turned and headed for home. I watched him for a few seconds before I also turned and walked to the front door of our apartment.

The screen door shut behind me with a bang as I entered the kitchen. As soon as I flipped on the light, a big old brown roach ran for cover. I took off my right sandal and smashed it before it could run under the sink. Ripping a paper towel from the roll above the sink, I wiped up the carcass and threw it in the trash can. "Damn, things," I muttered.

Roaches are disgusting creatures that have no useful purpose that I could understand. If there was a nuclear holocaust, the only things left alive would be the damn roaches, and they would get very, very big.

"Marci, you home?" I hollered into the dark interior of our ground floor apartment. Receiving no response, I hollered again, "Marci?" She had probably passed out drunk in bed and couldn't hear me. I only hoped that she hadn't found the bottle of Jack Daniels that I had stashed in the top cabinet yesterday. After my confrontation with the asshole out in the driveway, I needed a drink. I grabbed a kitchen chair and stood searching the shelf. "Hah, you missed them, Marci." I laughed. The two bottles sat right where I'd hid them. Snatching the closest bottle, I climbed down and stood by the sink. I found a glass and poured myself two fingers worth of the whisky. Downing it in a single gulp, I choked back the urge to spit it back out. I set the glass on the counter and let the warmth from the alcohol wash over me.

Marci's keys were sitting on the kitchen table, so I grabbed them and went back outside, letting the door slam behind me again. I unlocked her car and climbed in. Looking out the driver's side window, I could see the neighbor standing in the middle of his glass encased living room. He looked to be sipping a glass of red wine, probably a very expensive glass of red wine. Envy and bitterness not withstanding, I really disliked the guy. I needed to think of something to get even. Justice would prevail. I would see to it. I started the VW and moved it over into the driveway, thinking that Marci must have been pretty drunk to park that badly. She always seemed to be drunk these days. Sometimes she never came home at all, saying that she had passed out in one place or another. We were quite the pair. I climbed back out of the car and locked it. As I walked back towards the house, I glanced up to see my neighbor watching me. I gave him the finger and kept walking into the house. I caught the door this time before it could slam shut.

At the kitchen counter, I poured some more whisky into the glass. I needed a minute to think. When I talked with Marci, I wanted to know what to say. I didn't think I needed to tell her the whole truth about the Carmen situation. I was sure that the police would fill her in soon enough when they checked on my alibi. I also didn't see any advantage in owning up to the fact that I wanted out of our relationship until tomorrow. The last thing I needed was a revengeful ex-girlfriend making up things to tell detectives. A strange sound interrupted my thoughts. I listened closely, and a few seconds later I heard it again. A low moan came from somewhere back towards the bedroom. Something wasn't right. I downed the rest of the whiskey and headed for the back of the house.

I found the bed slept-in but empty. Confused, I scanned the room and noticed a light coming from under the closed bathroom door. I opened the door and shook my head at the sight that confronted me: Marci lay sprawled on her back on the cold tile floor. Her bright blue tank top was covered in vomit. A small puddle of light yellow urine was drying between her legs, a stain evident on her white cotton panties. "Marci, what are you doing, for Christ's sake." My first thought was to let her lie in her own mess and go back to the bar and find Annie. I was doing my best to keep my cool, but I wasn't the caretaker type. The thought of cleaning up vomit and piss was enough to make me gag. It was definitely a good thing that I had never had kids. "Oh, hell, Marci." I couldn't let her lie there like that. Marci was basically a good woman, and I did like her. So, I rolled up my sleeves, figuratively of course since Hawaiian shirts don't have sleeves, and found a roll of paper towels under the sink. I mopped up the vomit and piss from the floor as best I could. Then lifting her from behind by both arms, I sat her up with her back against the white bathtub.

"Hey, what the fuck?" Marci moaned. She had come alive during the act of sitting up.

"I'm trying to get you cleaned up. You passed out on the bathroom floor. Help me."

Taking the bottom of her tank top in both of my hands, I managed to raise it over her head. I threw it on top of the clothes hamper across the room. She was not wearing a bra.

Marci began to sob, slowly at first then with great gusto. "I can't do this shit anymore."

She was right about that, but I wasn't the one to help her with her problems. I had demons of my own to fight. "What shit is that, Marci. Getting fucked up, puking and pissing all over yourself?"

"Fuck you, Mason," she said in a slurred, whiny voice, trying to stifle her sobs.

I leaned over into the bathtub and plugged the drain before turning on the water. I needed to let her calm down and get her wits together so we could talk. "We'll get you some help tomorrow, Marci. You need to go to an AA meeting or something,"

The only thing I knew about Alcoholics Anonymous was that they had helped a ton of people get straight.

"Will you go with me, Mason?" She mumbled, her head falling to the side.

"Sure, Marci," I lied. "Let me get you cleaned up first. We'll go tomorrow."

"Promise?"

"Promise." I had no intention of keeping that promise. All I wanted to do was get her calm enough to sneak in a few questions about last night. Thinking the time was right, I asked, "What time did we get home last night?"

To my chagrin, I didn't get any response. Marci had passed out again. While we talked, the tub had filled enough, so I shut off the faucets and felt the water. It wasn't quite warm, but I didn't think she'd notice. I wanted to get this over with so I could finish asking my questions. I bent over and pulled off Marci's white cotton panties, snagging them on the big toe of her left foot. The task of navigating her left foot out of the tangled panties proved to be of greater dimension than originally planned, because by now I was getting quite drunk myself. The whiskey was doing its thing. When I finally managed to remove the soiled panties, I threw them in the sink. With great effort, I hauled up the dead weight of the passed-out Marci and slid her into the lukewarm water. Marci had been a cheerleader in high school and still looked good, but you could see that the wear and tear of her addictions were starting to take their toll. Her ribs showed through the once magnificent figure. Her firm, handful-sized breasts had given in to the gravity of the situation, no pun intended. I washed her completely, starting from her toes and moving up. As I was wiping a towel across her face, she stirred.

"I'm cold." Marci had returned from the depths of her alcoholism.

"Let's get you out of there. Help me."

She stood up carefully while I steadied her with both hands. I didn't want her to slip and fall. No matter how I felt about her at the moment, I didn't want her to get hurt. Once out of the tub, I wrapped a large towel around her shoulders.

"Mason, what's happened to us?" Marci had started to sob again.

"Hush. Let's get you to bed." I tried to urge her towards the bedroom, but she would have none of it.

"You don't give a shit about me anymore." Her shoulders shook with her sobs.

"Sure I do."

"You're a liar."

"Take it easy, Marci."

"No." Shaking the towel from her shoulders, she stood naked and defiant. She had stopped sobbing and seemed to remember something. In a cold voice she said, "I can't take your whoring around."

"What are you talking about?"

"Last night."

"What about last night?" Without knowing it, I had lost all control of the situation. My heart started thumping loudly in my chest. Fear of the unknown would soon be replaced with fear of the known. The answers would be forthcoming, but I wasn't sure I was prepared for them.

"Where did you go? Who the hell were you with?"

All the saliva had disappeared from my mouth. I had trouble forming words. All I could do was repeat myself. "What are you talking about? I was here sleeping."

"You know damn well what I'm talking about. When I woke up in the middle of the night, you were gone. Where did you go?"

I stalled for time. "What are you talking about? We came home together after last call. Didn't we?"

"Yes, we did. We went to bed. But when I woke up, you were gone." She pushed her way past me and into the bedroom.

I quickly followed, not wanting to drop the conversation, hoping that something would trigger my memories of last night. I watched as she stopped at the dresser and put on a pair of black panties and a white tee shirt, thinking how some things are just plain unjust. Marci drank almost as much as I did, but never had blackouts like me. She always remembered what happened. That had always been a good thing until now. "What time did you wake up, honey?"

"Don't honey me."

I backed off and waited for her anger to subside.

"A couple of hours after we went to bed," she finally answered.

"You're not even sure what time it was."

"It was still dark. I couldn't have been asleep for more

than a couple of hours. So it had to be three or four o'clock. You were gone."

"I wasn't gone, Marci. I was asleep in the hammock." The back porch of the house was set up like a Florida room, three sides were floor to ceiling screens. A huge double hammock offered a great place to sleep.

"Don't bullshit me, Mason. You were in the hammock in the morning, but where the hell did you go in the meantime?"

I was hoping that I could insert some doubt into her recollections, so when the police interviewed her, they couldn't rely on her statements. The thought scared me. I was thinking like a guilty man. Still, it seemed the reasonable thing to do. "Did you even look on the back porch to see if I was in the hammock?"

"Yes. You were not there. So where did you go?"

Backpedaling fast, I fell back on the only answer that would ring true. "I wanted to drink some more, so I went down to the boat." Running down to the boat is something that I've always done when I wanted to get away, so it seemed like a reasonable possibility. It might not even be a lie. I'm not sure she really believed me, but she had to give me the benefit of the doubt.

"Then you can go spend tonight on the boat too."

* * *

Cool night air is not something you find on the gulf coast of Florida in the summertime. At best, the temperature will get down into the mid-seventies. I had to piss terribly, and the sweat rolled down my face and neck as I pedaled my ass off towards the Sunset Beach Municipal Marina, which occupied the entire southern tip of the island. The three main dock areas were tucked in on the intra-coastal waterway, and it was just a matter of navigating around the very tip of the island through Sunset Pass and into the open waters of the Gulf of Mexico. Once I turned the corner onto Marina Drive, the three docks stretched out in front of me. A hundred or so boats occupied the slips, keeping time with the rhythm of the sea. My true destination came into sight a minute later. The bathroom was only moments away.

"Shit." It dawned on me that after midnight the bathroom facilities were locked. Luckily, the ride was downhill from here, so I stood on the pedals and coasted, trying to save some time by fishing the bathroom keys out of my pocket with my right hand, while still holding onto the bottle of Jack Daniels with my left hand. I might have pulled off the juggling act without incident, if the keys hadn't snagged on something. I glanced down at the keys and tugged as hard as I could until they finally broke free. Triumph turned to horror when I looked up in time to see the curb fast approaching. The bike hit the curb hard and launched me over the handlebars. I rolled head over heels onto the lawn in front of the bathroom and came back up on my feet. I checked the bottle of whiskey for damage. All was okay, but in my drunken state, I overcorrected and fell flat on my face. I still had to piss very badly, so I got up without looking and ran straight into someone.

When I checked to see who I ran into, I could not believe

my eyes. Standing directly in front of me was the same odd man I had seen twice earlier in the day: once in the parking lot at the beach, and once behind the crime scene tape at Carmen's. The caped crusader still wore the same shabby, graying dress shirt like a cape. The straw hat had fallen off his head when I ran into him, and now hung by the leather strap around his neck.

"Excuse me," he said.

"Sorry," I mumbled. I wanted to stop and talk to him but it would have to wait. I unlocked the door quickly. The bathroom was deserted, and I was able to relieve myself and be back outside in less than five minutes. But by that time, the man had disappeared. I was disappointed. I liked talking with odd ducks, especially when I was drunk. I had not seen him before today, so I figured he must be new addition to the zany mix that was Sunset Beach.

* * *

When I had first left the house, my spirits were in the dumper. I was sure that Detective Hall would have me arrested and thrown into jail. But as I thought about it, I realized that I still didn't know much about Carmen's murder, and neither did the police. After all, what did I really know for sure? I had been at Carmen's house with some beer, like many times before, and that I wasn't home when Marci woke up. She didn't know about Carmen, and the odds were that I had come down to the boat like a thousand other nights. Only one question still nagged at me: if I did go down to the boat, why did I go back home and climb into the hammock on a hot night, instead of just sleeping on the boat? I hoped my memory would return.

I picked up my bicycle from where it had fallen, and after a brief inspection, I could find no discernible damage. No longer in a hurry, I rolled it down the ramp towards C Dock and my boat slip. As I walked passed the boat next to mine, I spied a dead fish in the water. It looked to be a big redfish. I could see the black dot near the tail. "That's it." I had suddenly thought of an extremely childish way to exact some revenge on my asshole neighbor. There was a big redfish in the freezer at home. If I put the fish in a garbage bag and placed it under his front porch tomorrow night. By the next day, it would stink like hell, and he wouldn't know where it was coming from. I laughed like a kid who had been told a fart joke as I leaned my bicycle up against my boat. I was about to climb aboard the *Tramp* when I heard footsteps behind me. Before I could turn and look, I heard a familiar voice.

"Hey, bro. What's happening?"

"Arthur."

"Yeah, man. I had to come down and check on you. What are you laughing about?"

"You remember when my asshole neighbor called the police?"

"Sure." Arthur had been in attendance at the party.

"I know it's probably not enough revenge, but I thought I would place a redfish that I have in the freezer under his front porch."

Arthur laughed. "Should stink like hell within a day."

"Yeah. He won't know why his house suddenly stinks like shit." Practical jokes are cool, most of the time.

We'd been drinking since two hours before the Denver Bronco's football game started at noon. First pitchers of red beer at the Sports Page, then multiple beers at the game, followed by more beer and shooters back in the Springs after the game. I was in no condition to talk, let alone walk, so my good friends took me home.

Not wanting to confront my parents, they decided to prop me up against the front door and ring the doorbell until the lights came on. When my mother opened the door to see who it was, I fell in backwards like a dead body. I still remember my mother's screams.

"I need a drink," Arthur said.

"Sounds good, man. Come on aboard. I've got a bottle of Jack and maybe some beers in the refrigerator."

"Terrific."

"Let's go below. Get out of the heat." The Tramp's thirty-six foot length and almost twelve-foot beam provided plenty of room for both cruising and fishing. The helm resided on the fly bridge, which provided ample head room down in the main cabin. Three bunks, a head and shower, and a small galley complete with refrigerator provided all the comforts of home. I wasn't exactly roughing it when I came down here to drink and sleep. The air conditioner kept the cabin a cool sixty-eight degrees when docked. Arthur sat down at the galley table, while I poured a couple of whiskeys.

"Man, it's muggy tonight," Arthur said.

"Glad this boat has good air conditioning." I set two glasses of whiskey on the table as I sat down, sliding one in Arthur's direction. "Want to smoke a joint too?"

"No this is cool, Mason. I'm assuming you talked to Marci."

"Yeah, just barely. She was all fucked up. Passed out on the floor. I had to clean her up."

"You'll be next, if you have too many more of those," Arthur said and pointed at my glass.

"Since when have you become my keeper?"

"Since you can't do it yourself."

"I'm not like Marci. I can handle the booze."

"Famous last words. Haven't you learned anything today?"

"I'll be fine." I could sense the concern in Arthur. He was truly a good friend, but I didn't need to hear how bad my drinking had become. I was living the dream, wasn't I? Living on an island off the coast of Florida, surrounded by beautiful women, drinking with good friends. What could be bad with that?

"What did Marci have to say?"

"She said she needed help." Always the wise ass, I didn't want to get too serious about my situation.

"What'd she say about you, wise ass? Can she vouch for you all night?"

"No."

"No? You went home with her, didn't you?"

"Yes, but apparently I didn't stay long. She said she woke

up and I wasn't there."

"I thought you woke up at home?"

"I did, but I must have gone somewhere in between."

"Can you remember anything about last night yet?"

"No, nothing. Sometimes the memories come back and sometimes they don't."

"I don't understand the blackouts. Isn't there something you can to do to make the memories return?"

I had no answer for his question. There were blank periods scattered throughout the last several years of my life. No matter what I did, there were nights where I have no recollection whatsoever.

"What do you think you did?"

"I probably came here."

"You don't know that for sure, do you? What are you going to say to the police."

"Another good question. What can I say?"

"I guess you'll have to tell them the truth."

"I don't even know the truth, that's the hard part. I only know a piece of it."

"Will Marci cover your ass?"

"No. One thing about Marci, she's as honest as they come. She can't tell a lie. Not even to herself."

"Unlike you."

"Thanks, Arthur."

"I'm only trying to help."

Too bad Arthur couldn't go into my brain and unlock the mystery of the night before. The fear was beginning to creep back into my mind. Was I really as out of control as Marci?

Did I have something to do with Carmen's murder? I didn't like either of those questions.

Arthur must have read my mind, for he said, "You didn't murder Carmen."

"No, I didn't. But I bet I'll be the number one suspect after the police talk to Marci. I found the body, and I can't account for myself during the time of the murder."

"How's the boat running?" Arthur asked.

The question caught me by surprise. "The boat?"

"We could be in the Bahamas by tomorrow afternoon, my friend."

CHAPTER 6

The pounding reverberated inside my head. A giant of a man swung the axe swiftly, slicing a hole into the side of the large wooden cask. Rum ran rampant out of a dozen holes and onto the wooden floor. I slipped on the mess and fell, hitting my head on a table and almost knocking myself unconscious. As I came out of the fog, I found myself lying naked on the floor, an eerily familiar face staring at me through the porthole. "What the hell do you want?" I yelled at the noisemaker as I came around. Someone was pounding on the door of my cabin, waking me from my slumber. "Go away."

"Open the door. It's the police."

"Police?"

"Yes. Open the door. We want to talk to you."

My heart began to pound. I searched the floor and found a pair of black swim trunks and slipped them on. A flash of light came through the porthole where the face had been. I jumped up on the bunk and looked outside. A Sunset Beach police boat had pulled up across the bow of the *Tramp*. Off the stern, I could see two police officers standing on the dock. Behind them in the distance, two police vehicles were parked in the marina lot at the end of C Dock.

The pounding stopped for the moment, as a female voice ordered, "Open the door, Mr. Long."

It didn't appear that I had much choice. "All right, all right. Give me a second." I grabbed a dirty gray tee shirt from the top of the bunk and put it on over my head as I walked to the door. I slipped the dead bolt back and let the door fall open. As soon as it opened a crack, the door flew in upon me. Two people rushed in knocking me to my knees on the cabin floor.

"Get all the way down, face on the floor," a female voice screamed.

"Down now. Get down," a male voice yelled.

"What's this all about?"

Both officers kept yelling at me to get down at the top of their lungs, while the female pushed at me with her foot. I wanted to tell them that I could hear just fine.

"On your face, now. Clasp both hands behind your neck."

"Hands behind your neck, now."

"Okay, okay." I complied meekly, falling to the floor on my stomach and clasping my hands behind my neck. Rough hands slapped the handcuffs on me, first the left hand and then the right. I turned my head to the side, flat against the carpet. Nylon covered legs flowed up from a pair of women's pointy toed shoes and into a short black skirt. After the handcuffs were secured, the two strong hands yanked me back to my feet almost pulling my arms from their sockets. I stared at my tormentors.

"Are you Mason Prophet Long?" Detective Kendyll Hall asked.

"You know damn well that's my name. What's this all about?"

"You are under arrest. Mark, read him his rights."

"Wait a minute. For what?"

"For the murder of Carmen Lopez."

"Where's your warrant?"

"I don't need a warrant."

My mind hummed with activity. I couldn't sort it out. Between the hangover from last night and the adrenaline coursing through my veins, nothing made sense. I couldn't speak and was only vaguely aware that Hall's partner was talking to me.

"Do you understand?"

"Understand what?"

"Do you understand your rights?"

I stared at him blankly.

"Listen to me." Makowiak began, "You have the right to remain silent. You have the right to an attorney."

My mind tuned him out as I watched Hall and another police officer begin to rip through the cabin. I forced myself to relax. They could look all they want. My Valium and a couple of baggies of marijuana were stashed down in the bilge, and unless they tore the boat completely apart, they would never find them. I was only worried that Marci might have left some shit lying around in the open. I'd hate to end up in jail on drug charges because the cops made a mistake about who killed Carmen.

"Do you understand your rights?"

"Yes, I understand them." I'd seen enough cop shows to know the Miranda warning by heart. "I didn't murder Carmen. This is fucking ridiculous."

Kendyll Hall stood directly in my face, and said, "You can tell us all about it down at the station."

* * *

The hard plastic chair felt wonderful. My hangover was killing me, and the bastards had not given me a moment's peace since we arrived at the Sunset Beach Police station. First, I was dumped into a holding cell with some of the sleaziest human beings I had ever met. If those guys were indicative of the type of roommates I would have in jail, then I thought I would rather be dead. I couldn't even find a place where I actually wanted to sit. Then, the booking process was an exercise in humiliation. Fingerprints, blood and urine samples, pictures, a process overseen by county personnel lacking any feeling, save disgust. I shuddered at the memory.

My attention turned to my immediate surroundings. The room where I sat was as devoid of emotion as the booking personnel. A door occupied one wall of the eight by ten foot beige room, while a long mirror occupied the opposite wall. In between, a six-foot long beige table was surrounded by three off-white, hard plastic chairs. I was told to sit in the corner chair facing the mirror. I hadn't been allowed to speak with anyone. They kept telling me that I would get my chance, so I had kept my mouth shut.

Suddenly, the door opened and Detective Mark Makowiak entered the room. He stood at the head of the table and said in a friendly voice. "Do you want a drink?"

"Sure, I'll take a Budweiser." I was only half kidding. The longer I sat, the harder the hangover. I was shaking inside and out and would dearly love a drink to calm my nerves. I placed my hands flat on the table so he wouldn't see them shake.

"Very funny. I'll get you a soda if you'd like."

"What I'd like is to get out of here. I didn't have anything to do with what happened to Carmen. I'd like to know who really killed her myself."

"Then we're all on the same side," a female voice chimed in from the doorway. Detective Kendyll Hall stood in the doorway, smiling at me, resplendent in a short black skirt and white blouse.

My first thought upon seeing Hall was to wonder how anyone who looked that good could have such a black heart. Don't trust her for a second was my second thought. "I didn't do anything."

"We'll let you tell your story soon. But first answer a few simple questions?"

I remained silent, annoyed at the interruption.

"Would you like that soda?" Makowiak asked.

"Sure. Thanks." I leaned back into the uncomfortable chair, determined to rise above it all. My arrest was obviously a mistake, and I figured that if I cooperated I could get out of there. After all, I *wanted* to help them catch Carmen's real killer.

Hall came all the way into the room and stood near the end of the table. She flipped open a white manila folder and shuffled around some papers before she asked, "Do you live at 124 First Street here in Sunset Beach with a woman named Marci Glass?"

"Yes."

"Is she your girlfriend?"

"Yes."

"Is the Coconut Hut your favorite place to drink?"

"Yes."

"Do you drink a lot?"

I didn't understand what any of the personal questions had to with Carmen's murder, and I was becoming increasingly annoyed about everyone asking about my drinking. "That's none of your business."

"Do you think being drunk is an excuse for criminal actions."

"No." I answered truthfully. I was about to give her a piece of my mind, when we were interrupted by the return of Makowiak. I glared at her silently.

"Why don't you cool your heels for a minute and drink your soda?" Makowiak set the twenty ounce plastic bottle of orange soda on the table and slid it towards me. I wondered how he knew I liked orange soda. "We have to take care of few things, but we'll be back shortly. Then maybe we can get to the bottom of this."

I accepted the soda with a shrug.

Without another word, the two left the room. I sat alone at the table sipping on the orange soda, wondering how in the hell I got into such a mess, and afraid that I would never escape in one piece.

* * *

My bladder has seen better days, years of drinking beer and whiskey has taken its toll, and by the time the two detectives returned an hour and a half later, I had to piss something awful. My paranoia meter registered near the top because I was sure that my discomfort was the whole point behind the large orange soda. "It's about time," I said as the door opened.

Makowiak stepped into room first and asked, "About time for what?"

"You know for what, you son of a bitch. I need to go to the bathroom."

"Then play nice, and I'll take you."

Kendyll Hall said nothing. She stood just inside the door with a silly smirk on her face. I wanted to lay her out right there, but I decided I would keep my mouth shut, at least until I could relieve myself.

"Go ahead, Mark. Take Mister Long to the bathroom. I'll get settled here."

"Okay, Kendyll. Come on, Mister Long."

Innocent until proven guilty was something the courts believed in, but it did not seem to be the order of the day for my two detective friends. I was growing quite tired of the humiliation. As we walked down the hall towards the bathroom, I wondered if I would actually be able to go. I didn't like the idea of someone watching over me. "Do you have to come in with me?"

"No. I'll wait out here in the hall for you."

It felt really good to get up and walk, and even better to empty my bladder. I was grateful that my captors hadn't kept me waiting much longer. As I washed my hands, I studied the face in the mirror. I looked as bad as those other guys in the holding cell. My entire face seemed to sag. The longish, blond hair was all knotted and tangled like I hadn't run a comb through it for days. The blue eyes were all red and bloodshot. Very patriotic, I thought, red, white and blue eyes. The alcohol was killing me. I began to think that Arthur was right. I was every bit as out of control as Marci, and I needed to do something about it. What a strange place for a moment of clarity. I vowed that I would cut down on the drinking tonight, maybe only four or five beers after I got out of the police station to calm the shakes. I ran cold water over my hands and face, and then fought with the towel machine.

"Do you all really think that I killed Carmen?" I asked Makowiak when I returned to the hall.

"That's what were here to find out."

"Fair enough."

Back in my seat, I felt much better and ready to get on with the interview. Makowiak sat in the chair across the table from me, while Hall sat in a chair on the same side of the table facing me. I glanced into the mirror on the opposite wall, sure that we weren't alone.

"Are you ready to answer a few questions, Mister Long?" Hall asked before leaning over to switch on a digital voice recorder. "We're going to record your statement." She looked to me for acknowledgement. I nodded.

"Is your name Mason Prophet Long?" She asked.

"Yes."

"Are you talking to us voluntarily?"

"Yes."

"Remember, you can ask for a lawyer at any time and we will stop the interview. You found the body of Carmen Lopez in her home last evening. Is that correct?"

"Yes."

"Why were you there?"

"You know why." I was trying hard not to get annoyed, but Kendyll Hall had a way of making me angry.

"Answer the questions. You are trying to help? Aren't you?"

"I went to Carmen's house to pick her up and take her to TIA."

"The airport?"

"Yes. The airport."

"She was dead when you got there?"

"It looked to me like she'd been dead for awhile."

"The autopsy suggests that Carmen Lopez was strangled to death." Hall stopped and flipped through several sheets of paper in front of her before settling on one. "She died at some time during the middle of the previous night, probably in the wee hours of Friday morning. Do you know anything about that?"

"No."

"Where were you early Friday morning? Say between the

hours of midnight and six AM?"

Hall looked directly into my eyes. I glanced behind me to Makowiak who had remained silent through the interview so far. "Answer the question, Mister Long. We need to see if we can rule you out."

Or hang me, I thought, but I didn't see any reason to not answer their questions truthfully. I was sure that they had talked to Marci and Arthur by now and knew all the answers anyway. Unfortunately, my lack of memory was not going to add much to what they already knew.

"Let's start around midnight. Where were you around midnight?" Hall continued the interrogation.

"I was at the Coconut Hut with Marci."

"Were you drinking?"

"Of course, I was drinking."

"A lot?"

"Yes."

"Were you drunk?"

"Yes." Her line of questioning sure made me look bad, but I had to be truthful. The drinking was the obvious cause of my blackout.

Hall stopped a moment and wrote something onto the sheet of paper on the table in front of her. I saw her glance, first at Makowiak who remained motionless, and then at the mirror. I wondered who was behind the mirror. "What time did you leave the bar?"

"I think it was around closing time."

"What do you mean, you think?"

"I think. I don't know for sure. The bartender said that

Marci and I left the bar right before closing time."

"You don't remember?"

Embarrassment and humiliation took control of my biological functions and caused my face to turn very red and hot. Behind the heat, fear and doubt took control of my emotions. In response to the fear and doubt, anger raised its ugly head, and I almost lost control. But after my moment of clarity in the bathroom, I realized that I only had myself to blame for my situation, and I was the only one who could do anything to change it. I reaffirmed the vow to myself to quit drinking, or at least to slow down. "No, I don't remember." I replied in a barely audible voice.

"What?"

"No, I don't remember. I don't remember anything past shooting pool with my friend Arthur around 1 o'clock."

"How convenient." Makowiak piped in from across the table.

"Really, Mason, you expect us to believe that." Hall echoed his sentiments.

"Honest, I went into a blackout. I don't remember shit. Tell me that you've never gone into a blackout."

Hall remained silent. She scribbled a few notes onto the sheet of paper, all the while shaking her head back and forth. When she was done writing, she sat staring at me while tapping the pencil on the desk with her right hand. "What's the next thing you remember?" She finally asked.

"Waking up in the hammock on our back porch around noon."

"That's a lot of time unaccounted for," Makowiak stated

the obvious.

"You all talked to Marci. You already know what I'm telling you."

"True," Hall said, "but we want to hear it in your own words. She said you went out somewhere in the middle of the night. Where did you go?"

That was the million dollar question. The fear and doubt would haunt me until I could find the answer. "I don't remember anything. I don't even know if I did go out. Marci was very fucked up. She may be mistaken in her recollection." I was sure that Marci had admitted being drunk. For all I knew, she could be wrong, and for all they knew, she could be wrong. They didn't have any real answers at this point.

"But you don't remember staying at home either?"

"No."

"You don't remember anything?" Frustration had entered her voice.

"How many times are you going to ask me? Read my lips. I don't remember."

"You expect us to believe that?"

"It's the truth."

"You killed a woman in cold blood, and you don't even remember?"

"I didn't kill Carmen."

"We have your prints all over the house."

"Of course you do. I told you I had been there many times before," I interrupted.

"And as soon as the DNA test results come back we will link the semen we found in her body to you."

The statement hit me between the eyes like a thunderbolt. Did I do it with Carmen that night? We tried to never do it without a condom, but maybe we were in a hurry. I forced myself to slow down. I didn't know for sure whether I was there or not. One thing I did know for sure was that police would lie to get people to confess to crimes they didn't commit. "What are you talking about?" I protested. "I don't remember going to Carmen's that night."

"Why should we believe you? You lied."

"I haven't lied. I told you I don't remember."

"You lied about your relationship to Ms. Lopez. Your girlfriend told us that you were over there screwing around with her all of the time." Hall stopped to let the last statement sink in.

I wanted to wipe the smile from her face with the back of my hand. I didn't know what to say. It was a surprise to me that Marci knew about Carmen. I didn't think she did. No wonder she was so angry with me last night. "Okay, so I lied. I didn't think that my sex life was any of your business."

"Do you always cheat on your women?"

"That's none of your business either." Who was this woman? Her insistence on making me look bad seemed personal.

"It is my business. What else have you lied about?"

"I would never do something like that to Carmen." I defended myself. "I couldn't do that to anyone."

"I believe you." Hall leaned forward and scooted her chair closer to me. "It was unintentional. She told you no. You got mad and wanted to teach her a lesson."

"What are you talking about?" My voice had risen several octaves and decibels above normal.

"You accidentally killed her. You didn't mean to do it."

Her lines about wanting to find the truth, about wanting to get to the bottom of things, about wanting to find the real killer, were all part of an act. How stupid could I have been? I should have known and kept my mouth shut. True to her past form, Hall was looking to throw me in jail for Carmen's murder without any proof one way or the other. I needed to put an end to this interrogation. "Whoa, wait a minute here." I broke in, tapping the top of my left fingers with my right hand in a time-out gesture. "We're done talking. I want my lawyer."

CHAPTER 7

Thirty minutes later, my big brother arrived to save me from myself. Poco walked into the interrogation room like he owned the place. Dressed in an expensive, tailored, light gray suit, crisp white shirt, and pink tie, he looked the part of the high priced southern lawyer. I wasn't too thrilled with the pink tie. He was carrying a large yellow envelope, which he placed on the table. "Here's your stuff," he said.

"Thanks for getting here so fast," I said while opening the envelope to peek inside.

"Arthur's here too. He's waiting down stairs. I called him right after you and I hung up."

"Good." I felt better. The cavalry had arrived. But the good feelings were short-lived.

"What the hell have you gotten yourself into now, little brother?" Poco pronounced the words *little brother* with as much sarcasm and condescension that he could muster. The tone of his voice hit a nerve that had been raw for years. We were not very loving siblings. For at least the past five years, we were of the fighting variety, and I never talked much better to him than he talked to me. "Never mind the rhetorical question. You're always in trouble," he said. "Grab your stuff and let's get out of here."

I took my wallet and put it in my back pocket. The keys and cell phone ended up in my right front pocket. I quickly counted the cash, a hundred and thirty-five dollars, folded the bills, and stashed the wad in my left front pocket. "They think I murdered a woman named Carmen Lopez." I used the last name because I didn't think Poco knew Carmen.

"Don't talk, Mason."

"I didn't do it, Poco."

Poco stepped in close and grabbed me by my right arm, squeezing as hard as he could before saying in a quiet voice, "Seriously, little brother. Not another fucking word about anything until we're out of here." The condescension had disappeared from his voice. My big brother was here to protect me.

I took a final look into the envelope, which by now was completely empty. I could hardly believe that they were turning me loose. Poco must have worked his magic. "All right, Poco. I'm good to go." I threw the now empty envelope onto the table.

Poco led the way from the room and out into the second floor hall. We made our way quickly towards the exit at the front of the station, where the hallway opened into a high-ceilinged atrium. At the top of the stone staircase, I stopped Poco and pointed to Arthur standing at the bottom.

"Arthur's a good man, Mason. Don't drag him down with

you."

"I have no intentions of harming Arthur."

"I know you don't have bad intentions, but shit seems to happen around you."

No truer words were ever spoken. I seemed to attract the worst possible people, like the smallest kid on the playground attracts the bully. By the time we were halfway down the stairs, a very pretty bully appeared. I tapped Poco on the arm and pointed to the woman approaching Arthur. "That's Detective Hall," I informed him.

"I know who she is. You couldn't have done worse if you tried."

We continued down the stairs. As soon as we got close, Hall said to me in a low voice, "I know you did it."

"Not a word, Mason," Poco warned.

"It's just a matter of time, Mason. You'll rot in jail with the other killers."

"Talk to my lawyer." I replied, pointing to Poco. We slowed, but did not stop, so Arthur and Hall fell in step. The four us kept moving towards the door.

Poco turned his head long enough to say, "You're overstepping your bounds, Detective. If the district attorney thought he had a case against my client, he would have charged him with a crime."

"We will meet again," she said, not to be denied the final word.

Hall stopped dogging us as we neared the two glass front doors. We crashed through the doors and into the street, never looking back. Once we were far enough into the parking lot and out of earshot, we stopped. I took a deep breath of the salt air, determined to remain free.

"Hall wants your ass," Arthur said.

"No shit," I replied, putting my arm on Arthur's shoulder. "I'm glad you're here, man."

"I wouldn't miss it for the world," he grinned good-naturedly, "if it wasn't so scary, it would be funny. She's not going to let it go."

"What are you going to do now?" Poco asked.

"I have to get over to Croc's bar and talk to Marci." Marci had left several messages on my cell phone while I was otherwise occupied in the police station. Breaking up might not be as hard as I thought. She had mumbled something about money and having her bags packed. "Can you take me over to Croc's, Arthur?"

"Sure. Are you coming with us, Poco?" Arthur asked.

"No. You two go ahead. Come over to my place when you're done. Nancy will make us some supper."

"But . . ." I started to protest.

"No buts. We need to talk, and you haven't seen your niece in a while. I don't know why, but Jenny loves her uncle Mason."

"When?" I capitulated. There was a great big soft spot in my heart for Jenny.

"Say an hour? You're invited too, Arthur." Poco turned away and headed across the parking lot.

Marci worked as a bartender at a place called Croc's, located directly across Sunset Pass from the marina where my boat was slipped. On the nights when they had live bands playing,

I could hear the music from the deck of my boat. Normally, I enjoyed having a few drinks at Croc's, but things were anything but normal, and I was not looking forward to this meeting. Luckily, the place was nearly empty. Two guys sat by themselves at the far end of the bar. I could see Marci refreshing their beers. Arthur and I took seats at the opposite end. I waited patiently while Marci finished with the other patrons and headed in our direction. "Hi, Arthur." Marci said, ignoring me entirely.

"Hi, Marci. You're looking good today."

"Thanks, Arthur. Too bad your friend here isn't more like you. You need to find yourself a good woman."

"Maybe, you two would like to go out after . . ." I didn't know how to finish the sentence, so I shut up.

Marci made an exaggerated survey of Arthur, looking him over from head to toe. "That might not be a bad idea," she finally said.

Arthur never said a word. He wore his usual embarrassed, sheepish face. The one that appeared every time a woman teased him. I kept my mouth shut too, figuring that I would let her have her fun. In break up situations, I always found it easier to let the woman run her course. Eventually, Marci would get around to the task at hand. "Can we at least get a couple of beers?" If I had to listen to a ration of crap, I wanted to cop a buzz at the same time.

"Sure." Marci walked to middle of the bar and dug two cold long necks from the cooler. She opened both beers, came back and set one in front of each of us. "They're on me, gents. Call them goodbye beers, if you will."

We'll get to the heart of the matter now. I took a great big swallow of the cold beer. My resolution about cutting down on my drinking may have to wait until tomorrow. I had too much going on today.

"Goodbye?" Arthur mumbled.

"Yes, goodbye. My bags are packed and I'm ready to fly." The front door opened flooding the room with sunlight. A second Croc's bartender came in. I couldn't remember her name, but I'd seen her before. It was hard to forget the massive number of freckles and bright red hair. They must be expecting the Saturday evening rush soon. "Isn't that right, Erin." Marci asked the bartender who had just arrived.

"What's that, Marci?"

"I said my bags are packed and I'm ready to fly. I gave John notice last night, didn't I?"

"She sure did, and I'm not too happy about it. I'll miss you, girlfriend."

"I'll miss you, too," she said to Erin, who moved behind the bar, ready for work. "Can you cover the bar by yourself for a few?"

Erin looked at the two lonesome drinkers at the end of the bar and said, "I think I can handle it."

"Come on Mason, let's go in back and get this over with," Marci said and grabbed me by the hand.

"You're way too cheerful about this, Marci," I said as we settled into a booth near the back of the room.

"Seriously, Mason. You're a shit, and I don't want to be a couple anymore."

Feeling that I had to defend myself, I said, "I'm not that

bad. Maybe, I can do better." As soon as the words came out of my mouth, I worried that it sounded like I wanted to patch things up, which of course was light years from the truth.

"Do you really think we would have a chance?" She was baiting me.

"No, I guess not."

"I have to go, Mason. And you know what, it's not all your fault. I could probably even forgive you, I'm such an ass sometimes."

"Yes, but you've got such a likable ass."

She laughed. "We did have some great times on that score, didn't we? I'll remember them always. I'll remember you always."

"Me too, Marci."

"Oh bullshit, Mason. You won't remember who I was the day after I leave, which by the way will be tonight after I get off of work. I really do have my bags packed."

"That's a bit drastic, Ms. Drama Queen."

"It's like I started to say. This is not only about you. How did that old song go?" Marci hummed a few bars of something I couldn't make out. "Oh, yeah," she said. "I'm tired of you. I'm tired of myself. I'm tired of this town, and I'm going to get the fuck out of here while I still can."

"I can't say that's a bad idea."

"You see? Even you agree."

I had to admit she was right. We hadn't really been a couple for a long time. Most times, I didn't see the breakup coming, but this time it had been obvious. "Where are you going to go?"

"I don't know. All I know is that I need help. I need to straighten out my life and get free of the alcohol for a while. And if you were smart, you'd do the same thing."

"I wish you the best."

She looked at me cock-eyed.

"I really do. I don't hate you. I actually loved you in my own way."

"Which by the way sucks. No woman wants to compete with other women."

I had nothing further to say on the matter, so I bowed my head and mumbled, "Can I go now?"

"Not yet."

Great. She wasn't through with me yet. I wondered what else I would have to endure before she turned me loose.

"There's the little problem of the three hundred dollars you owe me."

"Shit." I had forgotten all about the money she loaned me to fix the boat a while back. "I don't have that much right now."

"You owe me the money, Mason. You better come up with it. How much do you have?"

I reached into my pocket for the wad of bills. Although my mind had been muddled by my visit to the police station, I seemed to remember that I had a hundred and thirty-five. "Here's a hundred and thirty-five. It's all I got."

She snatched the wad of bills from my hand and stuck them in her back pocket before saying, "That's not true. You have a hundred stashed in the freezer."

"You know about that?"

"Sure. I know more than you think I do."

Damn. The woman had known about Carmen. She knew about the money I had stashed in the freezer, but at least she didn't seem to know about the money I had hidden in the bedroom closet under some loose boards. What else did she know about? "Why didn't you take it?"

"Look I don't hate you either, Mason. I don't want bad feelings. I'm all about trying to get off the booze and find myself. Give me the hundred later tonight." That was Marci. She was as honorable as they came.

"Okay, but that only makes a little over two hundred."

"I'll take the rest in drugs. I'll need something to get through the withdrawal. I know you have some Valium and some pot stashed on the boat."

I saw no sense in trying to deny it. "Deal."

"I knew you'd come through."

The truth of the matter was that I did owe her three hundred dollars, and despite everything, I still liked her. If some of my stash helped to get her where she wanted to go, then so be it. "What time do you get off?"

"Closing time."

"You're really going to leave in the middle of the night?"

"That's the plan right now."

"I'll meet you at the boat."

* * *

The blond projectile leaped squarely into my lap, squealing with glee. Before I could react, a knee was planted hard into my crotch while two arms squeezed me tenderly in an affectionate bear hug. "Read to me, Uncle Mason."

"Sure, honey. Go get your basketball book."

"Okay," said Jenny. The eight year old leaped back off my lap and hit the floor running. I marveled at the energy of the kid, wishing that I could grab some of it for myself. "Be right back."

I could at least tolerate the children's sports book about the girl basketball player. The day had been tough enough without having to read a bunch of sappy, girlie crap. Poco poked his head through the doorway to the Florida room and said, "Dinner will be ready in a little while, Mason. You want something to drink? A beer?"

"Sure. That'd be great."

"I thought Arthur was coming back with you."

"He said he had to go over to cab company and take care of some kind of emergency."

"Emergency?"

"Yes, but don't worry. Everything is an emergency at the Tropical Cab Company. I bet one of the other dispatchers called in sick."

"Too bad he couldn't make it. I like having Arthur around. I'll send the beer in with the little one."

As my big brother disappeared back into the house, I thought about how much I wanted to thank him. For the moment, I was free. When I first arrived at the house, he explained to me that the police didn't have enough evidence to charge me with the crime, but that I would remain a Person of Interest, whatever the hell that meant. I didn't trust the police for a second, especially that damn Kendyll Hall, but Poco had come through in the clutch. Maybe, my predicament would have the beneficial side effect of bringing my brother and I closer together.

Jenny came bounding back into the room, her book in one hand a beer in the other. "Here's your beer, Uncle Mason."

I snatched her off the floor lifted her high into the air before sitting her on the sofa next to me. I took the beer from her before giving her a big hug. "How's school going, Jenny?" I popped the top and took a couple of drinks while Jenny rambled on about her teachers and her classmates, I wondered if my life would ever be normal. Opening the book, I settled in and began to read.

* * *

"Daddy, I don't want to eat anymore. I want to go play with Rusty," Jenny said, as she pushed the peas around her plate with her fork. Rusty was a raggedy old rust-colored stuffed bear that I had given her for her last birthday.

"Jenny, finish your dinner," Poco insisted.

"It's okay, Poco. Let her go," Nancy Long interrupted.

Jenny Long bolted from the table and was out the door before her mother finished the sentence. They all shared an easy laugh.

"She is quick," I said fondly, enjoying the peace and camaraderie of my family for the first time in a long time.

The proud parents beamed. The Long family lived on Isla del Luna in a very expensive home, fitting for one of the most powerful families in town. Poco set up practice in Sunset Beach after graduation the same year that my father and I moved here. He married Nancy a year later, and Jenny arrived the year after that. Nancy Long, nee Parker, born and raised in Sunset Beach, was the rare native daughter. The beautiful, blonde psychiatrist knew so many people, was so well loved, that she was seriously considering running for mayor in the next election.

"You're so great with Jenny, Mason. I can't help but think you should have some kids of your own," Nancy said.

"Hold on, Nancy. I'm not sure I'm ready for that. I'm not much of a caregiver."

"You're never completely ready for kids," Poco chimed in.

"I'd need a wife first," I said, laughing easily. "My life is in such turmoil now." I stopped laughing.

"We believe in you, Mason. Have faith," Nancy said strongly before changing the subject back to my love life. "What about Marci? She seems nice."

I really appreciated my sister-in-law not wanting to talk about the murder and the police. It was nice to know that there was someone who believed in you, even when you didn't have that much faith in yourself. But I didn't relish the conversation she had decided to pursue in its place. "No, Marci and I are history. In fact, we made it official an hour or so ago."

"That's too bad, Mason. I kind of liked her too," Poco said.

"Me too," I began. "But we're not good for each other. She's got more addictions than I do." I didn't want to go into the whole truth.

"I find that hard to believe."

"Don't be so hard on Mason, Poco."

"Come on, little brother, you have to admit you have a problem before you can do something about it." Concern was evident in his voice.

"You're right, Poco. I am going to try and take it easier with the drinking."

Poco opened his mouth to reply, but Nancy cut him off. I suspected that the reply would have been unworthy of his new role as my concerned big brother. "You need to find yourself a more normal woman. Someone who can help you build a normal life," she said.

"That would be nice."

"Do you ever meet any nice women?" Poco asked.

"Believe it or not, I have met someone nice. The idea took me by surprise last night."

"That's the way it happens," Nancy said. "It happens when you least expect it."

* * *

After the conversation over dinner, my mood had improved tremendously. Poco and I retired to his office with a couple of beers and were sipping them silently. I scanned the book titles on the shelf nearest me. To my surprise, most of the books were hard cover science fiction novels. "Light reading?" I pointed to the books.

"You bet. Occasionally, I need to escape from the law

books."

Sadly, it dawned on me how far my brother and I had drifted apart over the past few years. I had no idea that he liked science fiction. I vowed that I would never let that happen again. I seemed to be full of vows today. "Thanks for your help, Poco."

"No problem, Mason. You are my brother, although sometimes I think you forget that."

"You too."

"I'll concede that. Maybe we can change that around."

"And become brothers again? I think I'd like that, Poco. Dad would have liked it too."

"Even though he left the boat to you and not me."

Same old Poco, I thought immediately. I started to say something, but he interrupted me.

"I'm only kidding you, Mason. I know you appreciate the boat more than I ever could."

"Do you mean that?"

"I do. And don't take this the wrong way. If I wanted a boat, I could run out and buy one. I'm not that interested."

"You didn't always feel that way."

"No. I was jealous for a long time. I guess I'm getting older and wiser."

I smiled and nodded before stretching out my hand to my brother. He smiled back and grasped both of my hands in his. We kept contact for a few seconds before letting go. My brother and I were on the road back. "What do I do now, Poco?"

"Nothing. You didn't have anything to do with Ms.

Lopez's murder, and the police really have nothing."

"What will they do?"

"That's a different question. They will keep you as a Person of Interest, as they call it, but they can't keep arresting you without evidence."

"I don't trust the police for a minute."

"And you shouldn't, especially that woman detective Hall. She was acting on her own when they arrested you."

"How can she get away with that?"

"Police detectives have a lot of power."

"Yeah, and I bet a lot of innocent people have been convicted because of it."

"I won't let that happen, Mason. When all the evidence is in, you'll be cleared."

"I hope so." I was not as convinced as Poco, and I'm sure my face reflected the uncertainty. "Will I have talk with them again?"

"Not if you don't want to, but in the interest of putting an end to the matter, you should probably cooperate. Police don't like it when someone is not cooperative."

"I don't mind cooperating, but I don't know what else I can tell them."

"Do you remember anything about that night?"

"No."

"Then I'd cut back on this shit," he said and raised his can of beer to eye level, "before anything else bad happens."

CHAPTER 8

"Coquinas," I grabbed Annie by the hand and pointed to the commotion in the sand.

"Keynotes?"

The flurry of activity continued until the hundreds of tiny shellfish that had washed up in a wave had buried themselves back in the sand. Life on the gulf coast offered unlimited opportunities to stay in awe of Mother Nature. I never tired of watching the show. "C-O-Q-U-I-N-A, Coquina. They're little shellfish. They don't want to be exposed to predators."

"Wow, they're wonderful."

"They don't have shellfish on Long Island?"

"Nothing like these."

Turned out that Annie Jones hailed from a town called Wrightsville on Long Island, wherever that might be. She was twenty-eight years old and divorced once. She moved down to Florida for the beaches and sunshine, and although she wouldn't admit to it, I think the whole ex-husband thing had been a contributing factor to the move. We had covered a lot of ground as well as sand during our walk along the beach. I decided that I liked her a lot, and it appeared that it was mutual. "Let's sit for awhile," I suggested.

"I thought about you all day."

"You did?"

"And most of the night." She blushed and looked down as she spoke.

"I've been thinking about you too."

"I'm glad you decided to come by the Hut, Mason."

I had enjoyed my dinner with the Longs, but by the time Poco and I had finished off our after dinner beers, I was ready to escape the family nest, so I had him drop me off at the Coconut Hut. I was pleasantly surprised to find Annie waiting for me. Apparently, she had heard of my arrest and wanted to help if she could. Rather than try and talk in the noisy bar, we decided to take a walk on the beach and watch the sunset. "I bet they don't have sunsets like this on Long Island."

"Of course not, silly. The beaches face the other way."

"Good point." Sunset Beach faces due west, and the sunsets are magnificent, hence the name. We made ourselves comfortable in the sand and watched the show. Far off clouds hovered above the horizon causing the great ball of fire to grow redder and redder as it dropped into the sea. "Red sky at night, sailor's delight."

"Red sky in morning, sailors in mourning," Annie replied.

I laughed before gently correcting her. "Red sky in morning, sailors take warning."

"Oh, right."

"If you listen closely, you can hear the hiss when the sun sinks into the gulf."

"I can hear it." She giggled and wiggled in closer.

I wrapped my arm around her shoulders. Intellectually, I thought that this thing with Annie was moving way too fast. Marci and I hadn't yet completely ended it, although she'd be gone tonight, and I felt like I should also be mourning Carmen, at least to some degree. But emotionally and physically, Annie was touching places in my heart and soul that I didn't know existed, and if I ever tell that to some of my friends, they would tell me that they heard that before. The bell rang up at the concession stand, located immediately north of us. Tradition demanded that someone ring the bell as the sun sets into the ocean.

"This is nice, Mason."

"It's beautiful."

"No, I mean us."

"Yes, it is," I said and held her tighter. The hell with all that intellectual crap. Life is too short to pass up on something wonderful for fear of what other people might say. I was pleasantly contemplating how good our lives together might be when I felt her hand tug on the waistband of my shorts. Before I could react, she dumped something cold and wet into my shorts, not at all what I had hoped for. "What the fuck?" I mumbled, not knowing what else to do.

Annie slapped me right above the crotch, hoping to squish whatever the hell she had slipped into my pants. Without missing a beat, she was on her feet and running down the beach. I reached into my pants to find a handful of damp coral that had washed up onto the beach. I threw the coral down on the sand, and took off after her. "I'm going to get you," I yelled after her. I could hear her laughter, and it warmed my heart. By now she had quite a lead, but even out of shape, I was still pretty fast. I gained on her steadily, and within a minute or so, I was on top of her, tackling her in the sand. I rolled her over onto her back and straddled her. Pinning her arms above her head, I kissed her on the lips. Hungrily, she kissed back, locking onto my lips with great passion. I broke free for air and was going to kiss her again, but when I tried, she turned her head to the side. "What's the matter? Is my breath that bad?" I asked trying to make light of her reaction.

"No, Mason. I think you're great, but I'm not ready to take that next step while you're still living with another woman."

"Not to worry, Annie. Marci and I called it quits this evening, but I have to meet her later tonight to pay her some money I owe her. By tomorrow I will be completely free of Marci Glass and we can do whatever we want."

"Then I guess we should do something tomorrow to celebrate," she said.

"Like in a date?"

"Yes."

* * *

Back at the Coconut Hut, I put a couple more beers into me and was beginning to feel human again. I didn't know how many beers I had drank by that point. I no longer cared. Getting arrested for Carmen's murder had put the fear of God into me, but I was starting to put that memory in one of those nice little dusty places in the brain, where bad memories go to die. Pleasant Annie thoughts had begun to supplant the bad Carmen thoughts, and the bad Marci thoughts for that matter. The bar wasn't too busy for a Saturday night, so Annie and I could talk freely while she worked. She sat on the stool at the far end of the bar, while I sat on the stool next to her, enjoying her company. I hadn't felt that at ease with a woman for a long time. Two dudes that I had seen before, but couldn't remember there names, were shooting pool, and a bald guy that I didn't recognize sat at the far end of the bar, dressed in a white, sleeveless tee shirt. The only other person in the place was the owner Lenny DeCarlo, who sat in the booth behind us. That was it.

"Give me another drink." The bald guy yelled at Annie.

Dutifully, Annie rose from her seat and grabbed a beer from the cooler on her way to the other end of the bar. She took an empty from in front of Baldy and replaced it with the new one. He grabbed her wrist as she set the bottle down. I felt myself twitch when she snatched her hand back. They exchanged a few heated words that I couldn't hear, but she seemed okay when she returned to her bar stool. "What's up with that?" I asked her once she had settled down.

"Nothing, Mason. The guy is drunk. I probably should cut him off."

"Want me to take care of it?" I figured the answer would be no, but I thought I would offer.

"No. I appreciate you asking, but that is my job." She turned around in her stool and asked Lenny, "Should I cut him off after this one?"

"Yes, and if he gives you any trouble. I'll take care of it," DeCarlo answered.

Annie turned back to me. "See, it'll be fine." She didn't seem all that worried about the man. Her interest was in me. I couldn't help but think that Annie was different than any other woman I had ever met. She actually seemed to care. Most of the others let me do whatever I wanted as long as I didn't cause them too much trouble. They were all about themselves. I was betting that Annie would have a say in almost everything I did from this point forward. But you know what, I was thinking that was a good thing.

"What was it like growing up on Long Island?" I asked her.

"Cold."

"That's it. Cold?"

"Cold seems to invade most of my memories. I guess that's why I'm here in Florida."

"You better like the heat, living here."

"Even in the summer at Jones Beach, the water was cold. I always seemed to be shivering."

"I won't even go in the water until it warms up to at least the low eighties."

The man at the end of the bar interrupted our conversation once again. "Give me a fucking shooter."

I tensed, but Annie put her hand on my arm and said, "Don't worry, I'll deal with him."

"You sure?"

"Yes."

She approached the man slowly with a smile on her face. She talked to him quietly for a minute, before turning around and heading back in my direction. I noticed she didn't give him another drink. She stopped and stood facing me from across the bar.

"What did you do? Cut him off?"

"Yes. I told him to finish his beer and leave."

Suddenly, a shiny metal object rocketed through my field of vision. The round, chrome ashtray hit Annie squarely in the side of the head, dropping her to her knees behind the bar. It took me a couple of seconds to register what had happened as I rose instinctively into a defensive stance. I quickly took stock of the situation. Lenny DeCarlo had raced to Annie's side and was helping her to her feet behind the bar. Once I knew she was okay, my attention turned to the source of the attack. The bald man stood at the opposite end of the bar, shouting profanities at Annie. The scene slowed down as I watched the man reach for a second ashtray. I could see the sweat beads shining on the top of his shaved head. A single drop of sweat rolled down the left side of his forehead as I launched myself in his direction. The man's eyes widened as he realized I was headed his way. Until that moment, I guessed he believed that his actions would be without consequence.

He was wrong.

Now, I don't think of myself as a particularly violent person, but I try to live by a certain chivalrous code of conduct, and if that code is violated, then justice must be served. Men are not allowed to attack defenseless women in my world, especially in my hang out. When Baldy fully understood what I had in mind, I could see him trying to make a choice between his only two options at that point: stand and fight or turn and run. He turned and bolted out the front door, knocking down a woman customer who was trying to enter at the same time. He swept her out his way as if she were a piece of garbage. I was thoroughly annoyed.

I reached the door a second later and helped the woman to her feet. "You okay?"

"I'm okay. What the hell is going on?"

I didn't have time to answer her. Annie had cut the man off and refused to serve him any more drinks, but that was no reason to hurt her. The trouble was that he had decided to hurt her anyway, so I was determined to hurt him in return. An eye for eye was what the bible said. Once outside in the parking lot, I spied Baldy standing at the side of a beat-up, old red pick-up truck trying to open the driver's side door. I was determined to reach him before he could get inside the truck and make good on his escape. When he looked up and saw me bearing down on him, he dropped his keys.

I had him now.

"Son of a bitch," he said to the keys. To me, he shouted, "I've got a gun in here."

The statement sealed his fate. I didn't think it was true, but I wasn't about to let him get to a gun and shoot me with it. I'd beat him to a pulp first. "Too bad you dropped your keys then." I spat and quickened my pace. I was on him before the sentence had completely rolled off my tongue. I hit him hard with my right fist in a downward motion. He fell to his knees with both hands on the pavement. I stomped as hard as I could on his right hand, trying to make sure that he couldn't hold a gun, let alone shoot one. He grabbed his hand and screamed. I didn't know if I had actually broken it, but I was sure that I had hurt him bad. The thought made me feel good. This guy deserved what he got. I kicked him as hard as I could in the side and rolled him over.

"Please, man. I didn't mean to hit her. I was only trying to scare her."

"Well, you fucked up, didn't you?" The man was a sleaze, and I knew he was lying. He had every intention of hurting Annie with that ashtray. I kicked him two more times as hard as I could and probably would have really hurt him, except that suddenly someone grabbed me around the middle in a bear hug, pinning my arms to my sides. The hold didn't include my legs, so I kicked Baldy again as hard as I could.

"He's had enough, Mason. Don't kill him."

Arthur held me tight, dragging me away from the target of my anger. Baldy quickly realized that this was his chance to escape and managed to get to his feet, gingerly grasping his keys with his damaged hand. I watched helplessly as the man opened the door to the truck and climbed in, locking it behind him. At that point, I hoped that he had been lying about the gun. "Let me go, Arthur. The son of bitch deserves a beating." I strained against his grip.

"Let it go, Mason. The dude's not worth the effort."

Since Arthur had no intention of letting me go, I calmed

myself and decided that he was right. I watched as my nemesis wheeled the truck towards the south entrance of the parking lot without so much as a glance in our direction.

* * *

The flaming torches of the Hut's outside tiki bar beckoned to me like never before. Six yellow, beer-company flags waved straight in the wind, while the palm trees danced. The scene reminded me of a medieval warrior's return home from the war, island style of course. Overdramatic is my middle name. Once inside the door, bar owner Lenny DeCarlo greeted me with shouts of congratulations and a pat on the back for a job well done.

"You did good, Mason. That punk deserved to get his ass kicked."

Annie came over and took my hand, seating me at the head of the large bamboo table beneath the thatched roof. The flaming torches cast flickering shadows across our faces. "What does my hero desire?" Annie asked, smiling warmly. She didn't appear to have any lasting effects from the attack, save a round red mark on the side of her face.

"A beer, I guess."

"Anything else? I don't have to work tomorrow." Annie said with a sly grin. "Have you thought about where we can go? On our date."

"I'll go anywhere you want. Do you have something in mind?"

"I want to do something exciting, fun, different."

"That's a tall order."

"I don't want to just hang around a bar.."

I thought about that for a moment. Several things came to mind but I landed on one. "Road trip," I said smiling.

"Road trip?"

"We'll go ride some roller coasters."

Annie clapped her hands and laughed. "Wonderful. Where?"

"We'll go to The Gardens over in Tampa. Will you drive?" If Annie drove, I could drink more.

"Sure, I'll drive."

The idea did sound wonderful. I thought about holding her close on the roller coaster, easing her fears and mine. I smiled and said, "How about that beer?"

"Oh, I forgot. I'm so excited." She ran off for the beer.

Annie wasn't the only one excited. The thought of our date with her had me higher than the alcohol and drugs could ever manage. "Me too." I yelled after her.

Arthur came over and took a seat to my right. His face did not display the same happiness as that of our beautiful bartender.

"What's up, bro?" I asked.

"You're lucky DeCarlo didn't call the police."

"He was glad I kicked the dude's ass. He told me so."

"This time. But five will get you ten, if you guys had wrecked something in this here bar, DeCarlo would be looking for satisfaction through a police report."

I hadn't thought about that. But I rarely think at all when I get that angry.

"One of these days they're going to throw your ass in jail for good."

"Now, Arthur, Look at the joy I've brought to the Coconut Hut. Nobody wants an asshole invading their space and getting away with it."

"That's true, and I agree with you to a point. But someday you're going to go too far, and I don't want to be there to see it, Mason."

"Chill out, Arthur. I appreciate your concern, but everything turned out okay."

I was getting tired of Arthur being right all the time. My last comment did not ring true, even to me. If I were honest with myself, my violent actions would scare the hell out of me. Sometimes I feel so close to the abyss that one more thing could drive me over the edge, so I play along and pretend that all is well. Drink more, bury the anger, drink some more, and bury the fear. That's the ticket. My life had become a roller coaster of short-lived highs and deep down lows.

"Here, eat up." DeCarlo said as he came over and tossed several white bags down on the table. "Roast turkey legs and fries."

The low would have to wait as I realized that I was very hungry. I had to fight Arthur for access to the bag with the turkey legs. I finally snagged one and ripped at it with my teeth, wondering if the heroes of olden days had ridden the same kind of roller coaster.

CHAPTER 9

My daddy always taught me that life had its ups and downs, emphasizing that in order to succeed we must first understand. Then, we must trust in our ability to make the right decision based on that understanding. Very logical, my daddy. I could hear him clearly. "Let's review, Mason." Daddy would say that every time I made a mess of something. The practice had worked very well for me in the past, so I quickly reviewed the events of the day. Starting with my arrest, the day had gone steadily downhill, until Annie intervened and made me realize that there could be good in my life again. The bad times passed eventually, didn't they? And if I focused on the good, cleaned up my act, maybe I could get my life turned around.

The kitchen door slammed shut behind me with a bang, scaring me half to death. I couldn't help but think of how quickly the door was closing on my relationship with Marci. I hated to see things end, but some things needed to come to an end. Mainly, so that you can go out and start something new, try something different, turn your life around. I kept going back to the thought of once again becoming the person I had been while growing up in Colorado: a young man, seeing the world in black and white, the decisions clear, easy.

    I groped for the light, hoping that when I turned it on I didn't have to deal with any bugs. The light came on without incident, but the house appeared lifeless. It's amazing what the lack of a woman's presence will do to a home, even if it had only been a few hours. Things would be different now, Marci-less but Annie-full. Time to put an end to the old life, at least one part of it. My hundred-dollar bill, soon to be Marci's hundred-dollar bill, was stashed in the freezer wrapped in waxed paper and hidden beneath the frozen redfish. I hadn't put the single hundred with the other money I had stashed in the bedroom closet, because I figured it would be easier to get to in an emergency. I was real glad that Marci didn't know about the other hiding place. Being the kind of man not to waste any effort, I figured I would check the refrigerator for beer once I retrieved the money. Unfortunately, the refrigerator proved to be empty.

    As I was contemplating the lack of beer and what to do about it, the light coming in through the kitchen window from the house next door dimmed considerably. I peeked out through the kitchen window. My asshole neighbor must have decided to go to bed and turned off all the lights. His timing couldn't be more perfect. A mischievous grin crossed my face. I was once again a fun-loving teenager at heart, figuring that as long as I was here, I might as well take a few minutes and put the redfish under his porch. I clapped my hands with joy.

The sliver of a moon did not give me away as I snuck around the side of my house, through a gap in the bushes and into the back yard of my neighbor. I tightly clutched the opening of the black plastic garbage bag containing the poor redfish, holding it close to my chest. Unfortunately, the act of doing two things at once, holding onto the plastic bag and walking, had become too much for me. I had drank quite a few shooters after the fight, and in my drunken state, I tripped over my own two feet and fell headlong into one of the palmetto bushes, part of the xerascape that lined the neighbor's walk. Rolling, holding the bag over my head as I tumbled, I landed flat on my back in the grass. I stifled my laughter as best I could, shaking from the effort.

"Damn, that hurt," I whispered and checked the windows above me. No lights came on, so I guessed that I was safe for the moment. I scrambled back to my feet and made my way slowly around to the front of the expensive home. I stopped for a moment, caught my breath, and once again checked the upstairs windows for any sign of activity. There was none. "Up yours, old buddy," I whispered and raised the plastic bag toward the windows. I approached the front porch until I could walk no further, and then on all fours crept through the shrubbery until I could peer into the opening beneath the stairs. I opened the bag and dumped the redfish carcass onto to ground under the stairs. By late morning, the fish would start to stink. I was hoping that my neighbor wouldn't be able to figure out where the smell was coming from for several days.

I laughed silently as I threw the bag under the stairs before backing out through the shrubbery. I stood up straight and took a deep breath of the fresh salt air. Sometimes, justice does prevail. I shook my fist in triumph at the dark windows. Then I thought I'd better get the hell out of there before somebody caught me redfish-handed. The stupid pun set me off again. This time I could not stop myself. I started laughing uncontrollably, loudly, so I turned and bolted back down the neighbor's walkway towards my house. I ran through the palmettos and around to the side of the driveway. As I tried to step onto the driveway, I tripped over the garden hose; but before I could hit the pavement, I slammed into the back of my taxicab. The encounter with the trunk of the cab reminded me of the beers that I had stashed when I left Carmen's yesterday. I popped open the trunk. The four beers were just where I left them.

The breeze from the ceiling fan had begun to dry the sweat on my chest, making me feel clammy and sticky. The digital clock on the nightstand read: Friday, June 22, 3:45 AM. Plenty of time for a beer and another great round of sex, if Carmen was willing of course. I rose from her bed and started towards the door.

"Hey, lover. Where you going?"

"I'm going to get a beer. You want one?"

"No, I'm fine. Hurry back, I'm still horny."

I padded downstairs to the kitchen. The cold tile floor felt good under my bare feet, and the cool breeze coming from the air conditioning register felt good against the rest of my naked body. I took one of the five beers stashed in the vegetable bin of the refrigerator and walked over to the door overlooking the pool area. Popping the beer, I took a good swallow and thought that it might be fun to go skinny dipping later.

The flash of memory took me by surprise. Where did it come from? From of the depths of my blackout? I pulled one of the beers from the plastic ring and popped it open. A mighty swig of the piss warm beer almost made me puke, but I kept it down. The second drink didn't seem as bad as the first. The fear hit hard. I was at Carmen's on the night of her murder. The clock had read Friday, but I still didn't remember anything about the murder. I needed to know more, and the longer I thought about it, my initial fear began turning to hope. A bit of the blackout had lifted. If my memories returned completely, I might be able to prove once and for all that I had not killed Carmen. I closed the trunk lid of the cab and thought that I might as well head down to the boat and wait for Marci. With three-pack in hand, I climbed aboard my bike and headed for the marina.

* * *

The beer can landed squarely on my bare, big toe, then rolled across the deck of the boat, spewing beer as it rolled, until it came to rest against the aft wall of the deck. "Ouch. Damn it." I reached down and massaged my toe, trying to get the pain to subside. It took me a few seconds to realize that I must have passed out sitting in the deck chair. I shook my head, trying to clear out the cobwebs.

"What time is it?" I said to the dark, not expecting an answer. I received one anyway.

A voice spoke softly, "It's twelve thirty-five."

"Hey, thanks," I began, but when I looked up to see who had answered my question, my heart skipped a beat. The figure that had looked so comical yesterday had taken on a whole new dimension tonight. The man wearing the straw hat, and the graying, white dress shirt like a cape, unnerved me like nothing had ever done before. The same caped-crusader that I had seen at the parking lot at the beach, and then again in the crowd outside of Carmen's house, and then once again last night at the marina, stood on the dock looking down at me. But it wasn't his outfit that unnerved me; it was the look in his eyes.

He winked.

I damn near fell down as I scrambled out of my chair. "Who in the hell are you?" I teetered but stood tall on the deck, my hands balled into fists.

"I'm a bender," he said.

I don't know what I was expecting him to answer, but that wasn't it. I didn't know what to say, so I stood there mute, my mind racing. I stalled. "A vendor?" I don't think he expected me to not understand, having annunciated the 'B' quite clearly. He looked at me quizzically, trying to determine whether I was jerking him around or not.

"B as in boy. Bender." He shrugged.

"What is a bender?"

"I bend the will."

I had no idea what he was talking about, so true to my

nature I quipped, "Yeah well, I bend the elbow." The self-professed bender actually cracked a smile. I think he appreciated my wit.

"I bend the will until it breaks. You still have time."

I still didn't know what to do, so I asked, "Time for what?"

"Before you meet Marci."

"How do you know about Marci? What are you doing here?"

"I came to see you."

"Are you stalking me?"

"I'm watching you."

Now I was worried. The idea of being watched by a raving lunatic dressed like a – I couldn't even finish the thought. "Why are you watching me?"

"You need protection."

"Look, dude. This is not getting us anywhere." The guy was obviously a raving lunatic, and I had tired of the conversation. The more we talked, the less fearful and more angry I had become. "Don't ever come near me again."

"Your will be done." He winked again and added, "For the moment. You'll have more questions soon."

A chill ran down my spine. If he winked at me one more damn time, I'd let him have it. "Get lost," I replied with all the bravado I could muster.

"I'll be in touch." The man turned and walked away in the dark, his shirt-cape flapping in the breeze behind him. I watched as the self-professed bender walked down C Dock and into the night.

CHAPTER 10

The silly nursery rhyme kept running through my mind, rocking one baby after another in the tree-tops. I couldn't turn it off. The beat of the rhyme kept time with the motion in my head.

Marine Tow, Marine Tow. This is the Tricky-Tommy. Radio check please. Switch to channel seventy-seven for your radio check, Captain.

That explained the rocking. I was on the boat and forgot to turn off the damn marine radio. I wished that I had at least turned the damn thing down. The noise hurt my head, but thankfully it tuned out that damn song. How many times had I just thought damn? The fog in my brain was beginning to lift, and my head began to pound even harder. I wondered how much whiskey I had actually drank last night. I brought both hands up to rub my eyes, but my left arm hit another arm on the way up, and I realized that I wasn't alone in my bunk. I rolled over and opened one eye very carefully, trying hard not to let too much light in. It had to be around noon, judging from the way the sun was coming into the cabin. I could see long dark hair on the back of the head lying in bed next to me. Ribs showed through the pale white skin: Marci. We must have decided to get drunk and have sex one last time before she hit the road. We were very good at it. She was curled up on her side completely naked, and at least one part of me started to wake up. I ran my bare foot under her bare foot. "Damn, Marci you got some cold feet." I didn't get a response, so I shook her shoulder slightly. "Hey, wake up." Her shoulder was cold to the touch.

"Why are you so cold?" The air conditioning did not keep the cabin that cold. Something wasn't right. With that thought, the hair stood up on the back of my neck. Now fully awake, I rolled her over. One look and I jumped from the bunk like I had been stabbed with a hot poker.

"Oh, my God." I stood looking down at Marci. Like Carmen, ugly marks ringed her throat. "Oh, my God?" I checked for a pulse.

"What happened, Marci?" She couldn't answer. Marci was dead. Strangled on my boat. "Oh shit." This couldn't be. This wasn't right. This wasn't a horse's head in a movie. "Oh, shit."

I couldn't keep my feet still. A sudden rush of adrenaline pumped through my veins making me feel like my entire insides were on the move. I couldn't think straight. I didn't know what to do. I was afraid I would go into shock. "Calm down, calm down." Instead of calming down, I began to pace. Not far. The cabin wasn't that big. The single thought that I had been suppressing, since my realization that Marci was dead, erupted to the surface. Could I have killed her? My breathing quickened, hyperventilated. I couldn't catch my breath. I had never felt so scared in my life.

"Calm down, Mason. You're not a murderer." Sitting on the bed, I bent over and put my head between my knees and took several deep breaths. The deep breathing helped, but with my head between my legs, I realized that I was as naked as the day I was born. "Do something, Mason." What? "Start by putting on some clothes." The act of doing something mundane calmed me a bit, but this morning's activities did not resemble my daily routine in any way shape or form. I never woke up with a dead body in my bed before. As I pulled on a pair of black swim trunks, I looked at Marci lying peaceful on the bed. I wanted to cry. She deserved a better fate. I went over to the bed and pulled the sheet up to her neck. None of this made any sense. I threw on a black tee shirt and tried to think clearly.

>Attention all vessels. We have reports of a vessel in trouble, roughly thirty miles southwest of Egmont Key. The vessel is a blue and white forty-foot sailboat emitting smoke. We do not know if any crew or passengers remain aboard. Anyone seeing a vessel of that description in the aforementioned area, please notify the Coast Guard on channel sixteen. If you spot people in the water, attempt a rescue and notify the Coast Guard immediately.

Thoughts of the Coast Guard boarding my boat looking for a body leaped into my mind and terrified me. I jumped up and turned off the marine radio, thinking that at least the Coast Guard would be busy elsewhere. Thoughts of police intervention brought me back to my immediate problem. "What the hell do I do now." The whine of my voice surprised me, almost like I was listening from outside of myself. I sounded like I was going to cry any minute. I had good reason to cry. I really liked Marci, and she had been murdered. Her body lay lifeless in my bed. The Coast Guard alert had scared me to death and made me realize that I didn't have many options. If I called the police and reported the crime like I did with Carmen, they'd toss me in jail unceremoniously. Detective Kendyll Hall would make sure that I hung from a streetlight in front of city hall, probably by tomorrow morning. Marci's body made two dead bodies in three days. Then it occurred to me. I could dump the body overboard.

"That's sick." But no one was going to believe my story. Even I had trouble believing it. Dumping the body might be my only real option. I could do it easy enough, and the body might never be found. Marci had told everyone that would listen that she was leaving Sunset Beach. She wouldn't be missed anytime soon. I began to warm to the idea. "That might work." I started to pace again. I could take the boat out twenty miles or so, away from where the Coast Guard was searching, and throw the body overboard. No one would see me. If I dumped the body, I could buy some time.

No words existed for my current situation. Nightmares

occurred at night. Daydreams occurred during the day. Daymare might be a suitable word.

"Am I in a daymare, Marci?" No answer. Her eyes stared unblinking at the ceiling. "I wish you could tell me what happened. You always remembered everything. I don't remember anything past . . . " Bits and pieces of the night before flashed through my mind, jumbled together in an alcoholic haze: walking on the beach with Annie, fighting with Baldy, eating turkey legs with Arthur, putting the redfish under my neighbor's porch in the heat.

"I don't understand, Marci. Who could have done this to you? You were a royal pain in the ass sometimes, but I can't imagine killing you." I vaguely remembered asking Carmen a similar question a couple of days ago. Had I lost my mind? "I'm talking to you like I've lost my mind."

Something else lay just beneath the surface trying to break into the open. I tried so hard to remember that I began to get a headache, so to ease the pain I decided to concentrate on the business at hand. I pulled back the sheet and found Marci's panties, shorts and tank top on the floor. Getting behind her, I managed to slip the tank top over her head. After I struggled with the panties, I wiggled the shorts up over her hips and buttoned them. I found her shoes on deck and put them on her feet. I surveyed my handiwork. "I'm sorry, Marci. I really am sorry, but I have to do this. I need to find out what's going on." She was dressed for a day of fun on the water. I'd slip her into the sea. In her shorts and tank top, she'd look like she had fallen off a boat and drowned. I wasn't worried about her washing up on the beach any time soon. By then, all kinds of things might happen to the body. I shuddered at the thought.

Suddenly, I remembered the strange man on the dock last night, the lunatic who called himself a bender. "Did Bender do this do you?" I didn't know what else to call him.

No answers were forthcoming. "What's he got to do with all this?" The man had admitted that he was watching me, and if I remembered correctly, he knew about my meeting with Marci. His appearance last night was too much of a coincidence. He must have something to do with the murders. I clung desperately to the thought that someone else might be responsible for the crimes. Bender might be setting me up for these murders, but why?

* * *

The old fishing boat slid easily through the calm water as I maneuvered my way to the fuel dock. I was relieved that there had been no sign of the police boat that had boxed me in yesterday when I was arrested. As I neared the dock, I slowed the boat by shifting both engines into neutral. A slight turn of the wheel to the starboard, a short burst of the port engine, and there would be a gentle bump as the boat docked. But as soon as I engaged the port engine, I noticed the police boat across the pass tied up at Croc's bar. In my confusion, I never disengaged the port engine and hit the dock hard. I quickly shifted into neutral and avoided any real damage. Joe Moore, the fuel dock owner and old friend, eyed me with that expression that you deserve when you've done something really stupid. Nevertheless, he silently caught the rope I tossed onto the dock and tied off the bow. I grabbed the stern line and tied it off.

"Nice job, Mason. Are you fucking drunk?" Joe said and laughed.

"Not yet, but I'm fucking working on it." I replied, sharing in the chuckle. I didn't want to let on that the sight of the police boat had scared the hell out of me. I snuck a look. There seemed to be some sort of commotion that had captured the police officer's attention. "I thought I saw something happening over at Croc's."

"You're right. Something's going on."

Two men were engaged in a fistfight. One was circling the other, throwing punches while the police officer from the patrol boat attempted to intervene.

"Looks like a fight," Moore said.

The two combatants ignored the police officer. They wrestled, arms wrapped around arms, before they fell to the ground, continuing the struggle at the policeman's feet. I thanked my lucky stars. The fight would act as cover for my leaving port with Marci's body. "Joe." I yelled for Moore's attention. "I need to keep moving."

"Oh, yeah, right."

"Can I put a hundred on my tab?"

"Sure, Mason." Moore grabbed the hose from the gasoline pump and handed it to me, and after unscrewing the gas cap on the starboard side, I squeezed the trigger and pumped in fifty dollars worth. Switching sides, I started to top off the port tank. Back at Croc's, the two fighters were once again on their feet, but you could tell they were getting tired. The blows came less often and missed their mark most of the time. Taking advantage of the lull in the action, the police officer stepped in between the two men. He had one hand squarely in the chest of the fighter on his left and was pointing the opposite end of the baton into the face of the fighter on his right. The three suddenly stood as still as in a snap shot.

When the pump hit one hundred, I removed the handle from the tank, careful not to spill any gasoline on the side of the boat. I passed the handle over the rail to Joe. He walked it back over to the pump itself while I replaced the gas cap. "Looks like it's over, Joe."

"Looked like a good one though. I haven't been in a good fight in a long time."

"Me either," I lied, not wanting to get into a discussion about my fight with Baldy the night before. Moore thought I was crazy enough without giving him more ammunition.

"A hundred even, Mason." Moore read from the numbers on the gas pump.

"Okay, Joe. Thanks." I walked back to the helm and started both engines without a hitch. The drone of the engines comforted me.

"Catch, Mason." I turned at the sound of his voice and barely caught the can of beer that Moore had tossed my way. His timing was perfect.

"Thanks, Joe. I can use it."

"My pleasure, Mason. Bring me a grouper if you get any."

"You bet." I popped open the beer and raised it to Moore

in a toast. He gave me a quick salute and untied both bow and stern lines before tossing them into the boat. I glanced over to Croc's to see what was happening with the fight. All three participants of the fight stood in a small circle. The police officer had his back to me, which I thought was a good thing. The fighter to his right winked, and although it was hard to see details all the way across the pass, the identity of the man was unmistakable: Bender.

I quickly waved goodbye to Joe and slammed both engines into forward. I couldn't help but think that Bender was running interference for me, keeping the police busy while I left port. Was the fight simply a coincidence? I had more questions than answers, but I had no time to worry about it. The open sea stretched blue in front of me as I lurched from the fuel dock. The afternoon sun still rode high in the sky, and the wind blew gently on my back, a magnificent display of nature that Marci would never see again.

* * *

The waters of the Gulf of Mexico near Sunset Beach start a murky, greenish hue in the shallows, but turn to a clear, deep blue once out in deep water. The GPS/Fish Finder unit informed me that the boat's location was about twenty-two miles northeast of Sunset Beach in about seventy feet of water. Good enough. The dark water would swallow its newest prize silently. Or so I hoped. I killed the engines and went below.

"Damn, you're heavy," I said as I struggled with the dead

weight. Marci seemed to be twice as heavy as she had in life. Placing one of my arms under each of her arms, I dragged the body from the bed and up the three steps to the deck, her feet bounced loudly on each step in turn. I had read somewhere that a high percentage of newly dead bodies sank immediately upon entering the water. I sure hoped that Marci's body fit in that high percentage. I laid the body next to the rail and rested for a moment. "C'mon, Mason. You can do it." I found an inner reserve of strength and swung the body up onto the starboard side rail, the legs hanging over the side of the boat. Theoretically, the body would not float until decomposition took over and bloated it with gases. She might never be found. Two years ago, six of my fellow Tropical Cab Company drivers had chartered a fishing boat for an all day trip. The first day passed, the second day passed, weeks passed, and no sign of the fishermen. To date, no one knows exactly what happened to those boys. Maybe, sharks ate them. I didn't want to think about that.

I searched the horizon in every direction. I didn't want any witnesses. I wondered what the charge was for dumping a dead body into the gulf. Would they charge me with dumping the body even if they found me innocent of murder? "Okay, Marci, here we go." I lifted the body until her bottom cleared the rail. With a hard push, she went into the water, the arms rising straight in the air before disappearing beneath the surface. The body remained visible for what seemed like hours as it sank in the clear, blue water, the fingers pointing towards the sky.

PART TWO

The Chase

CHAPTER 11

The first hour of parking is free in the short-term lot at Tampa International Airport. An ungodly amount of money is charged for each hour thereafter, but this was one bill that would never be paid. I slipped the light-green VW into a spot between two enormous SUVs, which looked as if they could eat Marci's bug in a single gulp. The trip across Tampa Bay had been uneventful. Thank God, because I hadn't even thought about Marci's car when I slipped her into the gulf earlier. I wondered how many other things I hadn't thought of that would come back to bite me in the ass later.

My boat *The Tramp* had been safely berthed back in her slip and hosed down from stem to stern. The cabin had been mopped, dusted, vacuumed, scrubbed and a host of other cleaning verbs. I drank a cold beer on deck when I had finished, and then casually walked down C Dock towards the parking lot. As I turned the corner after exiting C Dock, my knees damn near buckled when I saw her car. Of course, Marci had left the car in the lot when she came to meet me, and I couldn't very well leave it lying around. After all, she had left me last night and hit the road, or so the world thought. It wouldn't do for the police to see her car safely parked down the dock from my boat. The good news was that the police didn't seem to be watching me, and I quickly escaped from the marina parking lot and across the bay to the airport without being seen. My skin erupted in goose bumps at the thought.

With little time to waste, I climbed out of the car and locked the doors, glad that I hadn't thrown the keys overboard with Marci. Luckily, Marci had kept her keys in her purse and not in her pocket. Now, the purse and all of her earthly belongings were locked up safely in the car, and with a little luck, the car would stay lost at the airport for a few days. I realized that I was thinking like a criminal, like a guilty man, but I knew deep down inside that if I didn't clear myself as a police suspect, no one would. I had no doubt about my earlier assessment on the boat. Detective Kendyll Hall and the justice system would have their way with me. There would be nothing I could do to stop the process at that point. Off to jail I would go, do not pass go, do not collect any money. The only way that I could think of to clear myself involved finding out how this Bender character figured into the whole mess.

With my ball cap pulled down tight to my sunglasses, I headed toward the terminal with keys in hand, wondering whether I should hang on to them or ditch them someplace. After a few seconds of indecision, it seemed best to simply get rid of the keys. If I couldn't clear myself of these murders, then it made absolutely no sense to help the police do their job. I tossed the keys into the waste bin by the door to the terminal. I was feeling a bit safer as I entered the terminal and turned towards the down escalator. I hadn't walked ten feet when my cell phone started to vibrate in my pocket, interrupting my thoughts and sending waves of shock throughout my system. You'd have thought there were a couple of thousand volts surging through the phone. Once I realized the source of my apparent electrocution, I fished the phone from my pocket and read the display: Annie. Great timing – at least she didn't call as I was dumping Marci overboard. How in the hell was I going to get through all of this and still act normal, by anybody's definition of normal. I wondered how serial killers remained in jobs and marriages, while all the time killing scores of people. "Hi, Annie."

"Hi, Mason. You got a minute?"

"For you, anytime." I actually meant that statement.

"I had an idea."

Oh, oh. Whenever a woman in my life had an idea, it usually involved me doing something I didn't particularly want to do. "Yes," I answered cautiously.

"I have a friend. Well, maybe it's not such a good idea. All she meets these days are bums. She hasn't had a good time in a long time, and she likes roller coasters. She needs to find someone who won't take advantage of her. And." She stopped for breath.

"What's the idea?" I jumped in while I could, wanting her to get to the point, but not wanting to make her feel bad.

"A double date."

"Double date?" A thousand guy fantasies ran through my mind in two seconds flat. "What do you mean?"

"You and me and Zoe and Arthur."

"Arthur?" That was one thought that had never entered my mind. "Arthur?" I repeated, my mind veering off into the past.

The Tilt-a-Whirl went round and round. October Fest carnivals are so much fun. Arthur and his girlfriend sat across the car from the two of us, laughing and carrying on. Their faces wore looks of excitement. Mine wore a look of worry. The beer, the brat, the sauerkraut went round and round. My stomach couldn't take all the motion. The eruption was powerful. It rose from the pit of my stomach, rising to my throat, before spewing out in long streams, whirling with the ride, splashing the sides of the car and everyone in it.

Annie was still talking. "Yes, Arthur. He seems like a real nice man."

I forced myself back to the present. "He is, but I'm not sure he'd be interested in a double date." In fact, I was sure that he would absolutely hate the idea.

"C'mon, ask him. It will be fun. Zoe is both fun and gorgeous."

"Gorgeous?" Okay, so maybe Arthur would go for gorgeous. "Dark hair?"

"Yes."

"Arthur likes dark-haired women. I'll call him."

"Terrific, I'll tell Zoe to be ready at eight."

"Now, hold on. He hasn't said yes, yet."

"But he will. You'll convince him."

"I'll try, but I can't promise anything."

"Zoe will be here, so swing by and get Arthur, and then pick us up at my house at eight."

"If he'll come."

"Don't worry he'll come. Make sure you tell him she's beautiful and friendly. It will be fun. I'm looking forward to it."

"I'm looking forward to it too. The Gardens has roller coasters, a zoo, and lots of beer and food." A few beers sounded good, but I had made up my mind to take it easy on the alcohol tonight. I didn't want to black out again, and if I eased up on the alcohol, perhaps my memory would return.

"Sounds yummy," said Annie.

"I'll see you at eight."

"Mason, you're a sweetheart.."

"Yeah, right. Bye." I put the phone back into my pocket. I wanted to get away from the airport as fast as possible. Visions of Marci's fingers pointing to the sky as she sank into the depths kept running through my brain. The place buzzed with travelers, and I was sure that everyone in the airport knew what I had done. I hurried to the middle of the terminal and down the escalator to the ground level and public transportation. I figured the only safe way back to Sunset Beach was on a bus. I didn't want to call a cab and have someone take note of me. On a bus, I'd be anonymous. Off to my right, I could see the sign for Ground Transportation. Behind the doors stood the bus I needed. I ran across the terminal and bolted through the glass doors, making it to the door of the bus just as the driver was about to close it. She didn't give me a second look as I paid the fair and sat down near the back. The bus lurched forward as we left the curb.

* * *

My companions were a motley crew. I wondered where they all came from and why they were on the bus. The young man seated directly behind the driver had placed his bicycle in the rack attached to the front of the bus. I could tell because he had placed the black bicycle helmet on the seat next to him. I had never thought about it before, but it would be pretty difficult to ride a bicycle from Tampa to St. Petersburg. Most of the bridges did not have bicycle lanes, and you rode at your own risk. Long straggly hair and two-day growth of beard, he looked the beer-drinking type, headed home after a long day, looking forward to that cold beer at the end of his ride. Then again, I could be totally full of shit.

The other riders were equally non-dramatic. Every one of the dozen or so appeared to be bored to tears, waiting to get home to friends and family. Each wore a look of resignation, like nothing exciting had happened in a long time and probably never would, which basically summed up my life until a couple of days ago. Now, I longed for the normal, for the daily grind, for the lack of drama. I thought of Carmen and Marci. How could this have happened to them? I felt real bad about their deaths. I felt like I should be honoring their lives by observing a period of mourning, but life does go on.

I thought of Annie and the future. Could we ever have a normal life together? I wanted that very badly, and in order to make it happen, I had to press on. I grabbed my phone again and dialed Arthur's number.

During the third ring, Arthur answered, "Hey, Mason. What's up?"

"Hey bro, what are you doing tonight?" I wasn't too excited about talking double dating with him. He would not be too receptive to the idea, but then again maybe by now he was ready for a date. It certainly had been a while.

"Nothing, man. What do you have in mind?"

"I have a favor to ask of you." If I put the request in those terms, Arthur would be more receptive. He liked to do things for me.

"What's that?" Suspicion was evident in his voice. He knew me too well.

"Annie called me earlier. We're going to The Gardens later, and we were wondering if you'd like to go along. You busy later, say around a quarter of eight?"

"I don't know."

"Come on, we'll all have fun."

"Who's we all?" He had me. He knew I wouldn't lie to him.

"Me and Annie," I hesitated a moment before adding, "and Zoe."

"Zoe? Who the hell is Zoe? I could hear something in your voice. What are you up to?"

"All right, I'll come clean. Annie called me and said that she had a friend who wanted to meet you, so I said I'd see if you were interested.

"Like in a blind date? No, I'm not interested."

"Not a blind date. A double date."

"What the hell is the difference? I don't want to go out on any kind of date with a woman I don't know."

"Annie said she had a great personality." I thought I would have a little fun with him and not tell him about the gorgeous part just yet.

"She has a great personality?"

"And friendly."

"No thanks, man."

I had to laugh. "She also said Zoe was gorgeous. Her word, not mine."

"Gorgeous?"

He was turning the corner. Like I said before, Arthur had pretty much given up on seeking women, but I didn't think he'd turn one down if she fell into his lap, so to speak. He wasn't dead yet. I pushed harder. "Long, dark hair, man." Silence. I had him. "What do you say, Arthur? You never know. You might have a great time."

"Or not."

"Come on, man. It will be cool."

"Okay, but we leave if I say so."

"Deal. I'll pick you up a little before eight." I hung up before he could say anything else. My face smiled back at me from the reflection in the bus window. Outside, the rail of the Howard Frankland Bridge between Tampa and St. Petersburg rushed by. To the north, I could see the jets taking off and landing at the airport. To the south, I could see the skyline of

St. Petersburg. On the far side of downtown St. Pete, as the locals liked to call it, the bay curved to the west, flowing under the Sunshine Skyway Bridge and into the open waters of the Gulf of Mexico. The gathering late afternoon thunderstorms stopped me from seeing anything further south, but in my mind's eye, I could make out the very top of the big bridge's bright yellow suspension cables, rising high into the air so the tall ships could come safely into the Port of Tampa. The incredible height made the bridge a favorite local suicide spot. As I once again surveyed my companions on the bus, I wondered what kind of impossible situation could lead someone to such a drastic act.

   Although recent events seemed to be closing in on me like this afternoon's thunderstorm, I wasn't ready to give up the fight. A sense of urgency had invaded my very being. I knew deep down inside that I had to hurry up and find Bender. He was keeping tabs on me and would appear again when he felt the time was right. That thought scared the hell out of me, and made we want to be much more aggressive. Because if I waited until he came to me, I was certain there would be another murder. I couldn't take that chance. With those thoughts in mind, I decided to make a quick stop at my brother's house before heading over to pick up Arthur for our double date. I bet Poco could get a hold of the police report of the fight at Croc's. At least then I might be able to find out the identity of the man.

CHAPTER 12

My bright orange taxi looked great against the well-manicured backdrop of the Long's lush, dark-green lawn. The home and grounds were meticulously well kept, but I was positive they paid someone to do it. That type of luxury came with money. I had to give Poco credit. He had done quite well for himself. As I walked along the spotless white picket fence to the pool area in back, I thought about on my own lack of prosperity. My educational experience barely reached beyond high school, and if you weren't born into money, the only way to get it was through a solid education. One day I should go back to school.

I heard laughter as I walked, so I stopped at the gate to see what all the merriment was about. Nancy Long and her daughter Jenny were sitting on the top two steps at the shallow end of the pool, playing some sort of patty-cake game. I watched as they clapped and slapped their hands together, giggling the entire time. The scene warmed my heart, but also depressed the hell out of me, adding contrast to the lack of good in my life. Jenny noticed me before I could unlatch the gate. "Uncle, Mason," she screeched, clambering out of the pool and running across the deck in my direction.

Opening the gate quickly, I caught her in my open arms as she leaped into the air. I held her high and spun her around. Her giggling turned to shrieks, reaching a volume and intensity that could only be attained by young girls. "How's my favorite niece?" I asked and set her softly back onto the deck.

"I love you, Uncle Mason."

"I love you, too, Jenny."

"You going to come swimming with us?"

"I don't have any swimming trunks with me."

"Go in your clothes."

"I don't think your mother would like that." I looked to Nancy Long for help. She had climbed out of the pool and stood by the side of the pool, smiling at her daughter and me. "Uncle Mason can go swimming next time," Nancy said.

Jenny smiled, seemingly satisfied with the response. "Okay, then watch me," she said. She ran over to the side of the pool and stood in a diving posture with her small toes on the edge. "I know how to dive. Watch." She did a not so perfect dive into the pool, bouncing up from the bottom as fast as she could to take a breath of air.

"Excellent," I hollered and clapped my hands together.

Her mother also clapped her hands loudly, smiling widely. "Very good, Jenny, but that's enough for now. Go get your father. Tell him Uncle Mason is here."

She gave her mom a sullen look, but said, "Okay, mama." Jenny climbed back out of the pool, struggled with a towel for a moment, and then disappeared into the house.

"She's really something, Nancy. You guys did great."

"She's a delight all right. How are you doing?"

"Oh, I'm all right. I'm trying to get back to some kind of normal routine while things sort themselves out. If that's possible."

"I'm sure things will be fine. You know, you can always come and talk with me if you'd like."

I assumed that she meant professionally as well as sisterly, after all she was a first-class psychiatrist. I appreciated the concern, but I didn't think I needed psychiatric help, at least not yet. "Thanks, Nancy. I really do appreciate the offer, and I may just take you up on it one day."

"Anytime, Mason, you are *my* brother too."

"Thanks." I stumbled in the process of calling her my sister. It just wouldn't roll off my tongue, and I wondered why. "Poco's home?"

"Yes, he's home. He was finishing up a report that's due tomorrow. I'll see what's keeping him and let you two be alone."

"You are the greatest sister in the world, Nancy." There I said it, and it felt good.

"I'll send him out." She smiled before turning and disappearing into the house the same way her daughter had a minute earlier. I walked over to the far side of the pool near the empty dock and thought how nice a boat would look tied up to the dock. I sat down at the table under the umbrella overlooking the canal. The canal flowed the entire length of the island and then out to the gulf through Sunset Pass. In fact, the Long's lived on the same canal as Carmen, whose house was two blocks further south. I really would miss her.

"Mason." Poco yelled from the back door.

I welcomed the interruption to my thoughts about Carmen.

"You want a cold one?"

"Sure." I wouldn't be a very good guest if I refused.

Within a minute, Poco had reappeared in the doorway. Dressed in a pair of cutoffs and a black sleeveless tee shirt, he didn't look like a lawyer. He looked like my brother. I smiled as he walked over to the table and handed me the cold beer. "Thanks."

He sat down across the table from me. "Are you hungry? We're going to throw some steaks on the grill in a little bit." He looked to the sky and added, "If we don't get rained out."

"The rain never lasts too long."

"Even if it does, we'll move inside. What do you say?"

"Thanks, but no thanks, Poco. We're going over to The Gardens later. There will be plenty to eat and drink, I'm sure."

"You going to ride the roller coasters?"

"You bet."

"Man, I'm jealous. I haven't done anything like that in a long time."

"You haven't taken Jenny?"

"No, not yet."

"You're not doing your fatherly duty, man."

"Point taken. I'll have to get us over there real soon. What's up?"

I popped open the beer and took a swallow, thinking that I might as well get right to the point. "I need a favor. Can you get your hands on a police report?"

"What kind of police report. About you?"

"No, no, not about me. There was a fight at Croc's earlier this afternoon. Can you get the police report on the fight?"

"Why?"

I hesitated, not wanting to risk sounding like I'd lost my mind, but after thinking about it, I realized there wasn't much point in not answering his question. After all, he was my brother and my lawyer for that matter. "I think I'm being stalked, being set up."

"What?"

I told him all about Bender and the fight at Croc's, about how weird the man dressed, about how coincidental it was that he seemed to appear every time something bad happened, about how I had seen him at Carmen's, about how I'd seen him at the marina, about how he had said he was watching me. I left out the part about him being a Bender and bending the will. I didn't know what to make of any of that shit myself.

"You think he has something to do with the murder?"

I noted the singular case of murder, not murders. His choice of words reminded me that for the most part I was on my own. I wasn't ready to tell him that I had found Marci dead and that I had dumped her body into the Gulf of Mexico. I felt like I was drowning myself, getting deeper and deeper into the depths of hell, grasping at the only lifeline available: Bender. "I don't know, Poco. But I don't like coincidences."

"I don't like coincidences either. But why don't you go to the police?"

"And tell them what. That this really weird guy is stalking me, following me around and then killing . . " I almost blew it by using the plural women. ". . . and then killing Carmen. Detective Hall wouldn't believe a word of it. She's not going to look any farther. She thinks she has the killer, me."

"She can't prove anything."

"That doesn't seem to matter to her."

"Unfortunately, you do have a point."

"As far as I know, until this afternoon I was the only one to have actually laid eyes on this Bender character. I'm thinking that the police report will at least prove that Bender really does exist."

"So tell her about the fight and that you saw the same man at Carmen's."

"And what do you think she'd do?"

"Investigate the man, bring him in for questioning."

"Or she does a half-assed job and spooks him. I don't think I want him to know that I'm looking for him yet."

"Even if there is a police report, it won't prove anything."

"What do you mean if?"

"Most of the time, they break up the fight and let everybody go. You should know that."

I gave him a dirty look before I admitted, "You do have a point. But I need to know for sure."

"All right, I'll see if there is one. It still won't prove anything."

"True, but I'm thinking that I might be able to put a name to the face. With luck, maybe they even have an address for him."

"Then what?"

"I kick his ass. I bring him down to the police station myself. I don't know." I was getting a bit exasperated with his playing the devils' advocate and asked in a voice louder than I intended.. "Can you get your hands on the report?"

"All right, all right. I'll make a few phone calls."

"Can you do it without alerting Hall?"

"Yes. She travels in different circles than the cops I'll talk with."

I stood up from the table and reached across to shake his hand. "I have to go, but I owe you, Poco."

"You sure this is what you want to do?"

"Maybe, I'm wasting my time, but I have to do something. This guy Bender is the only real clue I have. I can't sit around and do nothing."

"But doing nothing might be your best course of action. You're innocent. Let the justice system take its course."

"I don't trust the police or the justice system like you do. I really do have to go." I rose from seat.

Poco also rose from his chair and walked with me towards the driveway. He clapped me on the back as he opened the gate. "I should be able to get the report first thing in the morning. I'll have a friend fax it to me. Call me tomorrow."

As I climbed into the orange taxi, the rain began, rising in intensity very quickly. I felt bad that I wasn't being completely honest with my big brother. But what he didn't know couldn't hurt him. I was on my own. My decision to dump Marci's body into the gulf had set me on a course of action, and I had no choice but to follow it to the end.

* * *

After parking the taxicab in the only space left, I walked briskly across the wet parking lot toward the open door of Croc's waterfront bar. The short cloudburst had served to cool things down a bit, and I guessed they were letting some of the smoke out of the bar. The sky was beginning to clear, promising nice weather for our trip to The Gardens. Loud music blared through the open door, rocking anything and anyone nearby. A brown pelican, sitting atop a post on the boardwalk, appeared to be keeping time with the music. I slowed and watched the pelican dance, but continued to walk. I was on a mission. I wanted to further my pursuit of Bender. A quick beer or two didn't sound bad either.

When I left my brother's house, I started thinking that he could be right, and if there was no police report, then my only way to Bender would be through Croc's. It dawned on me as I was driving through the rain, that I had inadvertently lied to Poco. I really wasn't the only one to have seen the man. The bartender, the cop, and the other fighter had seen him too. They might even know him, or at least know of him. One of the bartenders on duty right now had probably opened the doors at noon and might be able to provide me with some details about the fight. I quickened my pace and entered the bar, refocusing my eyes to the dim light. The noise level drowned out any further thought. Walking up to a clear space at the bar, I nudged my way in between several people. The big man to my left gave me a dirty look, so I returned the same. He immediately looked away, and I was glad. I didn't need a confrontation right now. My focus turned towards the nearest of the three bartenders, the one with the bright red hair. Damn, it was the same bartender that had come to work when Marci and I were breaking-up. I thought about coming back later or tomorrow and was about to leave when she spotted me and came over.

"What do you want?" She asked above the music.

"A large draft." I pointed to the nearest beer tap, uncaring of what the brand might be. I wasn't sure if she had recognized me.

She returned a minute later with the beer and set it on the bar in front of me. "Aren't you Marci's boyfriend? I mean ex-boyfriend?"

The music suddenly stopped. "Yes," I yelled anyway.

"You don't have to yell," she said and laughed.

I laughed too. "Sorry."

"Hey, no problem. I hope they give us a break with the jukebox for a few minutes. My ears are ringing. Isn't your name, Mason?"

"Good memory. Mine sucks."

"Erin."

"I knew that."

"Sure you did." She laughed easily. A woman several seats

to my left called for her. "Excuse me, I'll be back."

That didn't go too bad. Marci must not have said too many bad things about me. I figured I could probably talk with her about the fight. She might know what happened. I took a sip from my beer and let my mind wander, content for the moment.

On The Tramp, Marci sat comfortably in one of the captain's chairs. I took a big drag from the joint, holding the smoke in my lungs as long as I could, before exhaling into the night air. I passed the joint to her and watched her take two short puffs, closing her eyes when the smoke assaulted them.

"Good shit, huh?" I asked.

"Not bad. How much can you give me?"

"Don't worry, Marci. I'll take care of you before you hit the road."

"Thanks, Mason. Do you have any Valium left? What size are they?"

"They're five milligrams. I'll give you ten. Will that settle the debt?"

"Perfect. In some ways you are a good man. In others, you suck."

"You look happy, Marci."

"I am happy. I'm glad to be leaving you and this town."

"Then let's have a nice good-bye party."

"A good-bye party sounds good."

"How are you doing?" Erin asked.

Lost in the memory, I didn't understand what she had

said. "What?" I asked. The memory had to be from last night, judging from the topic of conversation.

"I asked how you were doing."

"So, so."

"Breaking up is hard to do." It wasn't a question. It was the voice of experience.

"Marci and I had a good run. She's probably much happier now." I hoped to God that was true.

"I bet your right. She wanted a change. Sometimes, I wish I could be somewhere else."

"Been a tough day?"

"Kind of."

The change of topic was perfect for turning the conversation where I wanted it to go. "Your day had to be pretty tough, especially if you opened the bar this afternoon. What with the fight and all."

"How'd you hear about that? Word sure spreads fast around these parts."

Judging from her comment, Erin had probably opened the bar. I figured I might as well pick her brain if she'd let me. "Not really. I was headed out fishing earlier and stopped at the fuel dock in the marina. I had a ringside seat. Looked like a pretty good fight. What happened?"

"It was the oddest thing. This man came in and ordered a beer, but I don't think he even drank any of it. Before I knew it he had picked a fight with one of our regulars."

"Did you recognize the man?"

"No, I'd never seen him before."

"So what was the odd part?"

"He wasn't here two minutes before he walked up to Jason and started thumping him in the chest. Jason tried to back away, but the man kept in his face, calling him a pussy and shoving him towards the front door."

"Did Jason know him?"

"Now that you ask, I'm not sure. He might have."

"It might help explain a few things."

"Yes, it would. Wouldn't it?"

"It sure would. I've been in a few fights myself, but I always had a good reason." Using my right hand in a rolling motion, I urged her to continue her narrative of the fight.

"The man kept swearing at Jason. I couldn't understand much of what he was saying. He kept pushing and pushing."

"I would have punched him in the face by now."

"Jason isn't like that. I've never seen him in a fight, but this man wouldn't stop. It was like he was pushing the fight for some other reason."

"What do you mean by that?"

"Well, it was like it didn't matter who he was fighting, only that he fight someone."

I couldn't help but think that Bender had staged the fight for my benefit, to cover me while I motored out in *The Tramp* with Marci's body. How could the man be so aware of what was happening to me? "What happened next?" I urged her on.

"Eventually, we all ended up outside. Things heated up when the man hit Jason."

"What did Jason do?"

"I guess he had had enough. He hit him back hard, but it

didn't seem to faze the man."

"Is Jason a big guy?" I asked.

"He is pretty big. One of those, big jolly types."

"You would think that he would have flattened the small man."

"What small man?"

"The small man with the beard."

"Mason, I don't know who you're talking about. The man wasn't that small, and he sure didn't have a beard."

Now, I was confused. Was she referring to Bender? I was sure that her definition of a small man could differ considerably from mine, but the man either had a beard or he didn't have a beard. "Are you sure he didn't have a beard?"

"No, he was definitely clean shaven."

"Long, graying hair?"

"He was kind of gray. Anyway, I went back inside and called the police. I didn't see much of the rest of the fight because my boss called at about the same time. When I looked outside again, the police officer was sending them both packing."

I was glad that Erin had kept talking. I was still trying to figure out the whole beard thing. Bender might have shaved since the last time I had seen him, and I simply saw the beard because that was what I had expected to see. I would have more answers tomorrow after I saw the police report. "The cop didn't arrest either of them?"

"No, he broke up the fight and told them both to get lost."

"That's typical, I guess, for a bar fight."

"True enough. Excuse me, I better go see who else needs a drink."

The music started up again, but somebody had turned the volume down to a bearable level. At least we wouldn't have to yell. I had twenty minutes before I had to pick up Arthur, and there were still a few questions that I wanted to ask Erin. I bet she could tell me where Jason worked. I wanted to ask him about the fight, and I didn't want to hang around here in the hopes he might show up. He may have met Bender before today. At any rate, I was sure he could give me a better description of the man than Erin. I finished off my beer and held the glass in the air until I had Erin's attention. She brought me a fresh glass of beer. I placed a ten-dollar bill on the bar and pushed it towards her. "Keep the change, Erin."

"Thanks, Mason."

The beer was beginning to taste real good. I drained half of the glass before I asked, "Do you know where Jason works?"

"He works downtown at the Sunset Inn."

"That's convenient. You said you all ended up outside. Who else was here?"

"Why are you so interested?"

"The dude looked familiar. If it's who I think it is, he owes me some money," I lied. "I thought Jason might be able to help me find him. It sounds like he deserves a good ass-kicking."

"That's for sure. I didn't like him at all. He scared me."

"Was there anyone else here that might have known him?"

"The only other person here was Danny. He's a

fisherman. I don't know which boat though."

"Danny who?"

"Don't know a last name."

"Thanks, Erin." I finished off the beer and set the glass on the bar. I waved good-bye, turned and headed for the door. The conversation had answered less questions than it raised. Fear and doubt crept into my mind like a fog.

* * *

As soon as the door to the bar closed behind me, the atmosphere turned from party time to laid-back marina, the only sounds coming from the sea birds. The fog cleared. I felt my entire being relax, my shoulders slumped, my heartbeat slowed. I stopped, took a deep breath, and relished the salt air. My mind turned forward to my upcoming double date. During the drive over to Annie's, I could collect myself and at least resemble a happy human being. A slight smile crossed my lips until I spotted Hall crossing the parking lot, headed straight in my direction. "Damn it." I said louder than I wanted. I looked around for an escape route. Maybe, if I acted quickly enough I could get away without her seeing me. The trouble was that there was no immediate cover to disguise my escape. I had to face the heat, or in this case the damn bitch, who by this time had spotted me anyway. A wry smile crept across her face as she approached. I waited silently like a condemned man, which as far as Hall was concerned, I was.

"Well, well, well. Look who we have here." Hall said when

she was close enough for me to hear without raising her voice.

"What do you want, Hall?"

She stopped, standing with her hands on her hips, legs slightly spread. "If it's not the asshole I wanted to see."

I noted that since we were alone, she didn't feel the need to hide her hostility. "You're a piece of work, lady." I replied with equal hostility.

"I know your kind." She baited me.

"And what might that be?" Like a moron, I took the bait.

"A womanizer."

"I like women, so what."

"Who has turned to murder to get his kicks."

"I haven't killed anybody. What the hell do you want?" I was thoroughly tired of her insinuations and her insults. "Either get to the point, or get lost."

"You don't remember me, do you?"

"What the hell are you talking about?"

"I didn't think so. Okay, I'll get to the point."

"Too late, asshole. I'm leaving."

I turned and took a step, but was stopped by her hand on my shoulder. "You hold it right there. I have some questions for you. Are you telling me that you're not willing to cooperate with the police?"

Poco's words came back to me. I didn't have to cooperate with the police, but if I didn't it would make me look bad. I didn't care what Hall thought anymore. I was long ago convinced that she wanted to hang me out to dry, but she could not convict me alone. As long as I did my best to help, the rest of the police department might keep her at bay. I turned back around and faced her, staring silently, my own hands on my hips. We remained silent, face-to-face, two feet apart, hands on hips, both silently wracked by our own thoughts.

"I need to locate Marci Glass. I stopped by your apartment, but she wasn't around. Do you know where she is?"

I tried to read her face. How much did she know? Was she baiting me again? I wasn't sure, but I didn't think I had much choice but to answer her as honestly as I could. Of course, I would leave out the details about finding Marci dead and dumping her body into the Gulf of Mexico. "I don't know." I said, thinking maybe she'd leave it at that.

"She's your girlfriend, isn't she?"

Hall was not giving me any solid clues as to her real thoughts, so I said, "We broke up yesterday."

She didn't look surprised. "You mean she finally smartened up and decided to dump you?"

"If you insist."

"When was the last time you saw her?"

"Last night." I had to be honest, especially considering where we were. I knew now that she had been heading to Croc's to talk with the people Marci worked for. I decided to point her towards Erin the bartender, who I thought would probably give me the benefit of the doubt. "She came down to my boat late last night for some money I owed her. I gave her the money and she split."

"Just like that?"

"Just like that. Ask Erin. She's one of the bartenders here. She'll tell you the same thing. Marci was pretty happy about the whole thing."

"Now that I believe. I'd be happy to be leaving you to."

I wanted to tell her to go and fuck herself, but I bit my tongue. "Look, I'm telling you what I know."

"Do you know where she went?"

"I have no idea. She probably went home to mama. Maybe, she told Erin where she was going. Ask her."

"You better believe I'll ask her."

I was beginning to get the sense that Marci's leaving was news to Hall, and she didn't quite know what to make of the new development. She stood staring at me for a solid minute, not saying anything, making me feel real nervous. Finally, she asked, "You're not going anywhere are you?"

I saw no reason to answer her, so I remained silent.

"We will meet again." She turned and walked into the bar.

The calmness I had felt when I first walked out of the bar was completely gone. Hall was not going to let Marci's disappearance go. She would follow it to the end of time if she had to. Time was running out. I had to find Bender before it was too late. I walked slowly towards the dock, thinking that I had better collect my thoughts and calm down before I headed over to Annie's house. When I reached the boardwalk, I leaned on the rail and watched one of the fishing boats dock in its slip.

CHAPTER 13

"Do you remember Ricky Dean?" I asked Arthur, who had come over and stood next to me at the rail of the ape exhibit at The Gardens.

"I remember poor Ricky."

I couldn't help but think how everyone added the word poor before the name when talking about Ricky Dean, whose alcohol and drug use had fried his brain before he had even finished his sophomore year in high school.

The intensity in the dark brown eyes never varied. "You don't understand, Ricky."

"What don't I understand, Mason."

I could not answer his question. How do you explain things to someone whose brain no longer made all the connections? I would not lie to him. He'd been a friend too long. "She wants someone with a future."

"I have a future." The dark brown eyes began to tear up.

"She wants the American dream. Two incomes, two kids, a

big house in the suburbs. How you going to get that for her."

"I'll get a job."

Ricky never finished high school. The object of his affection wasn't about to start dating a kid like him. The look of anger and frustration in his eyes began to make my eyes tear up. I couldn't look any longer.

"That ape over there reminds me of Ricky," I said, pointing to a large ape squatting near the far left side of the glass enclosure.

"Too big and dark for Ricky."

"It's the eyes, man. Remember how Ricky would look at you when he didn't understand something."

"Which was most of the time." Arthur interrupted.

"That ape has the same look in his eyes, like he's angry but doesn't know why, like he long ago forgot the reasons for his anger."

"I wonder whatever happened to Ricky."

"I don't know, but I bet it wasn't good."

A beautiful, blonde-haired arm appeared around my shoulder. The old memories would have to wait. "Here, Sweetie."

I turned and accepted the cup of cold beer that Annie handed to me. "Thanks, baby. You're the greatest." I kissed her lightly on the lips.

She kissed me back and smiled. "Anytime, Lover."

The closeness I felt with Annie warmed my heart, making me wish that times like these would never end, and making me question why life had to be so damn hard at times. I hadn't felt this good in a long time. I watched as Zoe handed Arthur his beer with a smile. Arthur smiled back warmly. The exchange made me think that his half of the double date was going pretty well too, at least so far.

"I'm hungry," Zoe announced to us all.

"Me too." Arthur joined in.

"You're always hungry, Arthur," I joked.

"So what's your point, Mason," he replied and laughed.

We all shared in his laugh, feeling the camaraderie building between us. I started thinking that there might be a future together for all of us. "Check the map, Zoe. I know there's a food court in this place somewhere," I suggested. Zoe fished the map from her purse and unfolded it on the top of the exhibit wall. As she surveyed the map with Arthur looking over her shoulder, I leaned over to Annie and whispered, "It looks like it's going pretty good for them. I hate to admit it, but you had a pretty good idea."

"What do you mean, you hate to admit it." She punctuated her words by punching me hard in the shoulder at the end of her sentence.

"Hey, that hurt." I hated to admit it, but it did hurt.

"Good. "

"What do you mean good?"

"Listen, Buster, I have lots of good ideas. In fact, I have a great idea for later on."

"Yeah, what might that be?" I rubbed my sore shoulder. She rubbed a bit lower. "Oh."

Annie laughed easily.

"What are you too giggling about?" Zoe asked, her

attention taken away from the map.

"Nothing." Annie looked at me and smiled conspiratorially. "Mason was just being a silly boy." Zoe smiled and grabbed Arthur by the hand. "Come on, follow us."

Annie had been right about another thing: Zoe was indeed gorgeous. The woman had long dark hair, and blue eyes as big as quarters. When she smiled, the perfect white teeth gave the impression that she could be a TV star or model. But instead of taking her place on high and keeping her distance, Zoe instantly made you feel at ease, at home. The effect she had on Arthur was obvious. I smiled as I watched them walk towards the train station.

* * *

B'wani Station sat at the eastern end of The Gardens, one of four stations to service the railroad that circled the park. The trains offered an alternative to walking the sometimes long distances between exhibits and amusement rides. The train would take us to the food court. We began to run as we neared the station, realizing that there was a train already boarding passengers. We were only a hundred feet from the train when the doors closed shut. Through the window, I could see the conductor shake his head from side to side, indicating that we were too late. Begrudgingly, we slowed down and watched as the train started to pull out of the station. As the last car passed us by, I saw a familiar face smiling at me through the rear window: Bender.

My feet reacted by immediately bounding into a sprint. I ran the length of the platform before stopping at the end, slightly out of breath. When I once again looked for Bender in the rear window of the now rapidly departing train, he was gone, and I really wasn't sure if he had been there, or if his face had been a figment of my imagination.

"What was that all about?" Arthur had followed me to the end of the platform.

"I thought I saw someone I know."

"Who?" Annie had come up behind Arthur and stood next to him. Zoe was right behind her.

I felt embarrassed because I was not sure of what I'd seen, and I didn't particularly want to talk about it. They were not to be denied, however, and stood there expectantly. I thought that I might as well be as honest as I could, without going into great detail. "I keep seeing a strange little man. I think he's stalking me."

"Can we help?" Arthur asked. Both Annie and Zoe nodded affirmatively.

"Did you all get a look at him in the back window."

"I didn't see anybody," Arthur said.

"Me either," added Zoe.

I looked to Annie for an answer. She shook her head no. I was quite annoyed that no one else had seen the man, lending credence to the possibility that I had imagined the whole event. I didn't know what else to say. As an afterthought, I said, "If you see a short man, wearing a straw hat, let me know."

"What do you mean by he's stalking you." Annie asked

me, hungry for more details.

"I'd rather not go into that right now, if that's okay with you all. We're here to have fun. We can talk about it later, okay? Besides, I'm not sure it was him anyway."

"But, Mason." Annie still wanted more.

"Please, let's enjoy ourselves and get a little drunk tonight. I have enough crap to worry about. It will wait until tomorrow." I don't think they liked my answer, but appeared willing to let it go.

"You're still pretty fast, man. Almost as fast as in your football days," Arthur quipped.

"I am still pretty fast." In fact, I was quite proud of myself.

Both Annie and Zoe smiled at the change of subject, and thankfully the awkwardness passed as another train pulled into the opposite end of the station. We immediately moved toward the train, but my mind lingered on the visage I had seen through the window of the first train. Had I manifested Bender's face because I wanted so desperately to find the man, or had he decided to tease me and keep me on edge. I suspected it was the latter.

Arthur had walked hand in hand with Zoe, and once inside the train, he plopped down into the nearest available seat. She sat down in his lap. Annie and I took the double seat across the aisle from them. Once I was seated, I couldn't stop myself from causing a little trouble. "Arthur, don't let anything embarrassing happen."

"What do you mean?"

Zoe caught on quickly and slowly circled her bottom into Arthur's crotch. His face immediately turned red, but he didn't seem to mind. He grabbed her by the waist and held on tight as the train rolled out of the station. "I think he's starting to like me," Zoe said in her best deep, sexy voice.

"You bet I am," Arthur replied, emphasizing the word bet.

Zoe wiggled her butt one last time before sliding down into the seat next to him. I couldn't remember the last time I had seen a smile like that on his face. As the train wound its way through and under a maze of roller coaster tracks, we settled in for the trip to the next station. Without warning, the roar of a roller coaster interrupted our peace and quiet. The flash of several brightly colored cars, speeding upside down above our heads, the occupants screaming in unison, painted the inside of the train car with every hue of the rainbow. The roar subsided as fast as it had come.

"Wow. We need to get on that one." Annie said in awe.

"Let's eat first," said Zoe.

"Maybe, we should ride first," I offered, thinking of the memory I had earlier of spilling my guts all over everything.

"Okay. We'll eat first," Annie agreed. "You guys okay with that."

The decision had been made. I didn't see any sense in arguing the point. "Sure, as long as we can wash it down with another beer." My resolution to take it easy on the alcohol had apparently gone by the wayside.

The train rolled into the food court station as Annie said, "Deal."

We were all on our feet before the train had fully stopped, and within a minute, we were out the door and walking up the ramp. Many times in the past, I have felt like a spectator to my own life, almost as if I was watching a movie and could only sit still while the plot unfolded. I watched the four of us, young and in lust, happy to be together on a warm summer evening. But like in a movie, where you *know* something bad is going to happen, I was scared that all the happy-happy was a trick. I grabbed Annie and brought her into my arms. "Are you having as much fun as I am?"

"I sure am." We kissed, enjoying the moment. When we broke, Annie motioned toward the double-daters. "And it looks like Zoe is having fun too. Do you think Arthur is enjoying himself?"

"I've never seen him happier." I was exaggerating a bit, but not much.

Annie motioned once again towards Zoe, who this time was pointing her finger at something in the distance. She nodded her head in response to Zoe and said, "We're going to the bathroom."

Annie and I caught up with the double-daters, and the two women headed off up a slight rise toward the small brick house that contained the restrooms. Annie looked back over her shoulder and said, "Meet us over at the beer stand."

"Good idea." I yelled after her. "Come on, Arthur. I don't have to be asked twice."

"I'm in."

We ordered two beers from the young woman behind the counter, sipping on them hungrily once we had them in hand. "So what do you think of Zoe?" I had to ask now that I had him alone.

"She's all right."

"What do you mean, she's all right."

"She's nice."

"She's nice. That's all you can say. Looks to me like you're already crazy about her. You can't hardly keep your tongue in your mouth." I laughed, enjoying his reaction.

"Okay, okay. Yes, she's really great. But I've only known her for a couple of hours for Christ's sake."

"I'm glad it's going well, Arthur. You're a good man. You deserve some happiness." I was going to add a few more niceties, but Arthur interrupted.

"Stop or I'll puke," he said.

"I think she likes you too."

"Now how would you know that?"

"I can just tell. Besides we'll know for sure in a little bit. They're in the bathroom together, remember?"

"You think they're talking about us?"

I gave him the look I reserve for people who have said or done something utterly stupid. I didn't say a word.

"Of course, they are." Arthur admitted, a horrified look on his face.

We ordered a second beer. Arthur could hardly calm himself, wondering what Zoe thought about the whole thing. "You better fill me in later, Mason."

* * *

The young woman used the fingertips of her right hand to turn my chin slightly to the left. I obliged, and tried to remain as still as I could, glancing longingly at the cup of beer sitting lonely on the ledge next to me. I hoped that the young artist finished the caricature before my beer got warm. She tugged slightly at the brim of her *Rays* baseball hat. Several loose strands of blond hair fell from under the hat. "Hold it right there," she said, before sitting back down on the stool in front of her easel.

I could see Annie out of the corner of my eye, smiling her best snapshot smile, the kind of smile that people wear when they pose for a camera, the kind of smile they never wear otherwise. She turned her eyes toward me, and the smile in her eyes was much more genuine than the smile on her face.

"Where you guys from?"

"We live here," said Annie.

"No, I mean, originally."

"I'm from Colorado. Annie's from New Jersey."

"I'm from Chicago."

I guessed that small talk was a part of her artistic process. I wished that she would shut up and finish the sketch. I wanted to get back to my beer.

She must have read my mind because she said, "A few more minutes and we'll be done."

Annie had spied the woman's booth down the walkway as we gulped down our hot dogs and beer. The dogs were wonderful slavered with mustard and kraut, and satisfied me much more than posing while someone made artistic fun of our faces. I never have liked caricatures as an art form, but Annie had insisted. I thought that they always made people look stupid.

"Honest, it won't be too much longer now. Where in

Colorado?"

"Colorado Springs. Have you ever been to Colorado?"

"No, but I've always wanted to go there. Do you want your shoulders in the picture?"

"Huh?"

"Do you want your shoulders visible. Or just from the neck up?"

I looked to Annie for help, not wanting to answer any more dumb questions. "I guess shoulders would be nice," Annie said, shrugging her shoulders to me.

I nodded and said, "Sure, put the shoulders in."

A few more strokes of the hand and the woman stood up. She stepped back a few feet from the easel to survey her work. After a moment, she stepped up once again to the easel and adjusted something in the sketch. "There, all done."

"Can we move now?" Annie asked, rubbing the circulation back into her arms.

"Sure, come and take a look."

"Great." I smiled and grabbed my beer before following her suggestion and taking my place behind her at the easel. I knew I would hate the sketch, and I was not disappointed, but what surprised me was the look on Annie's face. Her smile had been replaced by a deep frown. "How much?" I asked the woman, ignoring Annie's reaction for the moment.

"Twenty dollars for the caricature. If you want it framed, we can do that for another twenty, and you can pick it up in about an hour."

Annie shook her head no. "No, thanks. We'll frame it later." I said, digging a twenty and a five from my pocket. I handed the bills to the woman. "The rest is for you."

"Thanks. I appreciate it. I hope you like it."

She handed me the sketch, but didn't appear convinced that her work was much appreciated. Apparently, she had noticed Annie's reaction too. She slipped the money into her pocket and turned her back to me, already trying to convince the next group of people coming down the path that they too needed a caricature of their experience at The Gardens.

Annie grabbed me by the hand and dragged me back towards the food station, where Zoe and Arthur had said they'd wait. I could see the two double-daters sitting and laughing at one of the picnic tables next to the beer stand. I raised the picture up in front of me as we walked, trying to see what it was that Annie hadn't liked. We both looked stupid, but that was to be expected. After all, that was the essence of the art of caricature. Looking at it closely, I thought that Annie's image actually looked rather cute. The artist had captured the smile and the eyes almost to perfection. "I think you look pretty cute." I said, stopping and holding the picture up so she could see it better.

"Maybe, but look what she did to you."

I wasn't sure what the hell she was talking about, so I took a closer look at the sketch of my face. I had to admit that it did not flatter me, but I couldn't put my finger on why. I gave her a dumb look.

"It's the eyes, Mason."

I scanned the sketch again, but didn't think that the eyes were that bad, except for the fact that they were drawn a bit dark. "I don't get it."

"The eyes make you look . . ." She searched for words. "Bad, sinister. I don't know."

"Sinister?"

"Maybe not sinister."

"Then what?"

She stood thoughtfully looking at the sketch for a minute before she said, "The eyes make you look like you're hiding something, like you're up to no good."

I could hardly believe what I'd heard. I looked at the sketch one more time and had to admit that Annie's assessment was accurate. I did look like I was probably up to no good. Unfortunately, the artist had captured the reality of my situation. I had indeed hid a few things: a dead body, a car, some drugs, to name a few. "Let's toss it in the trash," I said, thinking that the trash was the best place for the damn thing.

"But you paid twenty-five dollars."

"It's only money. Besides, twenty-five dollars is not a lot of money. We'll get another one done some other time."

"You would do that for me?"

"Sure, Annie. If it will make you feel better, we don't have to keep it." I never added that I didn't relish the idea of the sketch hanging around if it made me look guilty of something. "Should I throw it in the trash?"

"Yes."

About halfway back to the food court, I found a trashcan. I tore the caricature into several small pieces before throwing it in the bin.

* * *

My stomach pushed hard up against the back of my throat. The force of gravity performed great tricks as we dropped hundreds of feet in a few short seconds, while the car did a 360-degree roll. We rolled on, rolled up a rise, momentarily suspended peacefully, only to scream downward once more, splashing through a small river of water, before going on the rise again. Annie screamed with glee every time we roared down into the abyss. Pure joy was etched into her face. My screams were more of the – *oh my God, we're going to die* – variety. "Holy shit," I moaned. I hated roller coasters. Why the hell did I get on one? I always had the same thoughts in the middle of a ride. For reasons mostly unknown to me, I had a love/hate relationship with actions that flirted with death. I always seemed to need something to keep me on edge. I guessed that's also why I took up boating and fishing on the Gulf of Mexico. Docking a large boat in a fierce windstorm took all the nerve you could manage. Fishing all night in the dark, forty miles from the shore and civilization, made you realize how fragile life could be. Before I could pursue my thoughts any further, the roller coaster dove down another steep slope, gaining speed mightily. I closed my eyes.

Clear blue water lapped at the side of the pool in the night breeze, making the black divider line painted on the bottom appear jagged, like a staggering drunk had painted it. The underwater lighting gave the entire pool area a shimmering glow, fading to black in the shadows of the boathouse and dock.

Peering through the kitchen door, the pool sure did look inviting and I had pretty much decided that after Carmen and I were through making love upstairs, we would have to take a dip. I was about to go back to Carmen, when I thought I saw something move along the side of the boathouse.

"I must be seeing things." I finished my beer, crushing the can in my hands and throwing the carcass in the sink.

I looked to the shadows one more time, and this time there was no mistake. Something had moved and disappeared around the back of the boathouse. Shit, I thought. That's just what we needed: a fucking burglar to ruin our night. I put my hand on the doorknob determined to scare the dude off, but realized that I was naked. It wouldn't be my idea of fun to confront a burglar without any clothes. I walked quickly to the downstairs bathroom, hoping that I had left a pair of shorts in there, but no luck. The best I could do was a large pink bath towel, which I quickly wrapped around my waist.

Back in the kitchen, I steeled my nerves at the door for a second, then pushed it open and went outside. I wasted no time, and in a few moments I was at the front door of the boathouse. The door was left wide open; the thief must have been inside. A boat hook hung immediately inside the door to the right, so I armed myself. Weapon in hand, I slowly made my way around the side of the small structure, stopping when I reached the rear of the building. I peeked slowly around the corner.

The back of the boat house appeared deserted.

I was certain that I had not been seeing things, so I moved slowly to the opposite side of the building and peeked around the corner. To my astonishment, a man sat comfortably in a chair at one of the poolside tables, his straw hat barely visible beneath the green and white striped umbrella. The man's shabby, graying white dress shirt was unbuttoned except for the very top button. His arms were not in the sleeves. A big brimmed straw hat, khaki shorts, and flip-flops completed his ensemble. His hair was long and graying like his beard and his shirt. I had to admit it was one of the strangest sights I'd ever seen by a pool in the middle of the night. I approached the man slowly, boat hook in hand.

As I neared the table, the man asked, "What are you going to do with that?"

I assumed that he meant the boat hook, so I replied, "I'm going to hit you over the head with it, if you don't get the hell out of here."

"You're dressed in a pink towel." He smiled.

I did feel pretty stupid confronting the man dressed in pink, so to offset the image that I presented, I thought I would slam the boat hook down on the table top to emphasize my order to get lost. I raised the boat hook high with my right arm, but as I started to move the weapon down towards the table, the odd little man raised his own right hand in a stop motion, his eyes gleaming in the moonlight. I could do nothing but stand there and hold the boat hook, like the Statue of Liberty holds her torch.

My screams could be heard in the next county, and I was afraid that if I didn't stop the screams soon, I would never be able to silence them. Mercifully, they subsided as the roller coaster came to a stop at the platform. My knees and my hands shook, but I wasn't sure whether the shaking was due to our roller coaster ride on *The Beast*, or was due to my own personal roller coaster ride. Great waves of fear gripped my mind, knowing that both Bender and I were at Carmen's on that fateful night. Trying to shake off the fear, I climbed from the car and turned around to help Annie climb out of her seat.

"That was great, Mason. Let's do it again."

"What?" I was still caught up in the memory from the other night.

"What's the matter? Are you okay?" Annie seemed to sense my discomfort.

"I'm okay." I forced myself back to the present. "The hot dog seems to be doing strange things to my stomach."

Annie laughed softly. "Poor baby."

Arthur and Zoe exited from the last car when it pulled up, and Zoe immediately ran over to where we stood. A second behind her, Arthur came up and slipped his arm around her waist.

"Was that cool? Or what?" she asked, the excitement in her voice clearly evident. "Let's do it again."

"Works for me," Arthur said. "I don't think I've ever been on a fucking ride like that. Man, it screams. I almost pissed my pants."

Arthur's face turned red at the last statement, but Zoe ran her hand along his blue jean covered right thigh. "Nope, they're dry. You're okay." Zoe smiled, leaned over and kissed Arthur lightly on the cheek.

"Thank God." The red in his face disappeared as his smile widened.

"Maybe, we should have a beer first?" I hinted.

Annie began to say something, stopped for a moment, and then said, "I don't think I want one, but maybe a cold beer will help settle your stomach."

She was probably thinking that I was drinking too much, and I agreed. Unfortunately, I never seemed to be able to stop myself once I started. I don't think I ever drank just one beer. If I had one, I'd drink a hundred. I was thankful for her understanding and promised myself that I would do better tomorrow, both for her sake and mine. "How about you guys?" I asked Zoe and Arthur.

A silent exchange took place between Zoe and Arthur. I wasn't sure if he wanted a beer or not, but I could tell that he would go along with whatever she wanted. Zoe said, "I think I'd rather ride the roller coaster again. Arthur?"

"Me, too. We'll get a beer after the next ride. Go ahead without us, Mason. We'll get you for the next ride."

"Okay. I thank you. My stomach thanks you." I really wanted some time to sort out the memories that had returned so unexpectedly. "Annie, you go ahead with Zoe and Arthur. I'll go on the next ride."

"You sure that you don't want me to stay with you."

"No. Go ahead and have fun."

Arthur and Zoe nodded encouragingly.

"Let's do it." She leaned over and kissed me on the lips. "We'll be right back, Mason."

"I'll be right here." I watched as my three friends headed back to the line for the roller coaster, wishing that I could be done with the crap that was haunting me, but grateful that my memory was returning. Up until this point, I had *assumed* that Bender had been involved with both murders. I already knew he had been on C Dock on the night Marci was killed, but now I knew for sure that he had also been around on the night of Carmen's murder. Thinking that I might as well get that beer, I walked over to the beer stand at the food court and asked the bartender, "Can I please have a large draft?"

"Coming right up."

Once I had my beer in hand, I walked back to the rail that lined the perimeter of The Beast and watched as a group of cars screamed down into the water trap, wondering if my friends were in one of the cars. Friends not withstanding, I never felt so alone in my life. I didn't have anyone to confide in, not without dragging them down into my mess. I only hoped that they would stay with me while I figured things out. I leaned forward on the rail and sipped my beer, more determined than ever to find the evil little man who had invaded my life.

* * *

The sweat had dampened the pillow beneath my head, making it feel cold and clammy. I stared at the ceiling of the cabin, trying to catch my breath. I had never felt so alive. The boat rocked slowly in its slip, reminding me that there was always an ebb and flow to things. I had to hang on tight to the good. I wiggled my arm around and behind Annie's head on the next pillow, and pulled her close to me. "That was great," I said.

"Yes, it was," she agreed with a smile.

I had nothing else to say. Sometimes, words were useless, and this was one of those times. A hand snaked its way up my thigh. Here we go again.

"You're amazing," Annie said.

"You are too." Afterwards, I climbed from the bunk and grabbed us a couple of beers from the refrigerator. After handing one to Annie, I took a big sip and climbed back into bed next to her. We snuggled up close.

"Mason, I've been thinking."

"Yes?"

"And I know that you don't want to talk about it."

"Yes?"

"But I want you to know that I don't believe for a minute that you could possibly be involved in that terrible crime."

I was tempted to give her a hard time, to make her say the word murder, to make her uncomfortable, but then I thought what the hell was wrong with me. The woman had her heart in the right place. In fact, I realized at the moment that she probably loved me. "Thank you, Annie. I need all the support I can get."

"Mason, you're a good man. Anyone who really knows you, knows that."

"Some people sure don't think I'm a good man, and most of them belong to the police department."

"Can I ask you a question?"

"Sure, fire away."

"Who was the man on the train at *The Gardens*? Or don't you want to talk about it?"

I had to think about that question for a moment. I really didn't mind Annie asking me about Bender, but I didn't know what to say. "Annie, it's not that I don't want to talk about it with you. I figure I can tell you anything."

"You can tell me anything. I believe in you. I . . ." Annie stopped short.

I wanted to finish the sentence for her. I wanted to believe that she loved me. I wanted to believe that I loved her, but everything was happening too fast. Then again, they always say that when it's right, you know it immediately. "It's not that I don't want to talk about it. I really don't know who he is or how he is involved in Carmen's murder. But I am positive that he is involved, and I need to find out how."

"Is there anything I can do to help?"

Before I could answer her question, I heard footsteps on deck. Without missing a beat, I jumped from the bed and put my shorts on.

"What's the matter, Mason?"

I put my right index finger up to my lips in a shush gesture and whispered, "I thought I heard someone on deck."

"You're scaring me." Annie said in a very low voice. She looked beautiful. The sheet had dropped across her lap, leaving her breasts exposed.

If we made it through all of this, I would tell her I loved her and never let her go. "It'll be okay. I'm going to take a look.

When I reached the cabin door, I stopped and listened for movement from above, but heard nothing. I climbed the three steps and opened the door to the deck. Peering out carefully, I looked around, but saw nothing. I climbed up to the fly bridge for a better vantage point. I could see the entire surface of the boat and the better part of C Dock all the way to the parking lot. I could not discern any movement. I shook my head and went back below.

"What was it?" Annie asked when my face appeared in the doorway.

"My imagination shifting into overdrive."

CHAPTER 14

My head felt like it was in a vise and someone kept applying constant pressure. Sunlight poured in through the port windows. I wondered what time it was. Turning to my left, I could see the outline of a body under the sheet. My heart skipped a beat. I couldn't remember a thing after I had checked the boat for an intruder. The body rolled over. The sheet fell from the face. Annie smiled and said, "Good morning, lover."

I could hardly speak, my mind in shock.

"Did you have a good time last night?" Annie climbed on top of my chest, kissing me full on the mouth. She moaned softly and ground her belly into mine.

"What part of last night?" I ground my hips upward.

"All of last night, silly. I know the last part was great."

"I had a great time last night, each and every part. Want to do it again?"

"I would love too, but look at the clock. I have to get to work."

I glanced at the bedside clock, which read 11:22. Apparently, she was scheduled to open the Coconut Hut at noon. "You got time."

"No, I don't. But I will after work."

"I don't know if I can wait until then."

"Keep thinking that way. I want you more than you know." Annie kissed me once more before climbing out of bed. I watched amused as she hunted through the pile of clothes on the floor, taking delight as she struggled into her bra. It was probably a good thing that she had to leave, there were people I needed to see, starting with Jason at the Sunset Inn and ending with Poco at his office. I found myself staring at the bottle of whisky we had left on the table. "Mason, are you okay? You don't look so good."

"I'm okay. I'm just a little hung over is all."

Annie must have noticed my longing look at the bottle of whisky, for she said, "The last thing you need this morning is the hair of the mouse that bit you."

"You mean the dog that bit me?" I found her so refreshing, so real. I laughed softly, knowing she was right.

"You shouldn't drink so much." Annie laughed uneasily.

I guessed from the look on her face that she thought she had crossed the line, but for first time in a long time, I found myself willing to let someone else give me some advice about my drinking. I quickly rose from the bed and crossed over to where she stood. Taking her in my arms, I hugged her tightly. "You're absolutely right, baby. I'll do better today." We stood in the middle of the room holding each other tight. We kissed long and hard. I didn't want to let go. I wanted the feelings to last forever. "Hey, I was thinking. Do you want to go with me to my brother's later? I want you to meet my family."

"I'd love to."

"I'll pick you up after work. What time are you done?"

"Six. Aren't *you* working today?"

"No, there's a few things I have to take care of."

"Having to do with the man at *The Gardens*?"

I saw no reason to lie to Annie. "Yes. I need to clear myself."

"I'm here if you need me." She stood on her toes and kissed me on the lips. Taking her hand, I escorted her up on deck. She climbed down onto the dock, waving good-bye before turning and walking away. I watched until she got to the end of C Dock, where she turned and waved once more. Annie was right about one thing: I didn't need the hair of the mouse that bit me. I would have laughed at the thought if my head didn't hurt so much. I definitely needed to heed her advice and slow down the drinking. "Yeah, right. I've heard that before." I was beginning to sound like a broken record, an ineffectual broken record, but I vowed not to drink this morning at least. There were other ways to self-medicate. I watched Annie drive out of the parking lot before I leaned down and raised the lid to the engine compartment. Reaching under the port engine, I retrieved the magnetic box that held my stash. I had not given all of the Valium to Marci. Opening the little plastic baggie, I looked at all the colors and smiled.

"White, yellow, or blue. What should I do?" I took one of the large economy sized blue pills and put the bag back in the tin. Bending over, I returned the tin to its hiding place. The

Valium wouldn't completely stop the withdrawal pain, but it would ease the shakes. They were getting worse and worse as the days went on. With luck, the drug would also ease the fear. Fear and uncertainty had me in a vise grip. The truth was that I was having a hard time distinguishing what was real and what wasn't. Bender here, Bender there, everywhere a Bender. Will the real one please stand up?

* * *

"What do you mean there's no police report?" I was deeply disappointed with Poco's news. I looked at the cell phone in my hand like it had done something wrong. Poco was still talking when I put the phone back to my ear.

"No police report was ever filed on an incident on Sunday morning at Croc's. Read my lips."

"That would be pretty hard to do over the phone."

"My little brother, always the wise ass."

"I'm sorry, Poco. I was hoping that I could get a handle on the dude I'm looking for."

"I know, so I talked to the police officer that was on duty Sunday morning."

"Good man. What did he have to say?"

"Not much. I'll fill you in when you get here. Are you going to be here soon?"

"Why not tell me what the officer said over the phone?"

"I didn't want to tell you this over the phone either, but maybe it's a good idea to do just that. Then you'll have a chance to cool off a bit."

"What are you talking about, Poco?"

"Hall wants to see you this afternoon."

"Damn." The air rushed from my lungs as my heart picked up speed. I didn't want to talk to the police. I didn't have anything new to tell them. "What does she want?"

"She didn't want to get into it over the phone. They don't ever want to tell you anything."

Oh my God. I immediately thought they must have found Marci's body washed up on the beach, but that was unlikely, so I just as quickly calmed myself. I didn't want to raise an alarm on my brother's radar. Besides, the police were probably fishing. "I'll be there within the hour, Poco."

"Good." He hung up the phone.

The thought of having to talk with Hall nearly made me miss my turn, but I managed to swing the cab into the parking lot on my right. Once in the lot, I veered quickly to the left and wheeled the cab down the first aisle and parked in a vacant space directly under the tall yellow and brown sign that read *Sunset Inn*. "At least something is going my way," I mumbled under my breath as I climbed out of the cab. I wouldn't have to walk too far to the front entrance.

The Inn, as the locals called it, had aspirations of being a five star resort hotel, and although the place looked magnificent from the outside, with its unblemished white columns, its pale blue walls, and its driveways lined with palm trees, the accommodations and service usually fell short. Good people were always hard to find at the wages *The Inn* was willing to pay. Instead, the place usually attracted employees that would work for nothing and do next to nothing. As I walked through the front door, I hoped Jason didn't fit in that category. I didn't need any attitude, only answers. The young, blond woman behind the reservation counter looked pleasant enough, so I walked straight up to the counter and stood waiting while she finished up on the phone. I couldn't help but admire her trim figure and the cute dimples that appeared when she smiled.

"Can I help you?" She said, after she hung up the phone, displaying those dimples. Her nametag read Amy.

"I was wondering if I might be able to talk to Jason for a minute." It occurred to me that I didn't have any idea what Jason's last name might be. "I don't know his last name. He works here at *The Inn* somewhere."

"I don't know a Jason. Let me ask the reservations manager. Maybe, she knows. Hold on a minute."

I didn't believe her for a second. The minute I spoke the name Jason, a cloud seemed to come over her face. She had become nervous immediately. The dimples went into hiding. I wondered what was wrong, as I watched her walk through the door behind the counter and into the back room. I could see an older woman sitting at a desk in the far corner of the room. Amy went over and leaned her hands on the front of the desk and began speaking in low tones. She looked up briefly to point a finger in my direction. The woman behind the desk nodded her head briefly, stood up, and headed in my direction.

"Are you a friend of Jason's?" She asked once she stood across the counter from me, with Amy standing next to her. She did not wear a nametag.

"Yes. I'm a friend from Croc's." I lied, betting that most of *The Inn*'s employees had been to Croc's a time or two.

The lie seemed to satisfy her and she visibly relaxed. "You can't be too careful these days."

"Is something wrong?" I asked quietly, putting on my best concerned face.

"There was an accident."

"Jason was in an accident?" I had to prod her, for she had stopped speaking and tried to collect herself.

Amy didn't have the same problem. "Yes, early this morning. A hit and run driver. Hurt him bad. They took him to the hospital in an ambulance. We don't know what's going on now."

I immediately assumed the worst. I was sure Jason was dead, but I didn't know whether to feel sorry for him or for myself. "Whoa, slow down," I said. Although I was speaking to Amy, I applied the words to myself as well. "What happened?"

The older woman held up a hand for Amy to stop, indicating that she would be taking over. I was grateful, because it had been hard to fully grasp what Amy had blurted out.

"About two this morning, probably on the way home from Croc's. Someone hit Jason as he was crossing Sunset Boulevard. Apparently, they never slowed down and never looked back."

"Do they have any idea who hit him?" The woman looked at me funny. She probably thought I should have asked how Jason was doing, if I was a friend and all, so I quickly added,

"Is he going to be all right. This is so upsetting."

She seemed mollified. "It's not good. He was in the emergency room. He's at Bay Pines. Are you going to go and see him?"

I did not answer her question. The ramifications of the accident were beginning to sink into my mind. How convenient for Bender that my key witness suddenly found himself in a life and death situation. Nothing good seemed to happen where Bender was involved. I nodded to the two women behind the desk, turned and walked away.

* * *

The law offices of Bailey, Tyrone and Long, were nestled in the southwest corner of the municipal complex and occupied the entire fourth floor of the Bailey Building. Most of the buildings that made up the complex were of recent vintage, all steel and glass, configured into strange shapes and angles, and in my humble opinion, looking completely out of place in a small beach town. The elevator doors opened into the dark-red, carpeted lobby on the fourth floor. Since Poco and I hadn't been very close in recent years, I had only been to his office once before. An unfamiliar woman sat behind the reception desk. "May I help you sir?"

"Hi. I'm here to see my brother, Poco Long."

"Your name?"

"I'm sorry. The name is Mason." I held out my hand to her as she rose from her seat. She took my hand and shook it warmly.

"I'm Victoria. I'll tell Mister Long that you are here." She pressed a couple of buttons before speaking into the phone on her desk, "Mister Long, your brother Mason is here to see you." As she waited for a response, I checked her out. She reminded me of a true southern belle, long dark curls and all. Victoria oozed class through every pore. The firm had done well in choosing her to be the face of Bailey, Tyrone, and Long. Her slight southern drawl spoke of old money and times past. "He'll see you now." She rose from her seat, motioned toward the right hallway, and said, "Please follow me."

I would have followed her anywhere, but we didn't have far to go. Poco's office was the first one on the left with the door opened wide. As we walked into his office, Poco rose from his seat. "Hey, little brother."

I was getting a bit tired of the little brother comments, especially in front of a woman like Victoria, but I grabbed the hand that was offered and didn't say anything.

"Miss Victoria, would you please see that we're not disturbed."

"Yes, sir." She backed from the office, closing the door behind her.

I couldn't help but ask him. "Where did you find her?"

"She's something isn't she?"

"Man, big brother."

"She's got way too much class for you, Mason."

"You're probably right Poco." As if to prove him correct, I asked, "So what's this shit about no police report?"

"I told you there probably wouldn't be one. Police officers

don't need to spend their time writing reports about bar fights. They would never have time for anything else. Besides, I talked to the cop who broke up the fight."

"What'd he have to say?"

"I took notes," he said, picking up a piece of paper from his desk. "Not much. According to him, the fight was your typical bar fight. It started in the bar and spilled out into the parking lot, where he got involved. The fight didn't last long and nobody was really hurt, so he told them all to leave and to go somewhere else."

"Shit I was hoping for more. Did he know the guys involved?"

"He said he knew one of the guys from around town," Poco hesitated as he read the paper in his hand. "Somebody named Jason who works at the Sunset Inn. The other guy was a complete stranger."

"I knew that. I talked to one of the bartenders at Croc's."

"Then you probably know as much as I do."

"Did he say what the other guy looked like?"

"The guy you called Bender?" Poco checked the paper and read, "Six foot tall, medium weight, short graying hair, blue eyes, light complexion."

"Nothing about a beard?"

"No mention of any."

I couldn't believe my ears. My thoughts raced back to my conversation with Erin the bartender at Croc's. She told me the man was clean-shaven, when I knew he had a beard. Now the cop said the guy was without a beard and six feet tall. The man I was looking for was nowhere near six feet tall. The worst part was that police officers were usually pretty good with their descriptions. What the hell was going on? Something wasn't right. "I don't get it. He doesn't describe the guy who's stalking me."

Poco remained silent, shrugging his shoulders slightly.

"I don't suppose the cop had a name for him?"

"No, he didn't pursue it any further."

"Damn, I was hoping for something more to go on. I have one last chance. I've got to get over to Bay Pines hospital and see what Jason says."

"Jason as in one of the combatants? He ended up in the hospital?"

"Not from the fight. They told me at the Sunset Inn that he was nailed by a hit and run driver early this morning."

"His luck hasn't been very good lately."

"I'm not sure luck has anything to do with it."

"What's that supposed to mean?"

"I'm thinking that my stalker had something to do with it. I'll let you know if I find out anything."

"Can you be back here by four o'clock? Remember, Hall wants to talk to you."

"That bitch."

"Nevertheless, she is the cop in charge."

My mind suddenly flashed on something in the past, something I couldn't quite get a handle on, but it involved our dear detective Kendyll Hall. "Do I have to talk to her again?"

"No you don't, but she'll be even more suspicious if you don't cooperate."

"Shit."

"I'll go with you, so you don't do anything stupid."

"You can do that?"

"Of course, I'm your lawyer. If I tell you to shut up, don't say another word. You hear me."

"I hear you."

"You be here."

"Okay, okay, big brother. One more thing, what are you doing tonight?"

He arched his eyebrows. "Why?"

"I met somebody, and I want you and Nancy and Jenny to meet her. Why don't you do steaks or something?"

"You met somebody in the middle of all this shit?"

"What can I tell you? You never know when something like that will happen. She's the real deal."

Poco shook his head. "I've heard that before."

I knew that would be the typical reaction from the people who really knew me. "Honest, Poco, I think I want to spend the rest of my life with her."

"Oh, please."

"Come on, man. Jenny will love her." Poco couldn't refuse anything that might please his little Jenny.

"Oh, all right. I must be crazy, but I'll give you the benefit of the doubt."

"Annie gets off work at six. Is after that okay?"

"Sure, I'll call Nancy and let her know."

"You're the greatest, Poco. I have to go." I was out the door before he could change his mind. Miss Victoria smiled widely as I passed her desk. I smiled back.

* * *

The cold beer tasted great. I swallowed half the glass in a single gulp. After leaving Poco's office, I couldn't take it anymore. The Valium had worn off almost entirely, allowing the withdrawal symptoms free rein. I tried to be good, but that damn little devil sat on my left shoulder urging me on. So up over the bridge I went to Madeira Beach, where hopefully I wouldn't run into anyone I knew. I finished the glass of beer and hailed the bartender. "Hey, Mac. Can I have another one?" I didn't know his name.

"Sure, Dude. The name's Brian."

While I waited I watched through the open windows as a casino boat docked in its berth. A minute later, Brian deposited another cold beer in front of me, taking the money he needed from the stack of bills next to my coaster. I only wanted a couple of beers to ease the pain. Besides, I had plenty of time before I had to meet with Poco and Kendyll Hall. Out of the corner of my eye, I watched as a man approached the stool next to me.

"Anybody here?" He asked in a low voice that I could barely understand.

"No. It's yours, man."

The man sat down and motioned to the bartender, who brought him what looked to be a scotch or whiskey and water. He turned and smiled at me. I couldn't see more than three or four teeth. As he sipped his drink, I lost all interest in the man, preferring to wallow in my own misery. I was wondering what the police wanted now when there was a tap on my elbow from my bar stool neighbor. I spun the stool and faced the man.

"Jesus never turned a face to . . ." He mumbled so low I lost the remainder of the sentence. I nodded politely, hoping the man would go away and leave me alone.

"They called me Jesus. I made the water turn to scotch." The almost toothless maw grinned widely.

Oh, great. I seemed to attract the strangest people. Maybe, it was my face. Maybe, I should try and look meaner or something. I looked to the bartender for help, rolling my eyes in the toothless one's direction. Brian shook his head from side to side, looking to me like he was trying to hold back a laugh. I didn't think it was funny.

"I was over at the house across the way from McDonald's on the causeway. They had heroin. They wanted to give me some, but I turned them down."

"That's nice." I could have simply left, but I sure wanted another beer or two, so I tried to remain tolerant. I actually felt kind of sorry for the guy. "You could go to jail for heroin."

"I live at the VA hospital."

That figures, I thought. I looked into his eyes and jokingly asked, "Ricky are you in there?"

"My name is Angel."

"Of course it is."

He reminded me of Ricky Dean with the fried brain. That's two times in two days that I had thought of Ricky Dean. My bar stool buddy apparently had the same mental disconnect as Ricky. I hoped that if my brain turned to mush,

I would see it coming. I wouldn't want to live that way. "Brian, another one please."

CHAPTER 15

I hated hospitals. They were places of pain and death. Sure I was aware of the opposite perspective: that hospitals were a place of care and healing, but my experiences with hospitals were all bad, and I couldn't get past that. Besides they were filled with all manner of horrible sights and smells. Personally, I preferred to ignore the possibility of pain and death. Thank you, very much.

On the surface, the Bay Pines VA complex pleased the eye. The Spanish style architecture of the older buildings blended in quite well with the newer, more modern buildings. The designers had kept to the original color scheme of red tile roofs and light pastel colored walls. I stopped my thoughts at that point because I really did not want to know what might lurk beneath the surface. I entered the main building through the side entrance, thinking that I wanted to be in and out as quickly as possible. Although I had been there before and knew where I was going, I stopped a very pretty brunette nurse, and asked for directions. "Excuse me.

Can you tell me where the information desk is located?"

She smiled pleasantly and said, "Right around the corner over there." She pointed towards the main lobby. "The information desk is just inside the main entrance."

"Thank you." I watched as she walked away before continuing on to the main lobby. The woman behind the reception desk looked big and mean, strong enough to throw me on the floor and pin me down, in probably less than thirty seconds. I only hoped that the hospital didn't have strict rules about visitors because I was sure that she would enforce them to the letter. My goal was to talk to Jason for a few minutes, no longer. I was certain that the man's answers to my questions were going to disappoint me. I could see the writing on the wall. Bender was not the other fighter at Croc's that afternoon, and the thought of what that fact did to my theories, frightened me.

"Can I help you?" The big woman asked pleasantly.

I was as wrong about her disposition as I seem to have been about a lot of things. "I'm here to see a friend of mine, Jason."

"Last name?"

It suddenly occurred to me that I had no idea of Jason's last name. I shuffled my feet, looked down, then looked sheepishly at the receptionist and said, "I don't know his last name. We hang around at a bar together. I wanted to see if he was all right." I gave her my best hang dog look and smiled.

"I guess I could search by first name. When was he admitted?"

"He was hit by a car on Sunset Boulevard early this

morning. A hit and run."

"Oh, that's terrible. So, it would have been today?"

"Yes, ma'am."

"Here we go. Jason Scott. Room 314."

I turned to go.

"Hold on a minute."

I thought, oh no. Here's where she'll tell me that I can't visit him.

"You'll need this."

I took the offered visitor pass and stuck it on my tee shirt over the left breast. "Thank you, ma'am. I really appreciate it." I turned once more and headed for the elevator bank, which was located down the corridor behind the reception desk. The experience at the desk proved not to be like the horrors I remembered from my youth. I began to relax, thinking that everything might be okay after all.

* * *

After exiting the elevator on the third floor, I watched as several doctors and nurses hustled and bustled around the nurse's station directly in front of me. To my right and to my left, hallways contained multiple doors, some opened and some closed. Jason would be in one of those rooms, but before I could take a single step towards the nurse's station, my eye caught movement at the end of the hallway to the left. Bender had entered the hall through a doorway near the far end and hurriedly exited into what I guessed to be a stairwell. The people around the nurse's station had paid no attention to me at all, so after a moment's hesitation, I gave chase. Walking swiftly, so as not to attract attention, I made it to the stairway door in just a few seconds. Once through the door, I heard footsteps on the stairs below, quickly followed by the slamming of a door. Peering down the middle of the stairwell, I guessed that it had to be on the first floor, because from my vantage point I could plainly see the second floor door. I quickened my pace, making it to the bottom of the stairway in short order. With no hesitation, I hustled through the door and into the first floor hall.

A young man dressed in green scrubs stood directly in my path. I couldn't stop my momentum and slammed into him hard, knocking us both to the floor. I looked up to see what had happened to my quarry. He stood in the next intersection to our right, laughing and pointing a finger at me. I scrambled to my feet and apologized to the young man that I had bowled over. "I'm sorry, man. I didn't see you."

"Be more careful, asshole. You shouldn't be running in here."

"I said I was sorry." I didn't mean to run into him. I thought about giving the jerk a piece of my mind, but I had another pressing matter. I glanced toward the intersection, where Bender was once again on the move, hurrying out of sight down the hallway to our right. "Stuff it, buddy," I said in frustration as I resumed my chase. Quickly, I ran the length of the hall and rounded the corner where Bender had disappeared, this time slowing down as I made the turn. The hall opened up into the emergency room area. Gurneys stood on each side of the hall. Several nurses attended to a patient brought in by paramedics, who were standing near the door watching the nurses take over. I surveyed the emergency room quickly, looking down length of the admittance area and into the curtained areas that I could see. Not finding Bender, I ran through the automatic glass double-doors and into the parking lot. There was no sign of my quarry. I stood with both hands on hips, watching the parking area. Noisily, the automatic doors opened behind me as one of the paramedics, a young blond woman of about thirty, walked through the doors. I turned and said, "Excuse me."

"Yes?" She stopped and faced me.

"Did you see anyone run through here in the last minute?"

"No, I haven't seen anyone."

"Small man, graying hair, beard. He probably ran past as you all were working with the man on the stretcher?"

"No I didn't see anybody like that. How about you, Max?"

Her partner had come out the emergency room doors and stopped to join us. "No, nobody ran past us, period."

"Damn," I swore. "I thought I'd seen a friend of mine."

The last thing I needed was to get in a long drawn out conversation with paramedics, who by their very nature wanted to help. I didn't need their kind of help. I wasn't sure what I needed. Feeling dejected, I waved them off and walked back into the emergency room. For the heck of it, I asked the woman at the emergency room's welcome desk if she had seen anyone matching Bender's description. She had not.

My arm felt frozen. I could hardly breathe from trying to make it move. The boat hook fell harmlessly from my hand.

Bender sat at the table and laughed at the lunatic standing there dressed only in a pink towel. "You're quite the sight."

"Fuck you." At least my voice still worked.

"Enough fun and games." The laughter disappeared from his voice, which lowered and deepened. " She's not who you think she is."

I had no idea what he was talking about. He seemed to know me, but I had never seen the man before this very moment.

"She must be cleansed."

"Cleansed?" The man must have escaped from the insane asylum. "Who in the hell are you?"

"Didn't you witness the maggots of her soul? Didn't you see them?"

"All I see is a strange little man sitting by my friend Carmen's pool. You need to leave right this minute before I call the police." Since I apparently wasn't able to evict him myself, I resorted to threats.

"Police are ineffective."

"They'll cart you off to jail or shoot your ass."

"They wouldn't see me."

"I see you. What the hell do you want."

"I want nothing."

"Then why are you here?"

"I'm here to protect you."

"Sir, are you okay?"

"Uh, yes I'm okay. I was just thinking." The woman at the emergency information desk gave me a strange look and nodded. I smiled and walked away down the hall. The bits and pieces of my returning memories posed questions that confounded me. Bender was definitely at Carmen's. Was he real, or was he as imaginary as the object of my current quest. My logical nature was ill prepared for what was taking place in my mind. I was beginning to think that there was no logical resolution to this drama. Nothing in my experience told me what to do or how to act or what to do. Jason was the last chance to bring things back to order.

* * *

"Who are you? Are you a doctor or nurse?" The man in the bed asked.

Standing in the doorway of Jason Scott's hospital room, dressed in cutoffs and a tee shirt, I waved and gave the man my best million dollar smile. Laughing easily I asked, "Do I look like a doctor?"

"Now that you mention it, no." Jason smiled the smile of someone in pain trying to be polite. "Do I know you?"

"Not really. I'm sure you know my ex-girlfriend Marci and her friend Erin from Croc's."

"Oh, sure." His smile broadened. "They're great."

"They send you their best," I lied. "They'll be here later." What did I care whether that was true or not? From the way Erin had talked about Jason, I was sure that she would have sent good thoughts. As for Marci, I didn't want to think about that. "The name's Mason Long. Are you all right, man?"

"Not really, but I'll live." He pointed to the large white

cast that enveloped his right leg. "It's broken in like three places or something."

"Oh, man. That must hurt like hell."

"Yes, but they're keeping me pretty jacked up on shit."

"I heard you were hit by a car on Sunset Boulevard." He looked at me quizzically. "Amy over at the Sunset Inn told me you were here."

"Nice girl, Amy."

"Very protective of you. At first, she didn't want to tell me anything. What happened?" I said and gestured toward his leg.

"I don't know exactly. One minute, I was crossing Sunset Boulevard. The next minute, I was bouncing on the pavement watching a white minivan speeding off in the distance."

"He never looked back?"

"No, she *did* look back. I could see a horrified look on her face, but she sped up even faster. I guess she couldn't afford to be in an accident."

"She?" My paranoia had quickly roared out of control. Bender had nothing to do with Jason's accident like I had originally thought. What else was I wrong about?

"Yes, it was definitely a woman. I haven't seen her or the van around town. She must be a tourist. Anyway, outside of the broken leg, just some scrapes and bruises."

"You're lucky. Sounds like you'll be fine."

"I appreciate the good thoughts, Mason, but you have something else on your mind. I can tell."

"You're right." I would relate to Jason my version of the

truth, which would be a mixture of fact and fiction. I still had not posed my most pressing question. "I wanted to talk to you about the fight you were in at Croc's the other day."

"I don't remember seeing you there. How did you find out about that? Is there a big story going around town?"

"No, not that I know of. I was across from Croc's at the marina fuel dock when you were fighting the guy."

"Weird, dude."

"What do you mean by weird?"

"Weird like I'd never seen the dude before. Weird like I never even talked to him Weird like why'd he pick me?"

I had my own theory about the last question, but I thought I'd better wait and see what Jason had to say first. I urged him on, "What started the fight?"

"He did. There was absolutely no reason. Why are you so interested?"

I wanted a description of the man he was fighting, but I wasn't sure I really wanted the answer. I hesitated a moment before I answered, "The dude looked familiar. He looked like a guy who owes me some money. I was hoping I could get a line on him from you."

"I don't know if I can help you. I never laid eyes on him before that day."

"Let's make sure we're talking about the same man: kind of short, graying hair and beard, straw hat and sandals?"

"Mason, you must have your wires crossed."

"How so?"

"The jackass who started the fight with me was at least six foot and probably two hundred pounds, and I remember for sure that he had on a white tee shirt and jeans." The look on my face must have spoke volumes, for he added, "Are you okay, man?"

I fought to hold back my disappointment. "I'm all right. I was hoping it was the same man. I won't keep you any longer." I started to slowly back from the room.

"Well look, any friend of Erin and Marci is a friend of mine. Maybe, we can all have a drink at Croc's when I get out of here."

"I think that's a great idea," I said. The sad part was that I knew the friendly drink would never happen. "Later, Jason."

"Watch yourself, Mason. There's a lot of fucking weirdos out there."

* * *

The bright sunshine assaulted my eyes as I sat on the curb of the emergency room driveway. I couldn't remember making my way down to the parking lot from Jason's room. My insides were churning, while my brain punched out thoughts at a mile a minute. "Fuck." I yelled much louder than I had intended. An older grayed haired woman entering a car on my right gave me a dirty look. I deserved it.

To say that my nerves were shattered would indeed be an understatement. I had thought that there might be a chance to find Bender and get myself out of this jam. But now all seemed hopeless. I was having difficulty swallowing one very hard fact: no one besides me had actually seen Bender. Instead of finding someone to validate his existence, my search had proven the exact opposite. There was no sense in trying to locate the last witness to the fight. I'm sure the fisherman would give me the same answer. I couldn't sit any longer, I only had fifteen minutes to find Poco and walk over to the police station, so I rose from the curb and slowly walked across the parking lot in the direction of my taxi. I never felt so tired in my life. I walked like a dead man, preparing for the final act.

How could I reconcile the fact that I was the only one to see Bender? The time had come to look within, and that thought scared the hell out of me. I began to think that I was in deeper trouble than I ever could have imagined. The world had closed in on me without my knowing it. I felt like I was caught in a vise, unable to breathe.

CHAPTER 16

The door to the interrogation room opened and the devil walked in. I waited for her partner to follow, but he was a no show. I didn't think that was a good thing. "Gentlemen." Hall said, before turning in my direction to add, "I use the term loosely in your case."

I did not respond, but let the look of disgust on my face answer for me.

Poco leaned over and whispered in my right ear, "Remember, if I tell you to shut up. Then you shut up." Thank God, Poco was there to protect me from myself. "Do you hear me?" He nudged me in the ribs with his elbow.

"I hear you."

Poco returned to reading whatever the hell he was reading, ignoring Hall completely. His open briefcase contained what looked like a ream of paper, scattered in chaos. I could not determine whether any of it had anything to do with me or my case. As Hall took the seat across the table from us, he said, "Remember, Detective Hall. This interview is over if I say so."

"Of course, counselor. We're all here trying to solve a crime. Isn't that right, Mr. Long?" She returned my look of disgust. I said nothing, so she said, "Let's get started then. You are here to cooperate?"

"Whatever."

"We are taping the interview. Is that okay with you counselor?"

"Yes. Go ahead."

Hall dug a notebook from her jacket pocket and flipped it open. "Let me bring you both up to date on the state of the investigation." She read over her notes for a moment and then said, "Mason, you are still the only suspect in the murder of Carmen Lopez. All leads still point to you."

I bet she hadn't even considered that anyone else could have committed the crime, and I couldn't help myself from pointing that out to her. "I'll bet you haven't even looked at anyone else."

"Well now, who would we look at?"

I considered telling her about Bender, but the moment was brief. I wasn't sure if he really existed, or was a figment of my imagination. It was like talking about a ghost. Hall would laugh me out of the room. "I don't know who else yet. I only know that I didn't kill Carmen."

"Did you kill Marci Glass?"

"What are you talking about?" I did not have to act surprised. Had they found Marci's body? "I haven't seen Marci since she left me the other night."

"What are you up to, Detective. There's been no mention

of a second murder. We did not come here to get ambushed. Has there been another murder?"

"Not exactly."

"What do you mean not exactly? I don't like your tactics."

"Frankly, I don't care what you and your murdering brother like or don't like."

"There is no room for insults in this interview. I'm not fucking around with you anymore, Hall. If you don't get reasonable, we are out of here."

Hall's demeanor lightened, but the fire in her eyes did not dim. She bit her tongue. "Okay. Let's start over. It seems that we have a missing person's case in addition to the murder case. Marci Glass has not been seen since Saturday night. That's too much coincidence for my taste."

"Missing?" Surprise was evident in Poco's voice.

"Mason didn't tell you about Marci?"

Poco looked at me sideways.

"There was nothing to tell you, Poco. Marci and I broke up. It was no big deal." I pointed a finger at Hall. "She's just trying to cause trouble."

"Please explain yourself, Detective Hall." Poco said in his best southern lawyer voice.

Hall continued, "Marci Glass has been missing since the night she met your brother at his boat. You don't look surprised, Mason."

"I'm not surprised. Marci's a free spirit. She does whatever she wants."

Hall ignored me while she wrote something down in her notebook. Once again her face wore a look of disgust. I'd seen that look before somewhere, and then I remembered.

Alarm bells had been ringing in my mind since I first met her, but it was very hard to take a pass on a woman as sexy as the woman lying in the bed with her back to me. The small of her tanned back rose softly to a beautiful white butt, the likes of which I hadn't seen in a long time. But the most recent object of my affection seemed to have two personalities: one as sweet as white chocolate, the other hard and mean. A couple of nights would be as far as this romance would progress.

I climbed out of bed, trying very hard not to wake the woman. I started thinking about the old coyote ugly joke, where you want to chew off your arm so you don't wake the woman as you make your escape. I laughed louder than I wanted, but she did not stir. Of course, the joke really didn't fit because she was beautiful. I had to admit that I had enjoyed the sex as well, but I couldn't take her hard personality. It would drive me crazy, so I thought it would probably be better if I just left. Besides, I didn't like confrontations. She seemed like one of those types that would hold a grudge, maybe even stalk you.

I dressed as quickly and quietly as I could. I put on everything but my shoes, which I held in my right hand, a finger in each shoe. I slowly made my way to the hotel room door, gently turning the handle without a sound. Before exiting into the hall, I turned to take one last look. I wanted to remember that body. As if on command, the woman rolled over onto her back. The large, heavy breasts flattened, large dark nipples pointed to the heavens. Part of me wanted to go back and take Kendyll in my arms.

No wonder she seemed to hate my guts. How could I have forgotten a woman as sexy as her. Sometimes I drank way too much. Obviously, she had taken our brief tryst much more seriously than I had. If I remembered right, she had scared me bad, so I probably wanted to bury the memories. I fought my way back to the present, thinking that I didn't want to get into it with her now in front of Poco and whoever was behind the glass. "I've already told you all I know about Marci's leaving."

"I want to hear it again."

I took a deep breath and tried to keep my voice from betraying my words. "I told you. Marci broke up with me. She came down to my boat the other night for some money I owed her and then split. She said she was moving on."

"No one has seen or heard from Ms. Glass since that night, and as far as we can determine, you are the last person to have seen her. We spoke with her friends at Croc's. I got quite an earful from a bartender named Erin."

"I'm sure Erin told you the same thing I have. She was there when we broke up."

"You are right. She does confirm that you were the last person to have seen Marci."

"You're twisting her words."

"She did tell us that Marci had planned on meeting you at your boat after work. We have since talked with several of Marci's other friends and her mother. No one has heard from her. Her mother says that is very unusual. Have you heard from her?"

"No. I haven't seen or talked with her since that night."

"Do you have reason to believe that she might have planned a trip somewhere?"

"Duh, what do you think? She packed her car and left, so I suppose so."

"Okay, wise ass. Then maybe you can explain to us why we found her car at TIA, fully packed. Why would she do that?"

The revelation that the police had found Marci's car hit me pretty hard. I fought to keep my breathing even while I thought things through. At least they hadn't found her body. If they had, I'd already be in jail. I decided to answer the question as indirectly as I could. "Now how in the hell would I know why Marci would do that. I never understood why she acted the way she did when I lived with her."

"Very clever answer. I know you know something. Don't you think it would be better for all concerned if you would just come clean and fess up to what you've done?"

"I haven't done anything."

"Then tell me. You know her as well as anyone. Where would she fly off to?"

"Look, I'll be honest with you." Since they had found Marci's car, I'm sure they found the drugs stashed inside. I could use that to my benefit. "Marci was a drug addict. It was one of the things we disagreed on. Who knows where she went or what she's doing. She was fucked up most of the time we lived together."

The accusation didn't seem to surprise Hall. Erin had probably told her something similar. "Are you a drug addict too, Mason?"

"I don't do that shit." I lied.

"Yeah, right."

"You believe whatever you want to believe."

"I know you're lying. You're lying about a lot of things."

"You have no proof of that, Detective." Poco interjected.

"But we do." Hall gave the two of us a smug smile. She turned and stared at me, before returning her attention to my brother. "We found evidence of your client at the murder scene."

"What are you talking about?"

Hall took her time answering his question, relishing the moment by thumbing through her notes. "We found trace evidence of your client in Carmen Lopez's bed. His DNA matched hair and semen stains found on the sheets."

"DNA? When did you get a DNA sample of my brother?"

"When we arrested him. He volunteered."

Poco stared at me. He didn't need to voice the message that he felt I had acted like a complete idiot. "I didn't know what to do." I said lamely.

"Had you been having an affair with her?" Poco asked me.

"Yes."

"Originally, he told us they were just friends. He lied. What else is he lying about?"

Poco ignored her comment and asked, "Did you find any semen in the body?"

Hall hesitated and said, "No."

"Then you have nothing. The hair and semen on the bed could have been left days before the murder."

"Carmen and I got together quite often." I volunteered.

Hall gave me a dirty look but said nothing.

"If you had any real evidence that linked my brother to the murder, you would have him arrested. What do you hope to gain by this interrogation?"

What Hall wanted to do was shake me up, and it had worked. The vise kept tightening tighter around my chest. It was getting harder and harder for me to believe my own story.

"I thought maybe your client would do the honorable thing and own up to the murders."

"Murder not murders," Poco corrected.

Hall turned to me, "Or at least tell us what happened to Ms. Glass."

"I told you. I don't know what happened to her."

"Just so you both know. We are intensifying our search for Ms. Glass, but I don't feel good about finding her alive. The entire island has been canvassed. The Coast Guard has been advised to keep an eye out. Flyers are in the process of being printed and will be distributed later this afternoon."

"Can I help?" I asked.

My question apparently took Hall by surprise. Her mouth opened for a second before snapping shut. "What?"

"Can I help to find her in some way?" Although I was terrified, I figured that I should go on the offensive, "I would like to help. Marci and I may have broken up, but we're still friends."

"I can't believe the balls on this guy." Hall said to Poco.

My thoughts ran back to the time Hall and I shared. She would never let up. To me, she said, "Sir, you are a liar and a drunk. I can smell the booze on you now. You couldn't stay sober long enough to come to this interrogation straight. Sooner or later, you will screw up, and I will be there to make sure that you get what you deserve. I only hope that no other women get hurt."

Poco gave me another one of those looks that asked if I knew I was stupid.

"I had a beer with lunch," I lied and defended myself. The woman must have a nose like a fucking bloodhound. I didn't think that anyone could smell a few beers. There must have been alcohol left in my system from all the booze I drank yesterday. But who cares anyway? Her comments had begun to make me angry. If I wanted to have a few beers, I would have a few beers. "I don't need to listen to this shit, Poco." I rose from my seat.

"No, you don't." Poco also rose from his seat. "This interview is over, Hall."

Hall had the last word, "One day, your lies will do you in."

* * *

Lying wasn't something that was exactly new to me. In fact, I had lied to my brother numerous times over the years, but I seemed to be taking the lying to new heights. My entire life seemed to be caught up in a lie. I could not tell where one lie ended and another began, and worse, I wasn't even sure what was a lie and what really wasn't a lie. "No, I'm not hiding anything from you, Poco."

"Are you sure? Do you know something about Marci's

disappearance?"

Obviously, I couldn't tell him the truth about dumping Marci's body in the Gulf of Mexico. I quickly thought of the pros and cons of telling him about my prior connection to Kendyll Hall and decided that it was probably a good idea to come clean on that issue. It would also serve to divert him from further questions about Marci. "I did remember something while we were in the interview."

"You talking about Marci?"

"No about Kendyll. We did a thing several years back."

"What do you mean you did a thing?"

"We went out."

"Out? As in dating?"

"Yes."

"Did you sleep with her?"

"Yes."

"Well, that explains a few things."

"That's what I thought." The little secret that Hall and I shared explained quite a few things. My assessment of her personality way back then had been correct. She was the type to hold a grudge, for seven or eight years by my recollection. I didn't feel too happy about being right in this particular case. Maybe, if I had only hung around long enough to exit gracefully.

"You went to bed with her? Wow. How was it? No, don't answer that. I have to think about this."

"It was only a couple of nights. No big deal."

"It was no big deal to you, but women are different than us."

"No shit." I gave him the same are you stupid look that he had given me during the interrogation. "Now that I'm thinking about it. Isn't this some kind of conflict of interest?"

"It probably is."

"Shouldn't she have removed herself from the case?"

"Yes, probably."

"Will this do us any good?"

"Not unless we go to court, and hopefully you'll be cleared before that happens."

"We're not going to court. I didn't do anything." I was no longer as sure of that as I once was. The whole world seemed to be turning upside down on me. If I couldn't remember making love with a gorgeous woman like Kendyll Hall, what else didn't I remember.

"I didn't say you did do anything. Have faith, little brother. Things work out like they're supposed to."

That's what I was afraid of, but I didn't voice that thought. "I'll see you at your house later, Poco. I have some things to think about.

* * *

The sun felt warm on my back, threatening to force the coldness from my soul. Sweat beads began to form on my brow as I walked around the building toward the rear parking lot. Poco still had faith in his little brother, but faith was one thing the little brother could hardly attain himself. My current situation was no longer manageable. True, I had gotten myself in deeper than I should have, but I couldn't help but think how much Hall actually had to with my decision to dump Marci's body into the gulf. Hall would never have given me the benefit of the doubt. My cab was parked behind the building in the back lot, so I would have to walk around the side of the building; but no sooner had I made it to the corner, Detective Hall came out of the side door, apparently headed for her vehicle as well. My timing seemed to suck on a variety of levels these days. There was no avoiding her. I stopped as she walked my way.

"You remembered who I was during the interview, didn't you?" Hall said when near enough for me to hear.

"Yes." I wondered if I was that easy to read on other points as well. "I'm sorry that it didn't work out between us, but that was a long time ago."

"Didn't work out? You were a shit, leaving me like that."

"It was only a couple nights of partying. I can't believe you've been holding on to this for so long."

"I haven't been holding on to anything, you idiot. I remembered you when I saw you in the driveway at the Lopez house."

"So I immediately became a suspect?"

"Yes. You showed me your true colors."

"People can change." I thought about my new relationship with Annie. Even though we had only been dating for a couple of days, I felt different about her. I was not sure whether I had ever put anyone else's needs before mine. That was change, wasn't it?

"Mason, you are a selfish, self-absorbed liar and drunk, who takes advantage of any woman he comes in contact with.

That is not my personal opinion. Everyone I have talked to, with few exceptions, has you pegged. Why would I think you have changed?"

My face reddened. I always thought that people had a better opinion of me. Were they right about me? I was beginning to think they might be. The drinking must be taking its toll, but I didn't want to admit that to Hall. "You are something. Because I rejected you a million years ago, I must be a murderer. Where the hell is the logic in that?"

"You really are dumber than you look. That has nothing to do with any of this "

"Of course, it does." There was no going back with Hall. She would never believe anything I said, no matter how long we lived. "I'm sorry you feel that way, but I haven't done anything and that's the truth."

"The truth? You've never been truthful in your entire life. This is not about us, I know you're hiding something now, and I'm going to find out what the truth really is."

"I keep telling you. I haven't done anything." I turned and started to walk away.

"Mason." I stopped and turned back to face Hall. "You may actually believe that you're innocent. And I'm guessing that you are telling the truth about one thing."

"And what might that be?"

"That you can't remember much. And that should worry you. Because that doesn't mean you're innocent." She turned and walked towards her car parked near the front entrance of the lot.

Her words had turned me to stone. I stood and watched

as she got into her car, but she didn't start it right away. She sat there looking through some papers or something on the front seat. Once I recovered my composure, I decided to walk to over the Coconut Hut and let Annie drive over to Poco's. I didn't want to give Hall a chance to arrest me for drunk driving. I would never again see the light of day as a free man.

CHAPTER 17

"Go fish." Jenny giggled with glee. "I'm going to win." The young girl was beside herself with excitement. She loved a good card game.

"Not if I can help it, young lady." I said and giggled with her.

"Not so fast, you two." Annie joined in the merriment.

I picked up a card from the deck. It didn't help me, so I picked up another, and then another. Finally, I could make a play and laid down a pair of threes before discarding an ace on the pile. Annie took the ace and laid down a pair of them. She threw a deuce onto the pile, which Jenny immediately snatched up before laying down her remaining cards.

"I told you so. I told you so." She stood up from the table and began hopping up and down. "I win. I win."

I made a grumbling sound and tried to give the child a dirty look, but I couldn't hold it but a few seconds. I burst into a laugh with her when she jumped into my lap. "You're too good for me, Jenny girl."

"You see, Auntie Annie. I beat Uncle Mason all the time."

"I see that."

I watched the exchange between probably the only two people in the world I loved more than myself. Was I really starting to think in those terms? I surprised myself. The smile on Annie's face when Jenny called her "Auntie Annie" was a sight to behold. She looked completely happy and content. I wanted to see that smile forever. "Jenny, can you go and get us a couple of cold beers?"

"Sure, Uncle Mason." She leaped from the chair and disappeared into the kitchen. I could hear her say something to her mother who was probably doing the dinner dishes, but couldn't quite make it out.

"She's something, Mason."

"That's what everybody says when they meet Jenny." I beamed like the proud uncle I was.

"You're so good with her."

"Jenny is easy to be good with."

"I'd love to have a girl like Jenny some day."

That particular sentiment would have sent me packing in the past, but with Annie, I found myself agreeing with her, "I would too."

"Is that the truth, Mason?" She smiled before looking down, like she was afraid of what the answer might be.

"Come here." I grabbed her hand and urged her to sit in my lap. "Yes, it's the truth. You have made me think about things that I've never thought about before."

"I love you, Mason."

She had voiced a sentiment that I would have run from in

the past, but not this time. "I love you too, Annie." And for the first time in my life, I meant it.

Jenny came bounding back into the room and broke the moment. "Here are the beers you ordered." She gave a bottle to Annie and then one to me.

"Thanks, sweetie."

Jenny gave me a frown in return. "What's the matter, honey?"

"Momma said that I have to do my homework before I can play some more."

"Well, you better do what your momma says. We can play cards again some other time." I watched as she disappeared up the stairs.

The Long's house had a similar layout to Carmen's house, large and expensive. The interior was not as elegant as Carmen's, less glass and crystal. Nancy and Poco's house was done much warmer, lots of wood and earth tones. As if reading my mind, Annie said, "Nice house. When I was a girl, I always dreamed of living in a place like this."

"We could never afford something like this."

"Oh, I know. That was a girl's dream. I wouldn't want a house this big. There'd be too much to clean."

I laughed and said, "You have a point there."

* * *

The evening had proven to be quite pleasant. After dinner, Poco had retired to his study to work on a brief he had to file the next day, while Annie, Jenny, and I moved to the game room to entertain ourselves. I had really enjoyed the time with my two girls, but I was anxious to move on to the second reason, perhaps the real reason I wanted to have dinner here tonight. I hoped Nancy was almost through messing around in the kitchen. On cue, Nancy appeared in the doorway. The women must be hearing my thoughts tonight, and after a second, I realized that could be both good and bad.

Nancy addressed Annie first, "Do you mind if I steal Mason away from you for a few minutes? I need his help with something in my office."

"No not at all. You do have a lovely house."

"Thank, you Annie. It's sweet of you to say that. I must say you've made quite an impression on my brother-in-law here, and Jenny too for that matter. Come on, Mason. I need your muscles."

Annie rose from her seat on my lap, so I could get up.

"Make yourself comfortable, Annie." Nancy pointed to the hallway at the far end of the game room and said, "The bathroom is the second door on the right, if you need it."

"Thanks, Nancy. You're a great host."

I watched Annie curl up in the corner of the big stuffed sofa along the far wall as I followed Nancy out of the game room and into the great room. Before dinner, I had secretly asked Nancy to call me out when she had the chance. I wanted to talk to her alone, but I didn't want to make Annie feel like she was being left out.

* * *

Unlike her husband, the books that lined the shelves of Nancy Long's office were more technical than science fiction. Unless of course, you feel that the psychiatric profession deals mostly in science fiction. I was never much of a believer in psychiatrists, not wanting to get too close for fear of catching something. Even the reading of books about mental illness scared me, made me feel afraid that if I read about something like bipolar disorder, I would start exhibiting the symptoms. My sister-in-law waved toward a comfortable brown leather chair sitting in the corner of the room. "Sit, Mason."

I sat, fidgeting with my hands, picking at the nail on my left ring finger. I could hardly look up, I felt so uncomfortable and out of place. My discomfort was not due to the office mind you, which was very warm and inviting, all wood and leather. My discomfort also wasn't due to my sister-in-law, who I really liked. My discomfort was due to the fact that I was beginning to think I was losing my mind.

Nancy sat down on the brown leather couch that completed the l-shaped corner sitting area. "What's the matter, Mason? You can talk to me."

I looked up at the kind smile. "I think I may be losing my mind." I was terrified that she would either laugh at me or scold me, but my fears were groundless. No laughter. No accusations. No yelling. No humiliation of any sort, nothing at all like my confrontations with Kendyll Hall.

In a quiet caring voice, she simply asked, "What makes

you think that?"

I breathed a deep sigh of relief, happy to be able to talk to somebody. "I don't know where to begin."

"Begin at the beginning. Has it something to do with your current troubles?"

"I believe so, but then that's why I'm here. I'm not really sure about anything anymore."

"Tell me about it."

I let it all pour out about Bender, about seeing him at the beach, about seeing him at Carmen's when I found her body. I told her about seeing Bender at the marina. I left out the part about finding Marci's body and dumping it into the gulf. I told her about seeing him at The Gardens. I told her about my search for Bender the fighter that no one else had seen. I told her about my returning memories, about speaking in riddles with Bender by Carmen's pool. Nancy listened patiently, not showing much emotion one way or the other, until I was completely spent, drained of any emotion myself.

"Has anyone besides you seen this man?"

"No. I thought I could find him and prove he existed by talking with the other fighter, but instead I'm afraid I only verified the fact that I might be losing my mind."

"We don't know that yet, Mason. Don't leap to any conclusions."

"But Bender obviously wasn't involved in the fight. I must have been seeing things."

"Slow down. The eye sometimes sees what the mind wants it to see. That doesn't necessarily mean you are losing your senses."

I tried to calm down and stay in control of my emotions. I pointed to a small refrigerator in the opposite corner of the room behind a small bar-like table. "Is there a beer in that refrigerator?"

"There sure is. Help yourself."

I hauled myself up out of the soft chair and made my way to the refrigerator. After opening the door, I reached in and grabbed a cold bottle, before turning and asking, "You want one too?"

"Sure, I'll drink one with you."

I grabbed a second bottle out of the refrigerator and twisted the tops off of both bottles. I threw the caps into the trashcan and returned to my seat. I handed a beer to Nancy and sat back down. We both took good, long swallows of the beer.

"Are you drinking at lot?"

I instantly started to lie and said, "Not too much. A few beers here and there," until I realized that lying was not going to do me any good, and judging from the look on Nancy's face, she wasn't buying my lies anyway. "That's not true. I'm drinking a real lot."

"How would you define a real lot?"

"Like night and day, every day."

"You said you didn't remember anything about the night of Carmen's murder. True?"

"True."

"Blackout?"

"Yes."

"Are you having a lot of blackouts?"

"Most nights, to be honest." I had never told anyone about the true extent of my drinking and blackouts before. I mean sure, Arthur and Poco knew some things, but they didn't know the full story either. I wondered what she would think of me. I was sure that she would see me as someone weak, maybe even evil, and treat me with disgust.

Nancy must have read my look of fear. "It's okay, Mason. Alcoholism is a disease."

"Alcoholism?" I jumped forward to the edge of my seat, panic setting in deep. I immediately took back all the nice things I had thought about the bitch. Sure I drank some, and maybe I overdid it at times, but alcoholic? No way. "I am not an alcoholic."

"Calm down, nobody said you were an alcoholic."

"You did."

"I'm sorry if you took it that way. Why? Do you think you're an alcoholic?"

"No, I don't."

"Perhaps, you're only a heavy drinker. You can make up your own mind about that, but blackouts are often one of the symptoms of the disease of alcoholism. Withdrawal is another indication. Are you having withdrawal symptoms when you cut down on the drinking?"

Despite her efforts to be kind, I didn't at all like the conversation. If I did have a drinking problem, I sure wasn't ready to admit it. I wasn't ready to quit drinking completely. I could slow down maybe, but quit? No way. What would I do with myself? I wouldn't have any friends. No, quitting drinking was not an option.

"Mason?"

"What?"

"I asked if you were having withdrawal symptoms?"

I was beginning to think that Nancy Long was like all the rest, ready to tell me what to do, tell me how to live my life, make me abandon the one thing I really liked to do. I stared at her.

"Look, Mason. You don't have to talk to me at all. I didn't drag you in here. You came to me because you're having a problem." She rose from her seat and set her half empty beer bottle on the table next to the sofa. "We can forget all about it, if you like?"

She was right. I had come to her, and if I could get my ego out of the fucking way, Nancy would help me sort things out. "Sit, Nancy. Please?"

She slowly settled back into the sofa. "Are you okay?" She asked, still thinking of me.

"No, I'm not okay."

"You know I don't have any miracles, but let's see if we can sort some things out. That's what we do as psychiatrists."

"Okay. What we're you asking." I had to bite the bullet and admit to my problems or I would never see a time where I could lead a relatively happy life.

"I asked if you go through withdrawal when you cut down on the drinking."

"If what you mean by withdrawal is the shakes. Yes, I'm shaking when I wake up and keep shaking until I either pop a Valium or have a couple of beers or something."

"Your body is trying to tell you something."

"Will the shakes and shit get better if I quit for awhile?"

"Sure, they'll stop, but the strange thing about drinking is that no matter how long you abstain, most people pick up right where they left off if they start drinking again."

I knew she inserted the word drinking when she wanted to say alcoholism for my benefit. "So I'm destined to go through this shit forever?"

"Probably."

"What kind of other kind of bullshit can happen?" As soon as the words were out of my mouth, my thoughts flashed to Bender. "Hallucinations?"

"I don't want to be the bearer of bad news, but I don't want to give you false hope either. Things can get much worse. People have been known to hallucinate during DTs. You've heard of delirium tremors?"

"Yes." Of course, I'd heard of them. Were my sightings of Bender actually hallucinations?

Nancy was continuing with her answer. "Heavy drinkers can develop various states of mental disorder, including and up to almost complete brain loss."

"Wet brain?"

"Yes. But the good news is that all you really need to do to eliminate all the bad news is to stop drinking completely."

Like it or not, we had gotten to the place that I dreaded. My head hurt. I didn't want to think about it anymore, but I had to find out what was happening to me. "Is it possible that I hallucinated all those Bender sightings?"

"Yes, it's possible. But like I said earlier, let's not jump to any conclusions. Let me ask you a couple of questions."

"Go ahead."

"Have you seen other things that could be hallucinations?"

"No, I can't think of anything else."

"Are all the Bender actions within the realm of possibility?"

"What do you mean?"

"I mean. Could an actual human being have done the things you say Bender has done?"

"You mean like standing in a crowd, riding a train, sitting under an umbrella. Sure I guess that's true."

"Then we really don't know with any degree of certainty whether he exists or whether you are hallucinating."

"I already knew that. I came to you for answers."

"You have the answer. You're not willing to accept it."

She was right on the money, of course. I knew what she would say next before she said it.

"Your answer is to stop drinking. We'll know soon enough if that eliminates the symptoms or not. At any rate, it is certainly the first step of treatment for whatever else ails you."

"You are right. I don't like the answer. Are there any other possibilities that would explain these Bender visions, if that's what they are?"

"Of course, but that might mean you really are losing your mind."

* * *

Dessert consisted of strawberry short cake and whipped

cream. I passed on the coffee. I didn't need a stimulant. I didn't need anything that would increase my agitation. Instead of calming my nerves, the conversation with Nancy had served to increase my anxiety. Nothing short of a miracle would provide me with a quick answer to my problems. And the truth of the matter was that no miracles would be forthcoming.

Nancy stood next to me with the dessert tray in her hands.

"Do you want another piece of short cake, Mason?"

I looked down at my plate, covered with crumbs and smeared with whipped cream. Apparently, I didn't remember eating the first piece. "No thanks."

"I want another one Momma."

"You've had enough, Jenny. If you're good you can have more tomorrow night."

"Aw, momma."

"You don't want to get bad eating habits do you?"

"No, momma. I guess not."

"How about you Annie?"

"No, thanks. I don't want to get bad eating habits either."

Annie winked at Jenny, who immediately giggled. Obviously, the two had become fast friends while Nancy and I had talked.

"You are a great hostess, Nancy. Thank you for everything."

"I'm glad you enjoyed it."

"I really did." Annie almost gushed her answers.

I could tell that my new love was really enjoying herself, and for my part, I was doing my best not to ruin it for her.

But all I wanted to do was get out of there and drink a few beers. I knew Nancy was right about the drinking, and I didn't want her to think that her advice would be lost on me. Tomorrow would be my day of reckoning, but not tonight. I leaned over towards Annie and said quietly, "Let's go get my boat and go for a sunset cruise."

Annie immediately nodded yes, a smile wide on her face.

As I rose from my chair, I thought I saw the briefest of clouds pass over the face of our hostess. "We're going to go. Thanks for everything." I winked at Nancy conspiratorially. Her face beamed with hope and kindness. I must have been mistaken about the clouds.

CHAPTER 18

"You will pay dearly for your indiscretions." I chased Annie all the way to the stern rail of the deck before I caught her once again. Somehow, her bikini top had come off in the tussle, and I grabbed her around the breasts with my left hand, while I tickled her side mercilessly with my right.

"Please, Mason. I can't take anymore."

I relented. Turning her around, I put my arms around her waist and kissed her deeply on the lips.

"You'll get yours one day, buddy." She laughed easily when we broke the kiss. "You know what they say. Paybacks are a motherfucker. Or something like that."

I gave her a sly look and asked, "What can I do to make it up to you?"

Before Annie could answer my question, the fishing rod perched in the rod holder next to us began to sing. I had baited the line and set it in place when we first stopped. Since fishing was one of my lifelong passions, I developed the habit of setting a rod. It didn't matter whether I was on a fishing trip or not, and this was why. "Holy shit." The fishing rod was bent in half, the tip pointing towards the blue water, the pink line peeling rapidly off the reel. "Will you look at that?"

Annie stood silent. Obviously, she had never seen a strike by a big fish, and the violence of the strike had rendered her speechless. She stood watching the rod with a look of wonder on her face. Her mouth hung open. I knew it had to be big fish because of the way it had hit the bait and kept going. The pressure of the reel's drag had not slowed it a bit. It had to be either a big king or a shark. "I guess I better do something." I eased the rod out of the holder, pressing the butt of the rod into my lower abdomen and holding on with both hands.

"What the hell is it?"

"It's probably a shark."

"Shark?" She voiced in a fevered pitch.

"Yes, probably a bull shark or a hammerhead judging from the size."

"You're not going to bring that thing in this boat?"

"Of course, I am. They're good eating."

"It might eat us."

"Don't worry too much yet. I have to get it to the boat first." The heavy fish remained intent on staying on the bottom, and every time I managed to bring him up a few feet, he dove back down. The battle raged. My arms began to tire, but I looked around in awe and the near perfect paradise that surrounded me. The warm, dark blue water glistened with the setting sun. A faint breeze rippled the water slightly. Annie still stood next to me bra-less, a vision of beauty. The thought that she might actually love me gave me a peace I hadn't known since my childhood. A far off thunderhead, dark in its beauty was the only thing that marred the scene. We would get rained on later. As I finally started to make some headway with the fish, I had an idea. "Come here, Annie. It's your turn." I removed the butt of the rod from my belly and held it with both hands, offering to let her share in the fun.

"Oh, no. Not me."

"Come on, you can do it. You'll love it."

I watched as indecision swept across her face until she slowly began to reach for the rod. I admired her willingness to try something new, even though I was certain that she was not too keen on the idea. I handed the rod to her. "Take it with both hands."

She obeyed, grapping the rod with her left hand just above the real and placing the butt in her abdomen as she had seen me do.

"Pump the rod."

"What?"

"Pump it. Bring it up, then lower it and reel at the same time." I demonstrated the motion for her.

"Got it." She began to work the fish, actually able to take in some line and get it closer to the boat. "This is cool," she said with a smile.

I had been wrong about the type of shark. Ten minutes later she had the Blacktip shark to the surface. This fish looked to be around five foot long and weighed maybe fifty pounds. I grabbed the gaff from its hanging place under the port rail. With the gaff in my right hand I leaned over the rail in front of Annie. Taking the line from the fishing rod in my left hand, I used it as a guide until I could get a grip on the brass swivel, which had come out of the water. "Steady, hold the rod high, Annie." In one smooth, fast motion, I struck the fish hard under the jaw, impaling him to the gaff. Using both hands, I pulled up hard, dragging the shark over the rail and onto the deck, where it thrashed around mightily.

"Oh my God." Annie dropped the rod onto the deck and headed for cover, climbing on the top of the closest rail.

I had underestimated the vitality of the fish. I had thought that it was pretty close to spent, but obviously I was wrong. I hurried over to retrieve the small baseball bat that I kept with the gaff. I had to beat the shark over the head several times before it stopped moving. By then, blood had spattered all over the deck and the two of us.

"Did you have to kill it?"

"What was I going to do? I wasn't about to try and wrestle it back into the water."

"Good point."

"I won't have killed him for nothing. We'll eat him. You'll see it will be great."

"Look, I'm covered with blood." Annie motioned to her still bare breasts.

Shark blood had mixed with sweat generated by her fight with the fish and ran down in a tiny rivulet between her breasts. I just smiled. "You'll live. Let's hose off the deck and get the fish cleaned and then you can take a shower."

"A cold water shower doesn't sound too great."

"We haven't been out of port too long. The water won't be that cold. The water heater stays on when we're plugged in at the marina." She seemed mollified with my answer although her smile had yet to return. "Then we'll take care of some other business."

Her smile returned. I bet she had remembered the sly look I had given her earlier. "Now that sounds good. Where's the hose, Captain?"

"Under the stern rail. See it? The blue hose."

"Yes, I see it." Annie went over and pulled the saltwater hose from under the stern rail. "Do I have to turn it on?"

"No, press the handle."

She pressed the handle, squirting salt water all over me. "Oops."

"Hey, watch where you're aiming that thing."

She squirted me again, not letting up for a good five seconds before she said, "Pay backs are a motherfucker, ain't they?"

"Point taken." I smiled and watched her go to work washing down the deck with the hose. "You'll get yours later."

"Promise?"

"Promise."

While she continued to hose down the deck, I busied myself with the task at hand. Picking up the bloody corpse, I placed it on the cleaning table behind the captain's seat. Since I always picked up ice on the way to the boat, there would be plenty to ice down the shark steaks. Grabbing my sharpest filet knife from the right table drawer, I cleanly sliced open the belly of the fish and removed the innards.

When she finished cleaning, Annie shut off the hose and

came over to watch. "That's yucky."

"Yes, but when I cook some of this baby, you'll be wanting me to get shark every night for year's to come."

"For years to come? I like the sound of that."

"Yes, for years to come." I smiled at her over my shoulder. Scooping up the bloody fish guts with both hands, I threw them overboard. Next, I cut off the shark's head and tail and threw them overboard. Although we were miles offshore, several sea gulls materialized out of thin air, fighting each other for diving rights to the sinking shark parts. With both hands I centered the remainder of the shark on the cutting board and neatly cut the fish into one-inch steaks. "These are going to be great. We'll grill a couple when we get back to the marina. You hungry?"

"I'm starting to get there."

"I'm almost done here. Why don't you go below and get cleaned up before the water cools down anymore."

Darkness began to set in as I put the shark steaks into plastic bags and then placed them on ice. When I was finished, I watched the full moon low on the eastern horizon. I loved full moons. The sun went down, the moon came up, nature in all of its glory, staging the greatest show on earth.

* * *

While Annie showered below, I took the opportunity to relax a bit in the captain's chair. I put my feet up and sipped on a cold beer. Once the sun went down, the temperature dropped back into the tolerable range, and after rolling the cool can back and forth over my forehead several times, I actually felt comfortable. A cool shower and I would be ready to roll. My spirits were on the rise. I had placed all the bad thoughts into the wait until later bin. Thinking another one wouldn't hurt, I swallowed down the rest of my beer in a single gulp and crushed the can in my right hand. I put my feet back on the deck and rose from the captain's chair. The remainder of the beer rested comfortably with the shark steaks, so I went over to the cooler, opened the lid, and tossed the empty inside. I retrieved a fresh beer and closed the lid. As I popped the top, later came.

I couldn't believe my eyes. Surely, they must be playing tricks on me. Bender sat sideways on the stern rail, smiling at me. His legs were pulled up into the lotus position. It was almost as if he was posing for a magazine layout. I hadn't heard a sound, and for the life of me, I couldn't imagine how he got there without my seeing or hearing anything. He simply materialized out of thin air like the sea gulls after the shark guts. My pulse quickened at the sight, but I was not surprised. I wondered what had taken him so long to show his face, and at the same time I was terrified of why he had finally come.

Bender swung his legs down to face me and said, "You don't look surprised."

"I'm not surprised. What took you so long?"

The laugh that came from his mouth sent cold shivers down my back. My arms erupted in goose bumps.

"The time wasn't right."

My mind drifted back to the conversation I'd had with

Nancy Long earlier in the evening. Until this point in time, everything Bender had done had been humanly possible. He could have been some deranged character stalking me, trying to make my life miserable. But now it seemed that he was a more integral part of me than I wanted to consider, or he was pure evil, manifested in a clown-like apparition. Neither choice particularly thrilled me. I tried not to react without thought, better I should feel him out. "But now the time is right?"

"Yes."

Who the hell was I talking with? I still had no answers. The unknown always did scare me more than the known. I could handle myself in a fight, but sneaky things, unseen things like cancer, that could be eating you away without your knowledge, those things frightened me deeply. I didn't want to hear the answer to my next question, but asked anyway. "Why?"

"You need protection."

"You've said that before, from who?"

"From whom?"

"I asked first."

"No, Mason. The correct word is whom. Not from who, but from whom."

Now the son of a bitch had turned into my fifth grade English teacher. Where would this end? I didn't want to hear the answer to that question either. "Answer the question, Bender."

Bender did not voice an answer, he simply pointed to the cabin door.

If I thought that I was scared before, I was wrong. When Bender pointed to the cabin door, thoughts of Annie lying broken like Carmen and Marci ran through my mind like a raging hurricane. My fists clenched and every other muscle in my body tightened. The thought of someone or some thing hurting Annie had triggered such emotion, such anger, that I couldn't think or see straight. "What?" I mumbled.

"She's not who you think she is."

The words were the same he spoke during my memories of the night that Carmen was murdered.

"She's not who you think she is."

This time the words referred to Annie. I had to do something. Without thought, I scrambled over to the port rail and grabbed the club that I used to beat the shark to death. In one quick motion, I lunged at Bender and swung as hard as I could at the man's head, but he disappeared as quickly and as silently as he had appeared. The club flew from my hand, spinning like a boomerang, until it hit the water and sank, a hundred or so feet from the boat. The crack in paradise that I had noticed recently opened wide and swallowed me whole.

PART THREE

No Escape

CHAPTER 19

"Who were you talking to?" Annie asked as she walked up through the cabin door and onto the deck. I searched for an answer, but could think of nothing that made sense. Stalling for time, I noticed the moon looming large above the horizon, so I answered, "The moon."

Annie returned a strange look, but played along. "The man in the moon?"

"Yes." Her quip came as close to an explanation as anything I could muster. I turned away from her and pointed to the rising moon. "Incredible, isn't it?"

She climbed into the captain's chair. Her legs dangled over the edge, missing the deck by at least a foot. Magically producing a banana, she peeled it half way down before taking a bite. "It sure is nice being here with you," her face still turned towards the sky.

I wondered what such a good-looking, sexy woman saw in a guy like me, and I would have loved to have been able to chit-chat further, to enjoy some special time with her, but the truth was that all I could think about was how I had to get her away from me. After the visit from Bender, I needed to get her home and safe. A static-filled woman's voice interrupted my thoughts.

Tonight's forecast calls for lows in the upper seventies with an eighty percent chance of rain in the coastal areas. More details at ten minutes after the hour.

Annie must have turned the radio on to the news and weather channel. Looking west, the weather people appeared to be right for once. Storms were building. I could see the flashes on the far horizon. I wondered why the human body had such a limited comfort range for heat and cold. To me, anything below seventy degrees was cold, and anything above eighty-five degrees was hot. That left a comfort range of fifteen degrees. No wonder people complained all the time. Annie came up behind me, wrapped her arms around my waist, and pushed her hips close. I turned around and draped my arms over her shoulders. We kissed.

This just in, the body of a young woman was found floating off the coast of Sunset Beach. The woman's identity has not been released by police, pending the notification of family.

The voice droned on, but I heard nothing further. My body stiffened as the news hit me hard. I knew immediately that it must be Marci. It had to be. Annie felt me stiffen. She leaned back and looked into my eyes.

"What's the matter, Mason. You're scaring me."

"Shhh. Listen."

Two fishermen found the woman's body a short time ago about two miles directly offshore from Sunset Pass. Police are at the scene. Further details at eleven.

"Oh, my God. You think it's Marci."

Unfortunately, Annie had read my mind. I replied, "I don't know what to think, but you are right. It's awful coincidental."

"Nobody has heard from Marci?"

"No." How could I tell the woman I loved and wanted to spend the rest of my life with that her future husband had dumped the body of his ex-girlfriend into the Gulf of Mexico. What kind of person would do that? Before I could beat myself up any further, the cell phone in my pocket vibrated. I read the display, and then added, "It's Poco."

"You better answer it."

"Can you turn off the radio?" I didn't care about the radio. What I really wanted was a bit of privacy. I didn't want to have to talk to Poco in front of Annie.

"Sure." Annie disappeared below.

I answered the call. "What's up bro?"

"I've got bad news, little brother."

"They found Marci's body."

"You heard?"

"It was on the radio. Are they sure it was Marci?"

"Yes, there was an ID in her pocket. They haven't made it public yet."

Damn, I didn't think they would find her body, and I sure didn't think she had any ID in those short shorts. "I'm sorry to hear that."

"They've issued a warrant for your arrest." I pictured Poco at home in his comfortable office, still working on the report due tomorrow morning when the phone call came from the police. I felt a knife twist in my guts, while the poor me's raced through my mind. How did I manage to get myself into these things? What have I ever done to deserve such trouble? Why can't I have a life like my brother's? Poco brought me back, "Where are you?"

I hesitated. Poco was my brother, but he was also my lawyer and an officer of the court. If anything, Poco was honest to a fault. He would do his duty and then help his little brother. By then, it could be too late.

"Tampa." I lied.

"Did you have something to do with this?"

I didn't know how to answer his question, but it no longer mattered. I made the decision then and there to run. I did not want to take my chances with the legal system and Hall. I also didn't want to involve Poco any more than necessary, so I remained silent.

"Where in Tampa?" Poco would not let go.

"I can't tell you, Poco. I don't want to get you in trouble."

"If you know something, then you need to turn yourself in."

"It's not what you think. I didn't kill Marci."

"But you know more than you are telling me. How in the hell am I supposed to help you if you won't help yourself."

"I didn't kill her."

"Then turn yourself in. I told Hall that I would bring you down voluntarily if I could."

I knew Hall would be involved. "I can't do that."

"I'll be right by your side."

Annie reappeared at the cabin door. I smiled at her, before returning my attention to the cell phone. "I love you, Poco." I closed the connection. I hoped that Poco would understand and forgive me one day. I sat down on the port rail totally drained of emotion.

"What's going on?" Annie came over and sat on the rail by my side.

I tried to answer but couldn't. I lowered my head into my hands, keeping a hold on myself. My whole world seemed to be coming to an end.

Annie rubbed her hand along the back of my neck. "Mason, talk to me. You're scaring me."

I had to find some courage, at least for her sake. I raised my head and said barely above a whisper, "They want to arrest me."

"The body they found was Marci?"

"Yes."

"But you haven't done anything."

"They think I did." By now, I was sure that everyone but Annie thought I was guilty of something, and they were right. I was at the very least guilty of stupidity. "They don't believe me."

"I believe you."

I raised my eyes to hers. The love in her eyes made me wince. I didn't deserve her trust or her love. But I vowed then and there that the least I could do was protect her. Bender's reference to Annie earlier had scared the hell out of me. I had to make sure she was safe before I left town. I rose from the rail and turned to her, holding both her hands in mine. "I have to leave, Annie."

"What do you mean leave. As in run away?"

"Yes."

"You're not a murderer. Stay here with me. I'll help."

"No." The tone of my response left no room for further discussion.

I could tell that she wasn't happy about it, but Annie quickly accepted the fact that I had to make the decision for myself. Her ability to understand was one of the traits I admired most about her. She looked up at me with those big sad eyes. Finally, she broke her silence and asked, "Where are you going to go?"

"South. The Bahamas."

Annie jumped up suddenly and wrapped both her arms around my shoulders. "Take me with you."

"I can't do that to you, Annie."

"But, Mason. I love you. I don't want to lose you."

"I love you too. Too much to make a fugitive out of you." We stood for the longest time holding on to each other tightly, neither of us willing to be the first one to break the bond. I had never felt so bad in my life about having to leave someone. The moon had risen some while my world tilted, its reflection trailed across the water to the south. If I managed to get my hands on some money and enough fuel, I could follow the trail wherever it led.

* * *

John's Pass separated Sunset Beach on the south from Madeira Beach to the north, providing an outlet to the Gulf of Mexico. And like the town of Sunset Beach, the area around the pass kept one foot in the past and one foot in the present. As I maneuvered *The Tramp* through the narrow opening of the main bridge span, trying not to hit the two boats heading out to sea, and trying not to whack the starboard side of my boat on the protective bridge fenders, I couldn't help but marvel at the mixture. Several old fuel docks and an outdated marina still retained the look from its storied past as a fishing village and smugglers haven. The story went that the pass was created by a horrific hurricane a hundred years or so ago. John's Pass suddenly provided a safe harbor for fishing and pirate vessels alike. Now, a boardwalk lined the northern side of the pass, full of touristy shops and restaurants while the Sunset Beach side of the pass had seen better days.

The place always seemed busy. For one thing, the pass provided the only exit from the Intracoastal Waterway for miles from the north. Anyone who lived in waterfront homes with boats in Madeira Beach and points north had to go through John's pass to get out into the Gulf of Mexico, or travel even further south to Sunset Pass. Fishing boats used the pass on a regular basis. The casino boat tied to the boardwalk used the pass. A fake pirate ship roamed the intracoastal and called the pass home. The point was that we could get lost in the hustle and bustle. I didn't know many people who lived around John's Pass and doubted that anyone would notice me or the Tramp. But what choice did I have? My credit cards were maxed out. I couldn't head out to sea without fuel and supplies.

Once inside the bridge, I turned toward the dilapidated fuel dock on the southern side. Most of the locals used Skip's because he gave discounts to residents. Like at Sunset Marina, I kept a tab at Skip's. In fact, Joe Moore who manned the fuel dock at my marina also moonlighted here in the evenings. I hoped that he was working tonight, because Joe wouldn't ask too many questions and wouldn't give anyone else too many answers. If I docked the boat around behind the fuel shack, I thought that I could get in and out of town without incident. As I slowed the boat to dock, Joe came out of the beat up old wooden shack that served as an office. I was in luck. "Annie, toss Joe the bow rope."

"Okay," she said, and ran up to the bow along the starboard side rail.

"Mason, what are you doing up here in these parts?" Joe called and caught the rope that Annie tossed him. He secured the boat to the dock.

"You make it sound like we're a hundred miles from Sunset Pass."

"Seems like another world. What with all these tourists and such."

In truth, we were only a couple of miles from my apartment, and I figured that I could walk Annie to the Coconut Hut, and then stop at the apartment and get the money I had stashed.

"Who do we have here?" Joe gave Annie an old man leer before smiling broadly.

"Annie, Joe. Joe, Annie. You must not have been at the Hut recently. Annie tends bar there."

"I guess I haven't, but I'm sure to go more often now."

"I bet you flirt with all the girls."

"He does." I chimed in. "Can you fill her up and put it on my tab?"

"Sure, Mason."

"Do you mind if I leave the boat here for awhile. I have to take care of some business. I'll take care of you next time."

"No problem."

"Grab your stuff, Annie."

While Annie busied herself below, I took stock of my situation. As we cruised in I had formulated a plan. Joe was taking care of the first part by fueling the boat. Step two required stopping at my apartment. Step three entailed stopping by the cab company to see what money Arthur could give me. Of course, all this had to be achieved without running into any cops. Then I'd take The Tramp south, way south. I wouldn't stop until I needed fuel. The plan ended when I hit the Bahamas. I'd have to adlib after that, but I could deal with fending for myself in the Caribbean better than I could deal with jail.

"I'm ready." Annie had reappeared from below deck.

My heart ached when I saw the sad look on her face. I had to be strong. "Let's do it."

"I hate this, Mason."

"I hate it too." She looked beautiful standing there in shorts and a tank top. I could hardly make myself leave her, but I needed to protect her. I was afraid of who I was and what I might do. Too many things had been left unexplained. The safest place for Annie was with friends at the Hut. We climbed from the boat and began to walk.

* * *

The roof of the Coconut Hut appeared as if on fire. The flickering torches surrounding the tiki hut bar in back gave the entire place a soft aura. The warm red glow poured over the roof and onto Annie, who stood before me with her arms wrapped around my waist. I looked deep into those big brown eyes. All I could see was love. My resolve to leave her behind and safe, crumbled as easily as my feet sank into the soft sand.

"Please, Mason. I can't stand the thought of living here without you. I want more time."

Time always seemed the culprit. Before all of this happened to me, time moved slowly, like it should in a small lazy beach town. But since last Friday, time had picked up speed considerably. It seemed as if I was living several lives all at the same time, trying to juggle separate existences. The weeks spent with Arthur and Marci partying at the Coconut Hut now seemed like the distant past. "I can't do that, honey.

I don't want you implicated in the whole mess. You could be charged with a crime."

"I don't care. I know you feel the same way about me as I feel about you. Don't you?"

"Of course, I do. You know I do, but that doesn't change anything." How could I tell her that the law wasn't the only thing I feared? How could I tell her that what I feared most seemed to be a figment of my own imagination?

"Please, Mason. Think about it." Annie turned her head sideways and snuggled into my chest.

"You know I can't."

"Please, don't say no yet. Come back with the boat and say good-bye."

"I don't know about that."

"Please?" She lifted her face towards mine and pleaded with those eyes. "Please, please, please."

The idea did have some merit. As long as the police weren't watching the Hut too closely, I could sneak the Tramp up the canal in the dark and tie off behind the mangroves next door. Although it might be a stupid thing to do, I too wanted to meet once more. It might be a long time before I hugged her again.

"Promise me. Promise that you'll at least come back to say good-bye."

Knowing full well that I would regret my decision later, I finally relented and said, "Okay." As Annie hugged me tighter, the back service door opened, allowing a nameless reggae tune to escape into the night. DeCarlo came through with two large trash bags. After he opened the top of the trash bin, he threw them inside. I didn't know what to do, but when Lenny nodded silently in my direction, I knew it would be all right. He wouldn't turn me in. Lenny's sudden appearance fueled my fear. There was no telling who might stumble upon us. "I have to go. I'll call your cell when I'm on my way back. Don't let anybody know what's going on. Promise?"

"Promise."

I turned and walked away, looking back to wave a couple of times. Annie stood in the glow from the firelight, tears on her face, until I turned the corner and headed for what was once home.

CHAPTER 20

The lights were on in most of the houses on my old block, but the street was fairly dark. The only direct light came from the streetlight on the corner. The streetlight in the middle of the block had burned out weeks ago and hadn't been repaired. Now I'm not a cop, but wouldn't you think that if you were going to stake out a house, you would park in the middle of the block, in the dark. But no, two of Sunset Beach's finest had parked in plain sight close to the corner under the light. Go figure. Since they had the front of the house covered, I decided to see if anyone was watching the back of the house. I really needed the money and didn't want to leave without it. I figured that if no one was out back, I could sneak into the apartment and get my stash without turning on any lights. Cutting around the corner, I silently crossed my asshole neighbor's yard in the dark, careful not to fall over the hedge that tripped me up the last time. Nothing in the backyards seemed out of place, except for a very rotten smelling aroma. I smiled.

I guessed the cops had decided that watching the front of the house would be enough, and I made it to the back door without incident. I retrieved the key from under the mat and inserted it into the deadbolt lock. A movement from next door caught my attention. My asshole neighbor had appeared in his kitchen window. The one good thing about all of this was that at least I'd probably never have to deal with him again. I didn't how wrong that thought would be as I fiddled with the lock. I hastened my movements, hoping that he had not seen me. Another two seconds and I was in the door. Once inside, I closed the door behind me silently and leaned back for a minute to let my eyes grow accustomed to the dark. Enough moonlight and streetlight filtered in through the windows for me to see well enough. I knew that the bottle of whiskey still sat on the top shelf, so I moved a chair over below the cabinet and retrieved the bottle. I felt no need to stand on ceremony in my present position and drank a good swallow right from the bottle. I headed for the back bedroom with bottle in hand. The money was hidden in a loose board inside of the bedroom closet. This old house had multiple loose boards and apparently Marci had never found my hiding place.

A sound from outside stopped me dead in my tracks. I stood straining and listening for a minute but heard nothing further. I resumed my hunt, and within a couple of minutes, had torn open the board and put the five hundred dollars in my pocket. At least I would have enough money to last a few days while I tried to find some work, wherever I ended up. My nerves were almost at their end. This sneaking around in the dark, afraid of the police, afraid of my self, afraid of the future, had taken its toll on me. I sat on the edge of bed, trying to catch my breath and collect my thoughts.

The pillow framed Marci's head in the soft light. She was beautiful in all her nakedness. I couldn't believe the way things had turned out, that she was leaving me and running out of town. If only things had been different.

She wrapped her arms and legs tighter around me and said, "Come on, lover. Don't' stop now."

"I wish things had worked out differently."

"I don't want to hear that shit. Do it to me."

I looked down into her eyes and my heart damn near stopped beating. Down in the depths of her eyes, a movement caught my attention. I focused harder. Something appeared to be moving. No not something, some things appeared to moving, frantically darting to and fro. I told myself not to look any further, but I couldn't take my own advice. I focused harder, let my eyes and mind drift down into the depths of her being. Hideous worm-like maggots kept creepy crawling in a pile. I screamed.

The sudden memory caused me to drop the bottle of whiskey onto the bedroom floor. I stood up from the bed like I had sat on a hot coal. My mind must have decided to check out on me, without informing me of its decision. I picked up the bottle as fast as I had dropped it without spilling but an ounce or so. I was shaking and couldn't stop. Putting the bottle to my lips, I took a great drink. If there was a worst time for a memory to return, I couldn't think of one.

Thankfully, I didn't have time to think because I heard a noise from outside again. The instinct of survival took over and I ran over to the bedroom window. "Damn, that asshole." The trouble-causing neighbor had struck again. Apparently, he had seen me at the back door and was now standing next to the police vehicle talking to one of the officers. I could see him gesturing like a mad man and running his mouth as usual. He must have told them that he had seen me, for a second later, two unmarked cars came speeding around the corner headed in my direction. The first car screeched to a halt in front of the apartment as I headed out the back door.

I retraced the steps I had taken to come into the house, and as I crossed back across my neighbor's yard, I was treated to a glimpse of my arch nemesis exiting her police vehicle. Kendyll Hall had exited the car with gun drawn and was headed for the front door of the apartment. I ran as quickly as I could out the back of the yard, across the alley, and into the yard that faced the next street over. I knew the neighborhood very well after driving a cab and living in Sunset Beach these past ten years, and unless I was completely unlucky, I thought I could avoid capture. As I ran, my mind kept wandering back to the memory that had reared its ugly head in the apartment. If I wasn't so busy trying to escape, I don't think I could have gone on. Was I really going crazy? I had looked deeply into Marci's eyes many times during our relationship, and mostly what I saw was joy, even love early on. Granted the look in her eyes had gone sour over the last few months, but I never saw anything like the nightmare of her eyes in my memory. Were my memories truly returning, or was my mind playing god-awful tricks on me.

An approaching police car interrupted my thoughts. I had kept to the shadows so I doubted that I had been seen. Nevertheless, I ducked behind a hedge and let the vehicle pass. In my panic, I had at first thought about going straight back to the boat, but then I thought calm down and follow the plan. Arthur should still be working. I could hide out and let things die down before heading back over to the boat. Besides, I was sure Arthur would lend me some cash.

CHAPTER 21

Usually during the late evening hours, the cab company garage was deserted. I snuck in the side door while a lone mechanic busied himself under one of the cabs in the far corner. As I made my way back toward the office, a familiar aroma assaulted my senses; Chemo must be nearby. I had to be careful. Someone like Chemo would raise the alarm in a heartbeat, just like my asshole neighbor. I snuck around behind the row of parked taxis that were waiting for morning service. The oranges, yellows and reds reminded me of the brightly dressed women in the Sunday morning church pews of my youth. I stopped behind the last car in the row, nearest to the far wall of the garage and office. I rose up over the trunk of the cab and peeked inside the office. My nose had been right. Chemo stood in front of the teller window talking with Arthur. The scene made me think: good news, bad news. The good news was that Arthur was there, but bad news Chemo would keep me at bay until he was finished and left. I sat down on the cold concrete, behind the broken taxis, with my back to the wall. How fitting was that? It seemed my back was to wall in a host of ways.

Ten minutes later, the office door opened with a click. I held my breath, not from fear that Chemo might hear me, but because of the smell. I waited until the footsteps faded before I dared rise up over the trunk once more. The garage was completely vacant. Either the mechanic had quit for the night or went outside for a smoke. I better be careful because I wasn't sure which might be the truth. Seeing no one, I waved at Arthur. He didn't see me at first, but after some frantic hand gestures, he spotted me. He disappeared from the teller window into the depths of the office inner sanctum. Arthur was headed for the back door, and after checking for the mechanic, I made my way out through a side door. The parking lot was deserted. Nothing moved anywhere, so I cautiously sneaked along the side of the building towards the back lot. Arthur would be all about helping me, but besides lending me some money, there wasn't much else he could do. I had gotten myself into one hell of a mess, and I was the only one who could get myself free. Once I rounded the corner of the building, I could see him standing near the back door.

As I drew near, Arthur said in a quiet voice, "Mason what the hell are you doing here? They're looking for you."

"I know, dude. They almost caught me at the apartment."

"What the hell did you go there for?"

"I needed money."

"Why? What are you thinking, man? Running?"

"I have to."

His face morphed from concern to fear to anger to despair. I knew he didn't like the idea of not having me around. "I'll go with you," he said.

"I can't do that to you, bro."

"We always do things together."

"Not this time, Arthur." Arthur started to protest some more, but I raised my right hand in a stop motion.

He could tell from the look on my face that I didn't feel any better about the idea than he did. After a minute, he reluctantly accepted the situation and asked, "What's the plan?"

"The Tramp is over at John's Pass. Joe gassed her up. I'll head south. That's all I know."

"Freeport?"

"To start with. I'll get in touch with you as soon as I settle in a bit."

"Man, I can't believe this shit."

"Me either." We stood for a moment like we did earlier at the Coconut Hut, shaking our heads in unison. Life comes at you so fast. One minute all was well, the next minute I was living a nightmare.

"At least let me give you some money."

"I'll let you do that." I smiled.

Then Arthur astonished me by doing something completely out of character. He gave me a great big bear hug. We'd hung together for years, and the only time he would do anything like that was to stop me from beating on someone. The gesture brought a tear to my eye. I hugged him back. We stood there knowing in our hearts that the worst was yet to come. "You go wait in my car. I'll be off duty in half an hour or so." Arthur broke the hug and pointed across the lot to his SUV, while fishing the keys from his jeans pocket. "Here," he said and handed me the keys.

I stood there feeling as awkward as I'd ever felt. Even the debacle of my first slow dance with Kathy G in her basement when I was twelve paled in comparison. A flash of lightning, followed closely by a loud thunderclap broke the moment. The rain began in earnest as I bolted for Arthur's vehicle.

* * *

The inside of the humongous maroon SUV had to be at least ninety degrees. The hot Florida sun had baked the contents all afternoon. I couldn't understand what made some people think that they could leave kids and dogs locked up inside without dire consequences. If the interior was that hot now, imagine what it would have been like at two in the afternoon. Even after the sun goes down, it takes some time for a vehicle to cool down, especially on a hot night. Within minutes, the windows had fogged due to a combination of the cold rain on the outside of the windows and my hot breath coating the inside of the windows.

I put the keys into the ignition and cracked open both the driver and passenger side windows, providing some cross-ventilation and a bit of relief. I was tempted to open all the windows as wide as I could but didn't for two reasons: one, the rain had continued to pour down in windy sheets, and two, the fogged windows afforded me a bit of added security.

Prying eyes would be unable to see clearly into the vehicle. That was a good thing. I checked the time on the dash. It was almost ten-thirty. Arthur must be waiting for one of the other dispatchers to show up. He usually only worked until ten, and I had no doubt that he was waiting for the new asshole that worked nights, who seemed to be late a lot. I couldn't remember his name. I really didn't mind waiting. The last couple of hours had been tough on me, both physically and mentally. As I got comfortable in the passenger seat, my eyes began to close. From the looks of the storm, I would have to fight the wind, rain and waves all night in the boat, and I could use whatever rest I could get.

The alarm clock flashed the number 12:00 over and over again, a consequence of the power failure. The storm had knocked the power off for a few minutes, just long enough to make all the clocks go nuts. I wanted to smash the thing to tiny pieces. Carmen laughed loudly as I stumbled, trying to climb back into bed. I had lost my balance due to my drunken state. I fell hard across the bottom third of the mattress, as she giggled and pulled her bare feet to her bare chest. My open beer dropped to the floor and rolled, spewing its contents violently.

If looks could kill...

Carmen laughed at my silly rage about my lost beer. Her face contorted in an evil mask, appearing strangely enough like a gargoyle, monsters that adorned old mansions and castles. I wanted to smash the gargoyle to tiny pieces.

Bender stood atop the glass patio table top next to the pool. He was ranting and raving about something, but I couldn't make out a word he said. White foam came pouring from his mouth, like a washer with way too much laundry detergent. The foam muffled his words. I strained to hear, wondering what the hell was going on.

The pool shimmered in the moonlight. I could see shapes moving on the bottom, but I couldn't decide what they were. They looked like sharks, but they couldn't be, not in a freshwater pool loaded with chlorine. The sharks swam to and fro. There had to be four or five. They took turns swimming to the far side of the pool, before turning sharply and charging into the near side of the pool in a mad attempt to eat me. Each shark head made a loud thud as it hit the side of the pool.

Knuckles rapped on the driver side window. I could see a figure shrouded behind the foggy glass. I snapped my head forward as if I'd been asleep, but I wasn't sure if I'd actually dozed off or not. I had been in one of those twilight places, where the line between sleep and wakefulness is all in the imagination. I hoped that I'd been asleep, because if the place where I'd been was a dream, at least there was hope. I brought my mind back to the present. The figure behind the glass had to be Arthur. I leaned over and unlocked the door for him. My mind still struggled with the dream? The trouble was that I never remembered much from my dreams. For years I thought that I didn't dream at all. I suddenly felt cold and clammy, because if it was not a dream, I was losing my mind.

"Damn, Mason, what took you so long to open the door. I'm soaked."

"Sorry, Arthur. I guess I dozed off."

"Oh, don't worry about it. Reach under your seat and get me the towel that's under there."

I did as bid, and found the towel under my seat. One quick look at it and I decided to hold the soiled rag more gingerly. I didn't want my hands to touch it, and I sure wouldn't have wiped my face with it. The towel appeared to have resided under the seat for a great deal of time. I handed it to Arthur anyway. He wiped his face, arms and hands with the towel, seemingly oblivious to the dirt and grime. I guessed that when it was your dirt and grime, and you knew how it got that way, you could ignore the more ominous fears of contamination and disease. Or maybe, he had a higher tolerance for crap than I did. When he was finished, Arthur threw the towel into the back seat. "What the hell is happening, Mason. I'm worried."

"Me too, Arthur. I really don't know what else to do but take off. I can't do jail."

"What happened to the guy we saw at The Gardens?"

I noticed Arthur used we, and I didn't have the heart to correct him. After all, I was the only one to actually see Bender that night. "I tried to find him and couldn't. Nobody but me has seen him. I'm beginning to think he's not real."

"That's ridiculous."

"I don't know what to think. I was there when both Carmen and Marci were murdered."

"Marci?"

I guessed that Arthur had not heard about the fishermen finding her body. "Yes, Marci. They found her body floating in the gulf."

Arthur wore such a woeful look while he digested this latest bit of information. He had never in his life looked at me like that. It didn't last long, but it was long enough for me to realize how much everyone around me was being hurt by all of this. I strengthened my resolve to remove myself from the scene and save everyone the trouble of standing by me.

"What do you mean you were there? Did you murder them?" Arthur finally asked.

"I don't know. I still can't remember everything."

Arthur started the SUV while that last thought sank in. He put the vehicle into reverse but kept his foot on the brake. He turned to me and said, "So you really don't know whether you killed them or not."

It wasn't a question, but I answered anyway. The fear and frustration made it hard to talk. "No, I don't have any facts, but I'm sure that I'm involved somehow."

"I can't believe the Mason I know would kill anyone."

I thought that was true, but I was worried about the Mason that I didn't know. "I'm hallucinating, man. I don't know how to stop it." I was getting increasingly agitated as the conversation progressed. If I didn't calm myself, my head would pop off due to the pressure. "The mother fucker appeared on my boat."

"Did you throw him off?"

"We were a good twenty miles out. He simply appeared out of nowhere. Then disappeared from wherever the fuck he came from."

"You're not making any sense."

"Tell me about it. Let's get out of here."

Arthur backed the vehicle from its space and turned on the lights. He drove slowly out of the parking lot and made a left turn towards Sunset Boulevard. When we reached the boulevard, Arthur turned right and headed north towards Madeira Beach. After we had traveled a couple of blocks, he turned and said, "We'll get you some money. I probably have five hundred. You take the boat down to Freeport. I'll wire you some more in a few days."

I was too exhausted to argue. "Okay."

"There's one thing you have to promise me, Mason."

"Anything, Arthur. Thanks for being a good friend." No doubt, Arthur believed in my innocence, but I don't think it would matter to him if I were guilty or not. He would help me in any way he could.

He turned left on the first street after the John's Pass bridge on the Madeira Beach side, and then made a quick left into the bank parking lot. Sliding up to the ATM machine he withdrew the five hundred, and held out the wad of crisp twenties to me when he was done. I reached over for the bills and tried to take them from his hand, but he held firm. "I want one favor."

I nodded silently.

"After you get to Freeport, you lay low and stop drinking for a while. Personally, I think the alcohol is fucking with your brain. You can't think straight."

If everyone around me seemed to see that so clearly, why couldn't I?

Arthur tugged at the bills. "Promise me, Mason."

He knew that if I promised him, I would try my best to keep it. "Okay, I promise." What did I have to lose at this point? Didn't Nancy say that alcohol could cause hallucinations? I'd make a sober fresh start. Arthur turned loose of the money, and I stashed it in my front pocket as we pulled away from the ATM. "Arthur pull over. I don't want you getting any further involved. I don't want to take chance of letting the police see you with me."

"But I can drive you around to the boat."

"That's all right. I'll walk." I opened the passenger door once Arthur had stopped. At least the rain had slowed to almost nothing while we stopped at the machine, so Arthur climbed out and met me in the glare of the headlights. "You take care, bro." I said, tears threatening to burst from my eyes.

"You too." Arthur gave me a second big old bear hug. I could her a sniffle before he said, "What are we girls?" He laughed, a nervous laugh.

I broke the hug and shook his hand. I waved lamely before I turned and walked away, determined not to look back and let him see me cry.

* * *

The wind drove the rain in hard gusts across the surface of the pass. I could barely see the Sunset Beach shore, but I wouldn't have been able to see the *Tramp* tied up at the fuel dock from my vantage point on a clear day. My perch on the barstool gave me a good view of the wooden boardwalk and tourists. I slicked down my wet hair with both hands, trying to dry out a bit. When I left Arthur in the parking lot the rain had slowed, but by the time I made it to the bar, I was soaking wet. I wanted to have a few beers anyway before I shoved off, but now I actually had an excuse. With this wind and rain, the seas would be heavy. To be safe, I should at least wait until the heaviest storms passed. The bartender waved a what do you want in my direction. I motioned to the bar taps and said, "A large draft."

"Any particular kind?"

"No, I don't care."

"Coming right up."

I tried to make myself as comfortable as possible, which wasn't all that easy because my cutoffs were almost as wet as my hair and shirt. I didn't think the wait would be too long. "Thanks," I said when the bartender set the beer in front of me. He took the twenty I had laid on the bar. I tried not to worry. Nobody knew the Tramp was there. It was highly unlikely that anyone would notice. Once the weather calmed, I would put to sea, after a quick stop to say good-bye to Annie. With the rain and clouds, there wouldn't be much light at all in the canal behind the Hut.

"Thanks, man." The bartender had returned with my change.

I nodded. I could still hardly believe all that had happened in the last few days, and I tried to avoid thinking about the bad, but I cursed my luck. Who would have thought that I would meet somebody like Annie in the first place? Why did it have to be now? I knew I was going to have to disappoint her. There was no way I could convince myself that taking her with me was the right thing to do. After I said good-bye, I would head for the Bahamas and start a new life. With a little good luck, maybe Annie and Arthur would join me one day.

"Do you mind?"

"What?"

"Do you mind if I take the stool next to you?"

"No, go ahead." I thought why in the hell is this fool bothering me, but then I recognized the toothless grin. "Oh, God," I said louder than I wanted.

"No, not God." The man answered. "Some called me Jesus the other day. I knew they were mistaken. The name is Angel." He held out a hand that only had three and a half fingers. The ring finger was missing to the second knuckle.

Against my better judgment, I took the hand. His grip was firm even without all his fingers. "I remember you," I said.

He looked at me quizzically for a moment and then the toothless maw widened once more. At least he seemed able to retrieve his memories unlike yours truly. "You were here earlier. Back for more demon alcohol?" He asked.

"I prefer to call it the golden nectar of the gods." I raised my glass of beer.

The grin widened. "Demons or gods? A dilemma."

"Do you believe in demons?" I played along.

"If you believe in God, then you must believe in the devil and his disciples."

The lunatic had a point. And who was I to call him a lunatic, for there I sat conversing with the man like we were the best of buddies. I no longer knew what I believed in. The past few days had proved that at the very least, I had a posse of demons fucking with me. Nancy hadn't mentioned demonic possibilities. Can alcohol bring on the demons? I could now answer yes with certainty. I slugged down my beer. "Bartender. Another round for me and my friend. And give me a shot of Jack too."

"Do you have demons, friend?" Angel asked.

While the bartender brought us fresh drinks, I checked out the visage of the two new friends in the mirror behind the bar. I was shocked. I could hardly tell us apart. There must have been something wrong with the mirror. The twins seemed surrounded by an aura of darkness. I looked to Angel and back to the mirror. The aura had vanished. Two sad looking human beings had taken the place of the twins. "Seems like I have hundreds of demons."

"You have to believe." The maw smiled.

Believing had become a very difficult state to achieve. I slammed home the whisky and drank down half of my beer in a gulp.

"It's quiet now." Apparently, my friend Angel had moved on to another topic.

"What?" I could hardly believe that I sat there talking with the man, and even more incredibly, that I enjoyed it. I wasn't sure what that said about me.

"It's quiet now."

"What's quiet now?"

"Skip's."

At the mention of the name, he had my complete attention. "Wait a minute, wait a minute. What happened at

Skip's?"

"It looked like a light show. All the colored lights were so pretty."

"What are you talking about?"

"Red and blue lights everywhere, flashing and dancing."

"Red and blue?"

"Angel, look at me." I grabbed him by the arm and spun him around in his stool. "Start from the beginning and tell me what happened at Skip's."

The man frustrated me further when he turned back to take a big swallow of his scotch. But there could only be one reason for flashing red and blue lights at Skip's. The police had found the Tramp. I had to hear it with my own ears. "Angel, please. Tell me what happened."

He spun back towards me and said, "The police had a boat surrounded. They were all over it, but it's quiet now."

"What do you mean it's quiet."

"The boat is still there, but the police are gone. They think I'm Jesus."

I left a five-dollar bill on the bar as a tip and stashed the rest in my pocket as I was rising from the seat. I hurried towards the door, pushing it open when I got there. I looked behind me as I made my way through. Angel sat facing me, his toothless maw wore a surprised look. I bet he was wondering what he had said to make his new friend disappear. I hoped he wasn't offended.

CHAPTER 22

"What are you thinking?" I chastised myself quietly before I had made it halfway up the boardwalk towards the bridge. I couldn't simply walk across the bridge in the open. If my guardian angel was right, the police would be lying in wait, itching to arrest me as I tried to take off with the Tramp. Although it was still drizzling, the wind had let up some. I ducked under the overhang in front of a sandals shop. The window advertisements offered quality footwear at low prices. Don't they all? Wouldn't it be grand if I could turn back the clock and pursue such simple pleasures, but my immediate concern involved creeping up close enough to my boat to check out whether or not the police had her under surveillance? As I thought about how to get there, my mind drifted to the larger question: what do I do if they have the Tramp surrounded? A very good question for which I had no answer.

First the nose and then the dorsal fin of a dolphin appeared as it broke the surface. A second dolphin appeared immediately behind and to the left of the first. The wind had calmed for the moment and the surface of the water appeared dark and foreboding lit only by the surrounding shop and streetlights. In the afternoon the crystal-clear water beamed blue-green, the sun sparkling across the surface. At night, nothing could be seen beneath the surface. That thought once again reminded me of the police that were probably hiding beneath my radar. "That's it," I said, snapping my fingers. Under my very feet, beneath the boardwalk lived a boat rental business. It would be closed now, and the powerboats would not have keys, but I knew for a fact that there would be a couple of small rowboats tied up amongst the other boats. The tide was coming in. I could row across the pass and let the tide sweep me further from the bridge, out of sight of any police eyes. It wouldn't be too hard now that the wind had slowed.

There weren't many people on the boardwalk because of the weather, so I quickly made my way to the wooden stairway a hundred feet to my right. Once at the bottom of the stairs, I surveyed the windows of the boat rental place. The only visible light came from the nighttime security lighting. I peered in the windows to make sure they were closed. Seeing no activity whatsoever, I walked out on the dock that ran beside and behind the office. Sure enough, I could see two rowboats tied up at the very end of the dock. A pair of oars leaned against the back of building. I had everything I needed to make my plan work.

As I was about to climb into the boat at the very end, I heard someone walking on the other side of the office. The footsteps continued to the dock. I climbed into the boat and lay flat on the bottom. The footsteps stopped when the person reached the back of the building. Being very cautious, I peered above the gunwale of the boat. A lone police officer stood overlooking the rental dock. He glanced first left and then right. I ducked. A few seconds later, I heard the footsteps once again. This time they retreated back the way they had come. I thanked my lucky stars that I hadn't begun to untie the boat when he had appeared. Maybe Angel was still with me. Wasting no more time, I placed the oars into the locks, untied the boat, and shoved off. I let the black current take me away from the dock and from the bridge. I kept a low profile until I was twenty or thirty yards from the dock. Sitting up, I grabbed the oars and stroked, trying to keep both oars in the water at the same time. It began to rain harder again. The low visibility would help. I rowed faster.

"Stroke."

I pulled the oars through the water, then raised them above the water and pushed forward in mindless repetition.

"Stroke."

It took me a minute to realize that the voice was not in my head but coming from the figure perched on the stern of the rowboat. Bender sat facing me with a smile on his face. "I always wanted to be the leader of a rowing team. What do they call the dude who calls the cadence?"

"Coxswain," I answered.

"Cocks wane? You mean they fade? That's awful." The apparition began to laugh, slowly at first, and then with great gusto. "What if it's a woman?"

"Don't be juvenile. What do you want?"

At first, Bender tried unsuccessfully to stifle the laughter, his body shaking. Not able to hold it in, he laughed hard once more before quieting down enough to reply, "Want? You invited me."

"I never invited you."

His first appearance on the Tramp had scared me deeply, but this time I was not surprised. I might be able to escape from the police, but I had no illusions anymore that I could escape from Bender, unless I was able to solve the why and how of his mysterious presence.

"You invite me in every night and most days. You have for years now."

"You're crazy."

"That's for sure." The annoying man burst into laughter once more, pointing a finger and wagging it in my direction.

"Fuck you." It was the only reply I could manage.

"You wish you could." He laughed harder at my inability to say anything that made sense.

"Why don't you leave me alone?"

"I can't do that. My fate is linked to yours." Bender teetered on the transom and almost fell overboard as a large wake hit the small rowboat. With all the distraction, I hadn't seen the big cruiser bearing down on us, and obviously, the cruiser's captain hadn't seen us. He passed within twenty feet of the bow, pushing a wall of water in front of him. I pulled hard with right oar when the wake hit and we were up and over in a great splash of water. Bender's knuckles turned white as he hung on tight to the rail.

"Damn that was close," I said. "Too bad you didn't fall overboard."

"You're not going to get rid of me that easily."

Of that I was sure. I pulled hard with both oars and straightened the boat back in the direction of the Sunset Beach shoreline. Once we were straight, I rested both oars for a minute and watched the stern of the cruiser recede into the night. The rowboat continued to bob in its wake like a cork. Not knowing what else to say, I asked, "Did you kill Carmen?"

He seemed surprised by my question. "That's for me to know and you to find out."

"I will find out." Of that I was not so sure.

"You can run, but you can't hide."

"I can if the police are not watching the boat."

"We'll find out soon enough." He laughed again.

His last statement surprised me. I wasn't sure why, but I thought that he would know. He didn't seem to know anymore than I did. He might not be so clever after all. I smiled and began to row again.

"Why are you smiling?" Bender asked.

"You are not as powerful as you think you are." I closed my eyes and wished with all my might that my tormentor would disappear. When I opened them once more, he was gone.

* * *

By the time I finally reached the Sunset Beach side of the

pass, I had drifted probably half a mile inland. In front of me, the Sun Point condominiums sat in the dark. I stopped rowing and let the rowboat glide up to the sea wall. Holding onto the top of the concrete wall, I stood on my seat and climbed out, letting the boat drift back out into the pass behind me. No matter what happened after this, I didn't think I would need a rowboat again. I had to shake the Bender visit and concentrate on the task at hand. Too many forces seemed to be pulling me in too many directions in too little time, and the trouble was I couldn't understand how most of it had happened, or what it meant. Most of my memory had yet to return, making me dependent on whatever Bender decided to tell me. I walked slowly behind the building and out of the glare of the parking lot lights. I was soaked to the skin, but at least it was a warm night. Since the boat had drifted a far piece from the bridge, so I was pretty sure that if there were cops around, they had not seen me.

 I kept close to the buildings in the dark as I made my way back toward the bridge and Skip's fuel dock. Once I passed the access road to the docks, I snuck down the alleyway until I reached the old high and dry marina, a very large tin-walled warehouse for boats that had seen better days. In its prime, the place was always crowded with people coming and going with their boats. A couple of hurricanes later and half the walls were gone. The rest were in disrepair. I went inside and climbed the back stairs to the roof. On top, I made my way slowly, hoping not to fall through a weak spot in the roof. They really needed to tear this thing down. When

I reached the edge, I knelt down and let my eyes adjust to the environment. From my vantage point, I could clearly see the deck of the Tramp. She appeared empty. Methodically, I let my eyes roam over the light and shadows of the entire dock area. The police wouldn't have expected me to come from the waterside and down the bank. They would have expected me to come from the direction of the bridge. A glint of light behind Skip's caught my attention. I could barely make him out, but there he stood behind a large cruiser dry-docked on a lift for repair. I squinted my eyes to try and see better and realized that the flash I had seen came from the man's handcuffs. Angel had been right. Now what?

My back rested flat against the ledge, reminding me of the wet tee shirt that clung to me like a second skin. The rain had finally stopped entirely while I watched the police watching for me. The sky was clearing in pockets, allowing the moon to glisten off the puddles on the roof. I removed the wet shirt and wrung it out as best I could. The warm breeze felt cold against my bare arms and chest. I put the still wet shirt back on with a struggle. Once again I knelt behind the ledge and peered below, hoping against hope that the police had given up their stakeout. Unfortunately, the first officer had been joined by a second. They stood quietly in the dark talking. Too bad I was too high up to hear the conversation. The presence of the police had let all the air out of my plans to run to the Caribbean. I might have made it too. The sea's a vast expanse of loneliness, a place to get lost in when desired. With my knowledge of the local waters, I had no doubt that I could have avoided any police or Coast Guard vessels in the immediate vicinity.

"It's a moot point now," I mumbled to myself as I sat back down. I wasn't completely out of options yet. My cab had probably gone unnoticed at the municipal complex. It was parked in the back row. My earlier decision not to risk a DUI had turned out to be an excellent move. One of the few good decisions I had made in the last couple of days. But where would I go? I couldn't envision myself as a modern day Jesse James, riding into the sunset with the posse on his heels. Nor could I see Annie and I as Bonnie and Clyde, ready to do gun battle with the police at every stop. Let's be real. "Shit." I cursed a bit louder than I had intended, so I checked on my police companions. The first officer had disappeared, leaving the second to squat behind the cruiser in his place. They must be changing the watch every couple of hours. Apparently, he hadn't heard a thing. I guessed I was far enough away not to worry about my voice covering the distance. I sat back down to think.

What would I gain by running with the cab? Could I even get out of town without trouble? The answer to the first question was nothing, if the answer to the second question was no. I did not feel good about my chances in the car. I had to be realistic. There were too many police agencies, too many officers and vehicles, and too few roads leading north. Florida is a peninsula after all. At sea I could get lost in the dark, on land they would catch me in no time. And I'd be a fugitive. Hall could shoot me dead if she wanted. "What do you mean if?" I laughed quietly but uncontrollably at my joke. The laughter felt good. At this point, I didn't care if the policeman below heard me or not.

If I ran and they caught me, it would appear as an admission of guilt. The prosecutors would hang me with my own actions, and I really didn't think I could survive a long jail sentence. So getting shot by Hall might actually be a good thing. But right now, they had no proof of my guilt. I had no proof of my guilt. Sure, I had to admit I was involved somehow. Bender kept reminding me of that fact. But as Arthur had said earlier, the Mason he knew would not have killed anybody. I had to hold on tightly to that thought. While I might be guilty of lying and tampering with a crime scene, I was not a murderer. Poco was a hell of a lawyer. Surely, the courts would find me innocent. At any rate, what choice did I have? All things considered, the only logical thing to do was turn myself in. The cold logic of the decision made sense. I rose to my feet and made my way down the stairs to the first floor. I turned left after I exited the building, and slowly walked east along the intracoastal toward downtown and the municipal complex. Once I was safely out of earshot of the police, I fished the cell phone from my pocket and dialed Poco's number. He answered on the second ring. "Mason, where are you?"

"I'm in town."

"Are you okay?"

"Yes, I'm okay. I've decided to turn myself in, but I don't want to go to the police station alone. I'm afraid of what they might do."

"I'll be by your side, like I've always been."

Always would not have been my choice of word a couple

of days ago, but looking back on things I knew he was right. "I know, Poco."

"Can you get over here?"

"No, not the house. I'll meet you at your office in two hours."

"Two hours?"

"Yes, there are a couple of things I need to do. Let's say two o'clock."

"Are you sure?"

"No, but I don't have much choice."

"No you don't. I love you, Mason."

I broke the connection. Tonight might be my last night of freedom for a while. Consequently, there were three things I wanted to accomplish before turning myself in to Hall. I wanted to get as drunk as I could, I wanted to talk with Angel, and I wanted to see and hold Annie, not necessarily in that order.

* * *

Three of the four beers from Carmen's refrigerator were still in the trunk of the cab when I had opened it. Like I had figured, no one had noticed the cab parked in the municipal parking lot. The beer was warm as piss, but I was cold, so it didn't taste too bad. I stepped back to survey my handiwork after I put the last strip of black electrical tape in place. The cab number now read one twenty-nine instead of twenty-four. It was amazing what two little strips of tape could do. At least the change of number would provide me with a bit more cover as I made way around town.

Tossing the roll of tape and the empty beer can into the trunk, I closed the lid quietly. I still held the plastic ring with the remaining two beers in my right hand. My eye caught movement near the side of the police department directly across the parking lot from where I stood, so I quickly opened the driver side door and climbed inside. I slumped down in the seat until I could identify the movement I'd seen. Two figures had appeared from the around the corner and stopped to talk. I cursed my luck because of course one of the two figures was none other than Kendyll Hall. The other figure was her partner Mark Makowiak. I wondered briefly where the hell he had been. I guessed he had a long weekend off. "Son of a bitch. I can't cop a break." I would have to wait until they were gone before I could go anywhere. I opened another one of the warm beers and took a sip. It didn't taste nearly as good this time.

"Wait a minute." My devious mind had come up with an idea. I bet if I called Hall's cell phone, I could set up a time to turn myself in. She might even be stupid enough to ease up on their search for me and I could reclaim the *Tramp*. Okay, so I knew I was kidding myself about the boat, but I liked the idea of messing with her head. I might as well give it a shot. What did I have to lose? I opened the glove box and retrieved the business card Hall had given me in the driveway at Carmen's. I read the card and found her cell number. My call would surprise her big time. I dialed the number and watched her from my seat.

She suddenly reached for the phone attached to her belt.

"Hall speaking."

"My dear, Kendyll."

A few seconds elapsed before she said, "Mason, you shit."

"Is that any way to treat an old friend?" I was enjoying the exchange. I hadn't had any control over anything at all until this very minute. I also guessed that I was probably drunker than I had thought.

"You are not a friend. Are you ready to give up and turn yourself in? You don't stand a chance."

"Yes."

The air went silent for a few seconds. I didn't think she had expected that reply. Then I watched as she pumped her fist high into the air. "Good. Where are you?"

"None of your business. Call off the dogs, and I'll come in with my lawyer in a couple of hours. I have to do something first."

"You're not in charge here, Mason. You come in right now."

"If you could find me, you already would have me. I'll come in when I'm ready. That's what you want isn't it."

"Of course it is. You are a murderer."

"We'll let the jury decide that. Not you."

"They will see you for what you are. You'll be in jail until you die."

The thought of spending the rest of my life in jail did not appeal to me. I wondered if she was right in her assessment. I hoped not. I was still a young man, and I had a lot of living to do, but sitting in jail was not my idea of living. "Call the dogs off. I'll come to your office at two-thirty." Hall had no more choice in the matter than I did. Things were going to play out as they were supposed to. Once again I hoped that she'd make the mistake of bringing all her people in. Then I might have a second chance at escaping in the boat.

Her reply killed that idea. "If you think that I'm going to drop surveillance of your boat, you're out of your mind. You can forget that idea."

"It was worth a try."

"You'll be here at two-thirty?"

"Yes."

"Why should I believe you?"

"You have no choice." I hung up and put the cell phone back in my pocket. The two detectives stood for a minute slapping hands, enjoying themselves at my expense. For a few brief seconds, I considered starting the cab, pressing the gas pedal to the floor, and running down the nasty bitch. I didn't care whether I ran her partner down or not. After a couple of minutes of celebration, the two turned and went back inside the police station. I started the cab, rolled down the window, and gave the now vacant doorway of the police station the finger as I drove past.

CHAPTER 23

Once I left the parking lot of the municipal complex, I headed south through Isla del Luna and out the back way to the mainland. Using the Gulfway, I made my way east and then north to the Madeira Beach Causeway at the opposite end of the island from John's Pass. The night was dark. Traffic at the bewitching hour was light. I drove fast, like cabs always do. I didn't want to attract attention. The long way around took me almost twenty minutes, but avoiding the John's Pass Bridge was probably the smart thing to do. After all, I knew for sure that the police would still be watching over the *Tramp*. The thought of leaving my boat behind as I went to jail brought me down to a point I'd never been before. It's funny what we value most in life, but the boat was the only thing that was entirely mine, bought and paid for and all that good shit.

As I approached the causeway bridge, a figure down on the beach to my left caught my attention. A man stood on top of large tree stump. He was facing the dark water of the

Intracoastal Waterway, waving his arms in the moonlight. I couldn't be sure, but it looked like Angel. So once I crossed the bridge, I made a quick left into the empty seafood restaurant parking lot. The sign offered the fresh catch of day, a ten-ounce grouper filet. It occurred to me that I was hungry. I spun the cab around and headed back out on to the causeway bridge in the direction I had come. At the top of the bridge, I could once again make out the figure in the dark. If he wasn't Angel, the man certainly resembled him. I sped right towards the beach lot and parked facing the figure on the stump. The headlights of the cab shone on the side of the man's face. He turned in my direction and smiled a toothless grin. Unaccountably, I smiled. I felt real good about seeing Angel again. I needed advice. For a man in my situation, he was probably as good an expert on what it was like to be nuts that I could find. That was a scary thought. I turned off the ignition and exited the cab. I walked the short distance to his podium. He seemed to be orchestrating the vast, empty expanse of water. "Hey, Angel."

He turned and said, "What took you so long."

Was I that predictable? Angel was not the first one to say that to me tonight. I ignored the comment. "What are you doing?"

"They call me Jesus. They think I'm preaching, blessing the fish or something. But they're wrong."

"It looked more like you were conducting an orchestra," I offered.

"That's very insightful of you. What is your name anyway?"

"Mason Prophet Long."

"Prophet?"

"Yes. I was named after a country rock band. It's a long story."

"Oh, Mason Proffit. Good band. As I said, they're wrong. I am directing the music of the spheres, Prophet Man."

Oh boy, I thought. Here's another character I couldn't understand. But the last few days had served to convince me, that I too, belonged in that category. I hoped that Angel could provide me with a glimpse of what lie ahead.

"They think I'm crazy," he said.

"Are you crazy?" If I talked with someone who was already around the bend, maybe I could figure out if I too was crazy. I wasn't sure whether the logic of that thought worked or not.

The man shut his mouth with a snap, then the toothless smile slowly spread across his face. He looked both left and then right. In a low, conspiratorial voice, he said, "Of course, I am."

I smiled and in an equally conspiratorial tone, I asked, "How long have you been crazy?"

"Do you really want to hear my tale?"

"I do."

"I wasn't always crazy." He hesitated.

"What happened?"

"I don't know for sure. Would you reach into that back pack by the side of the stump and grab the pint of scotch for me?"

"Sure." I hadn't seen the backpack until Angel pointed to

it. I moved over and took it in my hands, unzipping the top of the pack in the process.

"By the way, the pint of whiskey is for you."

"How did you know I'd come?"

"When we were in the bar, the mirror reflected us as twins."

"I saw the twins too." Can two people share the same hallucination? I remained completely confused. None of this made sense, but if I was going insane, I was looking for logic in a place where there was none.

"Do you *think* you're crazy?" Angel asked, taking the bottle of scotch from me. He took a big swallow of the golden-brown liquid.

"I don't know." I found the bottle of whiskey in the backpack, a bottle of Jack. I ripped off the top, and like Angel, took a big swallow, grimacing as the heat hit my throat. "I'm not sure why all this shit has happened to me."

"I wasn't always crazy," Angel began his tale. "One day I woke up and nothing seemed right. Before too long I realized that I had passed over into a realm of being that had nothing to do with any reality I'd known before. I was doing weird things and talking to myself."

"Were you violent?"

Angel rubbed his chin and climbed down from the stump. I was glad because I was getting a stiff neck looking up at him. He sat down on the stump, and I joined him, happy that there were no mirrors.

"No I wasn't violent. I don't think I ever really hurt anybody, at least not intentionally."

"You are talking pretty sane right now." As soon as the words came out of my mouth, I realized that I really had no idea whether that was true or not.

"I've learned to live with being crazy. In fact, I use it to my benefit. Most people give me a lot of space and generally leave me alone. And then there are the do-gooders who help me. They keep me in a place to live, supply me with scotch. They are great enablers." He laughed softly.

Angel might be a lot of things, but he sure wasn't stupid. I took another shot of the whiskey, trying to digest all that he was saying and all that I was thinking. I always knew that human beings were capable of adapting to almost anything, but adapting to this new twist of fate would not be easy. I wondered if everyone who was crazy knew they were crazy. I didn't think so. I was pretty certain that there had to be levels of craziness, and I was determined to find out where I fit on that scale. "Did you ever see things, Angel?"

"What kind of things?"

"You know, like people who aren't there, but they're talking to you."

"No, I never talked with a," he searched for a word.

"Hallucination?" I offered.

"No I never talked with a hallucination that I know of. Of course, I have met some strange people who could have been hallucinations, I guess."

Now that thought tickled me. I started to laugh uncontrollably. I bet that most people at one time or another wondered whether they might be talking to a hallucination, someone just too bizarre to be real. A look of concern came over Angel's face, so I said, "I'm not laughing at you Angel. I've met some people over the years ago who might have been hallucinations. They were sure strange enough."

Angel laughed politely, but I'm not sure he understood my joke. However, he did seem convinced that I wasn't laughing at him, and he visibly relaxed once more. "I never talked to hallucinations as such," he said. "But I did hear voices for a while."

"For a while?"

"Yes. I heard them for almost two years."

"What happened then? Did they simply stop talking?"

"No I willed them to go away. It took me some time but I was able to make the voices stop."

My mind flashed back to the rowboat and the visit from Bender. I remembered that I closed my eyes and wished with all my might that he would disappear, and he did. The thought made me feel better, but then I realized that in order for me to make him disappear, Bender had to be a more integral part of me than I had ever imagined.

"You really didn't think you could get rid of me that easy?"

The familiar voice came from behind and to my right. I had to turn my entire body to the right to see where it had come from. Bender sat on a second stump with a shit-eating grin on his face.

"What the hell do you want?" I asked Bender.

"Who me?" Angel asked.

"No, not you. The man sitting over on that other stump." I pointed to Bender.

Angel looked at the stump and then to me before he asked, "Are you having one of your hallucinations?"

I nodded. Obviously, Angel could not see Bender. I was disappointed. I didn't know what I expected, but I guessed that I hoped at least Angel could see Bender.

"Will him to go away," Angel said.

"You truly are crazy if you think you'll be able to do that, Mason." Bender laughed. "I told you once before, I bend the will."

I thought back to our first meeting. He did say he bent the will, but I had to hope that he couldn't break the will. He did not appear all-powerful or all knowing. "And I told you then that I bend the elbow." I took a swallow of whisky and set the bottle down, trying to distract him. I closed my eyes and tried with all my might to will him away. When I opened my eyes once more, he still sat on the stump, grinning like a cat that had swallowed a mouse.

"I told you it would not be easy."

"Did it work?" Angel asked.

"No." The despair in my voice made him wince.

"Don't give up. Try again."

Bender laughed once more from his seat on the stump. "I will be able to make you do anything I want. I will take control."

I closed my eyes again, trying real hard to concentrate my mind on ridding myself of the nightmarish apparition. I began to feel dizzy. I felt as if I were no longer a part of myself. I was engaged in a battle of wills with Bender, mine against his. When I was about to pass out from the struggle, I looked up and he was gone. It had been harder to get rid of him than it had been in the rowboat, but at least I had managed to make him disappear once more.

Angel reached over and gripped my arm. "Is he gone?"

I took the bottle of whisky when Angel offered it. Closing my eyes, I swallowed mightily, coughing as the burning liquid hit the back of my throat. I began to shake slightly, trying to hold in the emotions that threatened to tear me apart. Like Angel had done before me, I seemed to have passed over a threshold into a reality that no longer had any real meaning. Bender had been right about one thing: I no longer felt that I had control over my destiny.

"It will get easier," Angel said.

Once the coughing fit stopped, I asked, "What will get easier?"

"Stopping the hallucinations."

"I hope so. I didn't realize until now that I actually had a choice in the matter."

"And if it doesn't get easier, you'll learn to live with them."

The last statement was certainly debatable. How bad were the hallucinations? I still did not have complete recollection of the nights since Carmen's murder. I knew for sure that somehow Bender and I were inextricably involved in the murders, but I was still unsure of how I fit in. My fear was that I was more involved than I could live with. "I'm not sure I can do that, Angel."

"But you have to."

"Do you?" I asked.

Angel stared at me. The words I had uttered appeared to

have no meaning in his world. "You must go on."

The man had grown on me in the last couple of days, and I didn't want to hurt his feelings. "You're right, Angel. Let's get out of here."

* * *

The moon appeared briefly among the clouds behind the buildings that lined the boardwalk. Winds rushed the clouds by fast, allowing another brief flash of the cold light. The storms were moving away. Soon the night would be hot and humid once more. I watched as Angel struggled with the joint. As soon as he had enough of the marijuana in the paper, he jiggled his fingers and dropped half of it back into the baggie in his lap. "Do you want me to do that?" I asked.

"No, I'll get it." If nothing else, he was determined. He seemed determined to live his life to the fullest despite his shortcomings.

"Some time tonight would be good." I said and laughed. He looked like he was almost done.

The toothless maw smiled back. "There," he said finally and held up the neatly rolled joint for my admiration. He quickly fished a lighter out of his pocket and lit the joint. He sucked heartily. The aromatic smoke blew by my nose in the breeze from the open windows as Angel inhaled deeply. Once he had filled his lungs, he shook the lighter swiftly, like he was shaking out a match, and then threw the lighter out of the open passenger side window and into the parking lot.

"What the fuck are you doing? That's a lighter."

Angel looked at me horrified for a second, then turned and looked out the window, then turned back to me and grinned the toothless grin that I was learning to enjoy before he burst into laughter at his mistake. "I must be more fucked up than I thought." He said and laughed harder.

I couldn't help myself. The laughter started deep and I reveled in it, enjoying the moment. "Well, go get it, Angel."

Angel giggled and held his hand to his mouth like a schoolgirl before opening his door. As he tried to get out, he slipped and fell out.

"Way to go, Grace." I laughed at my new friend, wishing the reality of why we were together was different.

After crawling for a moment, Angel sat up on the pavement, lighter in hand. "Got it."

"Well, get back in here."

He climbed back in the cab and shut the door. Once again we were in the dark, giggling between pulls on the joint. We finished it in short order.

"Did you kill them women?" Angel asked suddenly.

Surprised, I stared at him vacantly for a few seconds before I asked, "You don't miss much do you?"

"I hear things." He waited expectantly for my answer.

"You didn't see me on TV or anything?"

"No. I overheard some people at the corner store talking about the murders." He sat silently waiting for me to answer. The laughter had died.

"I don't know." I answered honestly.

"You don't seem like a killer to me."

"Thank you, I think."

"No, no. I'm serious. You don't seem the type. I've met some real crazy people over the years, one of which I'm sure was a serial killer."

"Where?"

"In a facility."

"You mean asylum?"

"I don't like that word." Angel lowered his eyes and frowned as he spoke.

"Sorry, Angel. You're right I don't think I'm a killer, but I don't remember much from those nights the women were killed."

"But you're not so sure about the invisible guy?"

"You hit the nail on the head there, man. I don't know why I'm having these hallucinations or how to stop them. I don't know whether they are real or not."

"Tough spot."

"Tell me about it." Angel had grasped my current situation in a matter of minutes. I guessed that came from experience. I searched my friend's face for signs of condemnation or disgust, but found nothing but empathy.

"It doesn't matter anyway." Angel said in a low voice.

"What do you mean?"

"If you're crazy, you are not responsible for your actions."

My mind reeled, speeding from thought to incoherent thought. For some time, I'd been doing my best to avoid thinking about the possibilities of Bender being a real part of me, a part of my very being. The Mason I didn't know. I shuddered.

"I don't take much responsibility for my actions." Angel

continued.

That was fine, if you were talking about taking a few free drinks or living for free on someone else's dime like Angel, but I didn't want to go through life like Baldy, who thought there would be no consequences for hurting a woman with an ashtray in a bar. I could not live like that. I didn't want to think about it any more, so I opened my door and said. "I need a cold one."

"Do you ladies mind if we sit down?" I said to two very pretty women who sat near the end of the bar. Three bar stools remained vacant to their right. "Don't' smile," I said quietly to Angel who was right behind me. He grinned widely. The faces of the women suddenly wore worried looks.

They answered politely in unison, "No of course not. We'd enjoy the company." The words did not match the looks. We sat down anyway.

"Bartender." I waited for the man's attention before adding, "Two large cold drafts."

"Coming right up."

I turned to Angel and pointed towards the two on my left, "I think they like you."

He grinned from ear to ear. "Yeah, right," he said, and then added, "Maybe, they'll like you."

I turned to the dark haired woman on the stool to my immediate left and gave her my best smile. "Are you two from around here?" I smiled at her blond friend and looked her in the eyes. "You all don't look familiar."

The dark-haired woman seemed much more friendly than her friend. Maybe the friend was afraid she'd have to entertain Angel if things progressed too far. I politely waited for an answer, doing my best to appear sincere. "We're visiting," the dark-haired woman kept her response short.

"From up north?"

"Michigan."

"Nice," I said and smiled again. I really possessed no information about Michigan, so consequently I couldn't add to the nicety. If the truth be told, I only had a vague notion of where Michigan was, although I was pretty sure it was cold there.

Angel leaned over and chimed in, "I've been to Michigan." The maw smiled widely.

"That's nice," the blond said uneasily.

I wasn't sure why I was trying to strike up a conversation with the two tourists. It wasn't like I had anything better to do, or nothing else occupying my mind. It must be the force of habit, I finally decided. I was about to make up some bullshit about how nice the beaches were when the front door of the bar opened. A man stood in the doorway. I poised myself, ready to run and hide if he turned out to be the police. "Oh, shit." I said as a recognized the figure in the doorway.

Angel saw the concern on my face and looked towards the door. After he turned back, he shrugged his shoulders in a question. "My tormentor," I said as Bender took a seat on the opposite side of Angel.

"You can handle him," Angel said.

"Sure you can, Mason." Bender said as he settled down on the barstool.

If I weren't so scared, I would have found the whole situation rather funny. In the mirror, I could see the three of us. One certifiably crazy, one well on his way, and the last a figment of the second one's imagination. "Why don't you leave me the fuck alone," I said to the empty stool, much too loud for the small room. Faces turned toward the three of us, as I realized that everyone else in the room saw only the two of us. The bartender eyed me suspiciously.

Angel came to the rescue, "Don't mind him everybody. He's crazy."

I bobbed my head and smiled, doing my best imitation of a bobble head doll. Polite smiles appeared around the room. No one seemed quite sure what to make of the two mad men who had appeared in their quiet bar. The two women on my left appeared horrified. I watched amused as the blond poked the dark-haired woman in the ribs. They began to drink faster, obviously ready to make their escape.

Angel put a hand on my arm and whispered, "Stay calm and get rid of him. You know how to do that. This will be good practice."

Practice? My entire life lurched out of control. I could hear my daddy's voice once again, "Let's review, Mason." There I sat, hanging out with a lunatic, a very nice lunatic mind you, but nevertheless a crazy person. Next to him sat my hallucination, a strange little bearded man with a large straw hat. How crazy was that? How crazy was I? I closed my eyes and tried my best to will him away. No luck. I tried again and again. No luck.

"Soon we'll be one." Bender chuckled.

I wanted to smash his face, but then realized that I couldn't do that. My old friend violence was as impotent in this situation as I. I rose from my seat and screamed at the top of my lungs, "Get out of my life."

Angel tried his best to diffuse the situation, pushing me back down on the stool and smiling towards the two tourists and the bartender, but events began to unfold fast. The two woman rose from their seats and couldn't get out of the front door fast enough, prompting the bartender to action. The man was rightly pissed at someone chasing off his customers. He headed in my direction.

I stood up and raised my hands to him, "Don't worry, man. I'm leaving."

He stopped and stood across the bar from me, his hands resting on the bar top. "We don't need you're kind here. Leave and don't come back."

I wanted to ask him what my kind might be. I was having a hard enough time trying to decipher my kind myself. "I'm leaving." I turned to Angel, grabbed his hand and shook it warmly, "Thanks, my man. Maybe I'll see you again one day."

Angel frowned deeply; the sad face did not smile. "Good luck, Mason."

I missed the toothless grin already as I turned on my heels and headed for the door. I was certain that Bender would follow, and I wasn't disappointed. We must have made quite a sight as I opened the door for him and allowed him to proceed me outside. Angel sat at the bar and waved, before draining the remainder of his beer. I shut the door behind me. The night air was warm and sticky.

* * *

The cab's back tires squealed as I rounded the corner and turned onto Park Street. I pressed my foot on the accelerator as hard as I could. The cab picked up speed. Maybe if I went fast enough, I could escape the demon that had invaded my life. The trees along the curb blurred together, passing by so quickly as to be unrecognizable. How fast did I have to go to outdistance the racing of my mind? A car stopped halfway into the intersection up ahead. I guessed the driver had not realized how fast I was going. I swerved around the front end and kept going.

Park Street wound its way along the mainland side of the intracoastal. The plan was to retrace my steps and return via the back door to Sunset Beach. My visit with Angel, along with the rude interruptions by Bender, had served to completely convince me that turning myself in was the right thing to do. I needed help. I would keep my promise to Annie and then head over to my brother's office. As I rounded a long curve to the left, I saw him too late and was by in a flash. The lights on the cruiser lit up brightly a few seconds later. My first thought was to stop and be done with it, but I really wanted some time to hold Annie in my arms, before I had to visit with her behind a glass wall in a prison. I hit the accelerator hard and spun the cab quickly to the left down a side street, not letting up until I neared the next corner. I turned right and sped the four blocks to Gulfway, hoping like hell that no one was driving or walking in my path. At Gulfway, I again turned right and pressed the pedal to the floor, speeding up and over the bridge to Isla del Luna. I turned at the first corner, and then again into an alley. I braked the cab to a stop and turned off the lights. I waited and watched the street for the police cruiser. Nothing happened for several minutes. I must have lost him back on the mainland.

"Damn that was close." I was probably okay. The mainland police would probably not be in close contact with the Sunset Beach police. I decided I could get away with taking a bit of a breather. I leaned back into the seat and rubbed my eyes.

"Nice job. Now we won't have to deal with the maggots anymore," Bender said. His face wore a look of both concern and amusement. It looked as if he would burst into either song or sobs. I stood in the room opposite of him as confused as the look on his face. The room looked familiar. I could see one of the posts of the four-poster mahogany bed frame. It occurred to me that we were at Carmen's house, but what was Bender doing in her bedroom. The windows were dark, the only light coming in from the pool area.

"You should be applauded." Bender clapped his hands together several times before leaning forward and clapping me on the back. He was dressed as usual with the straw hat, dingy gray shirt and khaki shorts.

"What?"

In contrast to the dark windows, the room was brightly lit. The semi-gloss, sand-colored walls increased the brightness. Carmen liked it that way. She always considered rooms painted in dark hues to be depressing. I didn't necessarily agree with her, but I did think that her room was nicely decorated. Darker furnishings completed the contrast between light and dark. I scanned the room until I saw her on the bed.

"What did you do?" I screamed at the comical figure.

Bender first smiled and then laughed heartily at my discomfort.

The naked figure lie dead on the bed, her dark hair framed that perfect sunless face.

Sweat poured down from my brow and into my eyes. I was shaking and moaning, "No, no, no." There had to be a mistake. I could not for the life of me imagine that I actually had something to do with Carmen's murder. Bender's words came back to me. "Nice job." He had said.

"Did I murder Carmen?" I fought back the urge to cry and the urge to vomit and host of other bodily functions that threatened to do me in right were I sat behind the wheel of the taxicab. The police would find me in the morning, hands still clenching the steering, dead from fright, a pale and horrified look etched into my face. Not knowing what else to do, I started the cab and sped down the alleyway, turning a hard right into the street. I lost control of the vehicle, the wheel slipping from my hands, and bounded up and over a curb. I sped hundred feet into someone's front yard before regaining control, narrowly missing a palm tree as I came to a stop. As the adrenaline continued to course through my veins, I put the cab into reverse. One coherent thought had popped into my mind: find Nancy.

CHAPTER 24

"Mason, what are you doing here?" The door stood open about two inches. Nancy clutched the edge of the door, not wanting to open it further. "It's after one o'clock in the morning."

"I know, but things have been happening to me that I don't understand. I need help."

Nancy hesitated, indecision obvious in her expression.

"Please. I need some advice. I've decided to turn myself in." The last statement seemed to ease her fears. She might have been in bed when I called Poco and didn't yet know of my decision.

She opened the door a bit further. "Poco wasn't upstairs, maybe he's in his office."

"I doubt it. He's probably waiting for me in his office downtown."

"He is?"

I guessed that Poco must not have wanted to wake her with the news. "It's you I want to talk to."

At last, she relented and opened the door, motioning for me to follow her inside. The great room was dark, and I couldn't see any light coming from under the door to Poco's office. Nancy walked over and opened the door anyway and peered inside. "You're right he's not here. I probably should call him."

"You don't need to do that. I'll see him soon." She ignored my statement and continued into the room. Through the open door, I watched as she walked over to his desk and turned on the light. She picked up the phone and dialed. I eased my way out of her vision and approached the door to the office. I wanted to hear the conversation. Once I reached the door, I leaned my back against the wall and listened.

"Yes. He's here now." I could not hear his reply, but he must have asked her if he should come home, for she replied, "No, not yet. He wants to talk to me."

I did want to talk with her. My recent hallucinations of Bender had put my sanity in doubt. I kept listening, trying to hear what Poco intended to do. I didn't want a confrontation with my brother right now. "If I don't call you back in half an hour or so, come home." I heard him say. Good, I had some time. I didn't blame her for wanting to make sure she was covered. She hung up the phone, so I quickly made my way back towards the middle of the great room. I stood there innocently and tried to smile. I failed miserably. When she reappeared, she motioned for me to follow her down the hall to her office. Once inside the office, she turned on the bright overhead lights and sat down behind her desk. I took my place on the leather couch as I had done before.

"You don't look so good," said Nancy.

"I'm not," I replied. Nancy would try and help me if she could. She was that way. My brother was a lucky fellow. "I need to do something. I can't go on like this."

"Like what?"

"You asked me the last time we talked if everything my stalker did was in the realm of possibility."

"You called him Bender, right?"

"You have a good memory."

"So, what is the answer?"

"Unfortunately, the answer is now no. He appeared tonight out of nowhere on the back of my boat. We were way out in the gulf."

"There's no way he could have come by boat?"

"No."

"Is that the only time he appeared?"

"No he appeared a few more times since then. I'm seeing things. I must be going crazy."

Nancy leaned forward in her chair, picked up a pen and wrote something on a sheet of paper in front of her. She rose to her feet and came over to sit by my side on the couch. She brushed some errant blond hair from my forehead, like my mother used to do when I was a child. I waited for the poor Mason comments, but they never came. "It's not the end of the world," she said.

"It's the end of the world as I know it."

"There's life after mental illness."

The words mental illness hit me hard. Before tonight, I had never, ever considered that I could have a mental problem. People like Ricky Dean had mental problems because they abused drugs, or people were born that way, missing a few pieces. "The future terrifies me. What could be wrong with me?" I asked in a whisper.

"We've already talked about the most obvious possibility: the alcohol."

"I can't stop." I thought that was probably the first time I had ever admitted that I couldn't stop drinking.

"We can get you help with the alcohol."

"But we don't know for sure that's what it is. Could I be losing my mind?"

"That's not an easy question to answer."

"I need answers, Nancy," I said in a loud, angry voice.

"It's okay, Mason." She brushed the hair from my forehead lightly. "I didn't say there weren't answers, but it will take time. We need to talk in detail and do some tests to see if you have some sort of chemical imbalance."

"So it could be physical rather than mental."

Nancy put her arm on my shoulder and said, "Nothing is ever simple. There could be combinations of issues. The alcohol is certainly a contributing factor. Still, many people lead productive lives. There are drugs to control symptoms and the anxiety that accompanies them."

I thought about Angel and how he learned to cope with his problems. I didn't think that I could live like him, but that was probably a moot point anyway. My freedom would be gone soon. My returning memory had shown me that I was guilty of something. I was at the very least an accomplice to murder, and at the very worst I was the murderer. In either case, I figured that legally I was no longer an innocent man, and I had some very urgent questions about my future. "Nancy, you don't understand."

"What don't I understand?" Care and concern filled her eyes.

"I'm guilty."

"What do you mean? Did you kill those women?" She rose from her seat and quickly put a bit of distance between us. She kept moving around behind her desk. I wondered if she kept a gun in one of the drawers. If she shot me dead, I would no longer have to deal with all my problems. I shuddered and brought myself back to reality.

"I don't know."

"How do you know you're guilty then?"

"Some of my blackouts are lifting. I know I was there in the room with Carmen's dead body. The only other person in the room was Bender, and if Bender is a product of my mind." I couldn't pursue that train of thought any further and asked instead, "Could I do something like that and not know it?"

Nancy tried valiantly, but she couldn't keep the look of horror from taking over her face. To her credit, she quickly recovered and once again became the concerned sister-in-law. But the look on her face for those few moments would be etched into my mind forever. "We'll do whatever it takes to get you the help you need."

"You didn't answer my question. Could I do something like kill another human being and not realize that I had?"

"The mind is an incredibly complex organ. Mysteries

remain no matter how long we study the human brain."

"What do you really mean?"

"If I had to answer truthfully?"

"Yes."

"Then the answer is yes. There have been documented cases of multiple personalities. People that have lived split lives, but that is very rare."

"But possible?"

"It can't be proven with certainty."

"But possible in your opinion."

"I can't rule it out."

The idea of a second personality hanging out in my brain without my consent or knowledge made my head hurt. Pun intended. I didn't know whether I believed such crap, but I had to admit that it would explain a few things where Bender was concerned. I had to hope that was not the case, because if it was true, I was guilty of murder.

Nancy watched me think with one eye on the door. I was sure that she was hoping that I would leave and never come back. She was no longer convinced of my innocence, and quite frankly, neither was I. "You know the law, Nancy. What are they going to do to me?"

"You don't know for sure whether you committed murder or not, do you?"

"No, but humor me, what if I am guilty?"

She shuffled a couple of steps closer to the door and answered, "You might be able to claim diminished capacity or plead innocent by reason of insanity."

"Oh, shit." I began to shake inside. My stomach hurt.

None of this was good news. I did not want to face the consequences of my actions. I didn't even know for sure what my actions were. How in the hell did I get into such a state? Wasn't life supposed to be good, simple. If this life was my future, I didn't know if I could go on. "And then what?"

"There will be interviews and examinations by me and other psychiatrists. If we find that you are legally insane, then you can be placed in an institution rather than in prison."

I raised my right hand and said, "Jail." Then I raised my left hand and said, "Asylum. Some fucking choice."

A sniffling noise came from behind us. We turned simultaneously in the direction of the door, in time to see that Jenny had come into the room, clad in bear-covered, white pajamas with feet. "Is that you, Uncle Mason?" She rubbed the sleep from her eyes as she moved in my direction.

"Jenny." Her mother was on the move. She quickly came out from behind the desk and snatched the girl up in her arms, presenting her back to me, a mother protecting her baby from the bad man.

"Mama." The girl admonished her mother. "I want to give Uncle Mason a kiss."

Nancy stood rooted to the spot. Obviously, the psychiatrist sister-in-law was willing to give me a chance, but the mother would not. She would take no chances with her daughter. I could understand her fear. It was time to leave.

"Hi, Jenny. I have to go." I moved toward mother and child until I was close enough to lean over a plant a kiss on Jenny's forehead. "I love you, Jenny."

"I love you too, Uncle Mason."

A single thought crystallized in my mind: if they locked me up, at least I couldn't hurt myself or anyone else. Tears began to run down my cheeks before I had made it out the front door and into the darkness.

In my teary state, I barely saw the car coming straight at me out of the darkness. I swerved the cab in time to avoid a collision. The driver of the other vehicle gave me a look that could kill. It was Poco. I didn't stop. Thirty seconds later, the cell phone rang on the seat beside me.

"What the fuck are you doing?" Poco asked when I answered.

"I've got something to do."

"Is everyone all right?"

"If you mean Nancy and Jenny, of course they are. I would never hurt them." I wasn't as sure of that as I sounded. I hung up. A sense of urgency had taken over my being. I didn't know how long I could keep it together before the moving walls of my mind snapped shut. I didn't know where to turn. Should I run? Should I drive down to the police station and lock myself away? I could hardly see straight. The only light in my life at this point waited for me at the Coconut Hut. I hoped it was all a dream and that by some miracle, Annie could take away all the pain and fear.

Driving carefully, I crossed over Sunset Boulevard and turned on the street that ended at the water and the Hut. Once I reached the end of the street, I slowed down to a crawl and surveyed the scene. I didn't want to walk into a police trap. A few minutes alone with Annie had become an obsession, and I was not about to give it up. In fact, I was no longer sure I wanted to turn myself in. Going down in a blaze of glory had become an attractive alternative, but no police were lurking in the dark. The blaze of glory would have to wait. I turned into the lot and parked behind the building. I turned off the headlights and tried to catch my breath. I seemed to be running on pure adrenaline. After this night was over, I knew I would sleep for a long time.

* * *

The decision had been made. Annie would not be privy to all my thoughts and deeds. She needed protection, and if I had been smart, I should never have come back to the Coconut Hut to say good-bye. But here I stood, like a lost puppy, in love with a dream that I could never attain. At least, the dark would hide my true self, the one that I had become all too familiar with during the last few hours. I needed her, badly. But I was determined that she wouldn't be hurt any more than necessary. I hugged her tightly and whispered in her ear, "I decided to turn myself in."

"I think turning yourself in is a good thing. You'll be cleared and then we can get on with our lives." Her big eyes shown with love, at least I think it was love. I really had no prior experience with anything that resembled the joy and sadness I could see in those lovely eyes. I cursed the fates that had brought us together under such dire circumstances.

Reminding myself to keep my true thoughts in check, I answered. "I hope you are right, Annie. I'd love to spend the rest of my life with you." That much was definitely true. I could think of no better way to spend the rest of my life. Certainly my first choice would not be jail or a crazy ward in a shitty mental hospital. We embraced harder, hugging for all we were worth. I wanted to close my eyes and never have to face the reality of my situation.

"Who let the cat out of the barn? I mean, what made you decide do take your chances with the police? I mean, what happened? I expected you to come by boat. I was watching the canal for what seemed like days."

I had to laugh one last time at her way with words. Annie was capable of making me laugh even in a bad situation. It was too bad that we hadn't met years ago. Maybe I wouldn't be in this situation. "The police found the boat. I didn't think my chances of running with the cab would be very good. "

"Aw, Mason, it will be all right. It has to be all right. Love fixes everything, doesn't it?" With her right hand, she brushed a few blond hairs from my forehead, like Nancy had done a short while ago.

I could understand Annie's comment about watching the canal for what seemed like days. The few short hours since our sunset cruise on the *Tramp* seemed like forever ago to me. Things were happening so fast, and paradoxically, that seemed to slow down time. What I couldn't understand was the comment about letting the cat out of the barn. I had to laugh again while I returned the gesture and brushed her forehead lightly. "I'm not so sure. The powers that be seemed determined to bring me down."

"What do you mean, the police?"

"Them too, but I mean like the universe, fate, the gods,

call it anything you want."

"You're having a streak of bad luck. It will get better. I promise."

I didn't think luck had anything to do with it, and I sure didn't think that her promise was one she could keep. Nevertheless, I was grateful for her support and hugged her more tightly. We kissed lightly at first, and then we kissed deeply, exploring the depths of our budding relationship, a union that seemed as doomed as Romeo and Juliet.

"I know we haven't known each other long, but I love you, Mason. I've loved you since the first time I set eyes on you at the Hut. I never told anyone, but I hoped for a long time that you and Marci would breakup."

She had gotten her wish. Now there was some irony. That very same wish was what would doom us in the end. "I love you too. Please always remember that."

"I don't like it when you say things like that. We will be together some day."

Out of the corner of my eye, I caught movement by the back door. Someone was moving around in the dark. The figure moved in our direction. I braced for an assault and broke the connection with my lover. Before I could react, the figure emerged from the dark. I breathed a sigh of relief when I recognized DeCarlo. He nodded at me and waved before turning around and leaving us alone once again. I was glad that I still had a few friends.

"Come here." Annie took my hand and drew me close. "I want you to stay with me forever."

"I really wish I could stay forever, but this is hard on both

311

of us. Maybe, I should go." Going to the police station was the very last thing in the world that I wanted to do. My insides churned at the thought of spending a single night in jail, let alone of spending the remainder of my life locked in a hole somewhere. I began to shake. In response, Annie held me tighter. She kissed me deeply on the lips. When we broke, I looked into those deep brown eyes one last time. "Annie, I love." The thought was cut off in mid-sentence. When I looked deep into her eyes, I saw movement. On closer inspection, the same worm-like creatures that I remembered seeing in Marci's eyes filled Annie's eyes. They moved to and fro in a pile of wiggly gelatin.

"Oh my, God," I yelled, shoving her away from me.

"Mason, what's wrong?"

I backed away and could no longer see into the depths of her eyes. All I could see was the hurt and confusion in those beautiful brown eyes.

"You must kill her. Protect yourself."

The voice came from the shadows behind the Hut immediately followed by the appearance of you know who. Bender moved to my side and grabbed my by the right elbow urging me forward. I responded like a zombie with no mind of my own, in a trance-like state where I seemed to have no control over my actions. I reached forward and snatched Annie by both of her hands, drawing her toward me.

"What are you doing, Mason." A look of horror had twisted her face into a caricature of my lover.

My hands reached for her throat, wrapping strong fingers around the soft neck. They squeezed hard trying to choke the life breath from her body. She choked out a few unintelligible words as the fingers drew tighter, bruising the flesh. Her eyes pleaded for me to stop. I remembered the stump and closed my eyes tight. With all my might, I tried to force the presence of Bender from my mind. My will had to take over from his will. I had to make that happen.

"You must protect yourself. Squeeze harder." Bender remained at my right elbow, urging me on.

I wrenched my right arm free of Bender's grasp, but I was unable to release that beautiful throat. Annie and I tumbled to the ground. She made a gurgling sound as we hit the sand. All I saw in those eyes was the love she had shown me in the last few days. I closed my eyes again as the tears streamed down my face. I was more determined than ever to free myself from the power that had taken over both my mind and body. With a sheer power of will, my mind broke, and I released her. Rolling free, she scrambled to her feet and began to scream. I reached for Annie to comfort her, to tell it was all right, to tell her that I still loved her, to tell her that wasn't me that tried to kill her. She kept screaming and ran towards the back door. I began to follow, but before either of us reached the door, it opened. The bright light lit the figure in the doorway.

"What the fuck is going on here?" DeCarlo said.

"It wasn't me. It was him." I pointed towards Bender, but of course he was gone. The ease of his coming and going in my mind terrified me.

"Him who?" DeCarlo caught Annie when she reached the door. He wrapped his hairy arms around her shoulders.

"You're okay, Annie. I'll see to that."

"I didn't. I didn't. I didn't." I repeated, trying to defend myself, trying to convince Annie and DeCarlo, and most importantly myself, that I had nothing to do with what had just happened. But of course that was untrue. I had tried to strangle the only woman since my mother that I could say had really loved me.

"Mason didn't mean it, Lenny." True to her spirit, Annie defended me.

"Bullshit," DeCarlo spat." He would have killed you if I hadn't come out when I heard you scream.

"That's not true," I began, "I had already let her go."

DeCarlo returned a threatening look "You've gone too far this time, Mason."

To make matters worse, as if that were possible, Arthur came through the door and watched the drama unfold.

"He was strangling her, Arthur."

"I didn't. It wasn't me."

"Bullshit," DeCarlo said again.

A noise at the door caught his attention. I couldn't make out who stood in the door in the dark. "Should I call the police?" The hidden figure asked.

"Yes, right now." DeCarlo said. He pushed Annie towards the door. "You get inside."

"But Lenny, Mason and I are . . . " Annie gave me one of the most sorrowful expressions I'd ever seen from a human being. My heart broke in pieces at the sight. How could I have let things get so out of hand. The artist at The Gardens had sketched the true me. I had an evil inside of me that was barely beneath the surface. DeCarlo did not let her finish the sentence, ushering her through the door instead.

I finished the sentence for her, " . . . doomed."

DeCarlo began to move in my direction, but Arthur stopped him.

"No, Lenny," Arthur said. DeCarlo didn't argue and stopped his advance. The three of us stood mute while the seconds passed like an eternity. I watched as the tears streamed from Arthur's eyes for the second time tonight, but this time the reason for the tears was entirely different. The look in his eyes told me that my best friend no longer believed in me. I would never be able to forget that look. It devastated me. I had hit rock bottom. There was nothing left but to turn and run, so I ran to the cab and started it. With one last look at the place where I'd had so much fun, met so many people, met the love of my life, I drove away. I was damned and could never return again to that life in paradise, no matter what transpired in the future

I sped from the lot and turned towards Sunset Boulevard. The police would react quickly to the call from the Coconut Hut, but if I was fast enough I could buy myself some time to think. I had no idea where to go or what to do when I got there. I made the right onto the boulevard and floored it. The cab sped towards Isla Del Luna and parts south. As I passed First Street, my mind drifted to the past.

The room felt like a meat locker, the coldness seeped into my very soul. I opened my eyes and looked deep into Carmen's beautiful brown eyes. The worm-like things kept crawling, piling

on top of one another until they blended into a single creepy mass. My hands tightened around her throat. She made no noise, silently cursing me with those beautiful eyes until she died.

I leaped from the bed and bumped into someone standing beside it.

"Nice job," Bender said.

I looked at the corpse on the bed, not believing that I had done something so horrible.

Carmen's bedroom disappeared and was replaced by the cabin of the Tramp. "No, Mason. Don't. What's the matter with you?" Marci cried. She stopped talking when my thumbs choked off her air. She died quickly; her strength had disappeared long ago with the drug use.

The cab slammed into a silver Mercedes parked on the right side of Island Drive. I could both hear and feel the crunch of metal on metal as I scraped along the side of the other car. I turned the wheel hard left and broke free, but at my rate of speed the cab couldn't hold the turn and careened to the left side of the street and slammed into a Ford pickup. The cab's left front fender crushed the passenger side door and bounced off. My speed had slowed and I was able to regain control of the vehicle and set it straight. I hit the gas again not wanting to admit what I'd remembered. The world would be better off if I rammed the cab into a pole and killed myself, but with my luck I wouldn't die. I'd rot in prison forever thinking about how I killed Carmen and Marci. I didn't understand. I loved them both. Sick to my stomach with guilt and heart-broken over my actions, I turned the cab south on Interstate 275. The twin yellow pyramids of the Sunshine Skyway Bridge loomed large in the distance.

CHAPTER 25

The tanker faded to black as it navigated through the channel and beyond the Egmont Key light into the open Gulf of Mexico. I was jealous of the men aboard the ship, headed for exotic ports of call. I wanted to be with them, but if anything, the last few hours had proved to me that there was no escape. I could try and run all I wanted to but I could not outrun myself.

"Let's review, Mason." My daddy's voice popped into my head.

"I already did that, Daddy. And it didn't do any good this time."

Sitting on the western rail of the Sunshine Skyway Bridge afforded me one of the most dramatic views in nature. I wasn't sure exactly how high the main span rose above Tampa Bay at this point, but ten, fifteen story tall tankers past underneath without a problem. I heard stories about when the old bridge fell into the bay after one of those great big tankers hit a supporting column. The story goes that a guy in a pickup truck fell straight down and onto the deck of one of those ships.

And lived.

Maybe, I should have jumped onto the deck of that passing ship and took my chances. But even if I survived the jump, there was still no escape. I was absolutely certain that Bender would still be with me, still controlling my fate, still urging me on. I was shocked to learn that I had actually killed both Carmen and Marci. What had snapped inside of me that had enabled me to commit such nefarious acts? I still didn't understand fully, but I did know one thing: I could not live that way. I had to accept my fate. Unlike Angel who at worst was a bit, okay so maybe a lot, eccentric, I had killed two people. Hurting myself was one thing, but hurting others was a whole different matter. One way or the other, women like Annie had to be protected from me.

The proof is in the beef stew," Annie said.

I laughed as she shook her head at her own misstatement. She was a treasure. The Tramp bobbed slowly in its berth, the gentle wind keeping us dry and cool. I had recovered from my roller coaster experience and never felt so close to anyone in my life, not even my mother.

"You'll see. One day we'll have a couple of kids, and we'll need rocking chairs installed on the back of this boat."

I laughed at the thought and said, "I don't know about the rocking chair part."

Annie laughed easily. She rose from her seat a crossed over to where I sat. Taking me by the hand, she said, "Come on, lover.

Let's go below."

Flashing lights stole me away from the wonderful memory. The pattern of lights had changed down in St. Pete. It was quite interesting to watch as the number of flashing blue and red lights grew and spread east from the beach. They would be at the northern end of the bridge soon. No matter. It would all end soon.

"Hey."

I turned left and faced the voice. Like me, Bender sat perched on the rail. He was smart enough to keep enough distance between us so I couldn't knock him off and send him on the long flight down to the bay water.

"Oh, it's you. I was expecting you."

"You'll never be free of me."

"I know that now."

"It could be worse."

"I don't think that's possible." I ignored him. I wanted to remember the good times, the times before him, the times when I was truly Mason Prophet Long, and not some imposter who murdered women in their beds.

The river slowed into a left turn before straightening towards Canon City. The prison loomed on our left as we rounded the bend. I grabbed the fishing stringer tied around my inner tube and retrieved the six-pack from the cold water. Removing a can from the plastic, I tossed it to Arthur, floating next to me in another inner tube. Summer on the Arkansas River was always great.

Arthur snatched the beer from the air and said, "Thanks, man."

"No problem." I grabbed a beer for myself before dropping the others back into the river to keep cool. I opened the beer and raised it in Arthur's direction. "Here's to you, good buddy."

"Cheers," Arthur replied. "

"It doesn't get any better than this."

The flashing lights had made their way to the bridge. They seemed to fill the entire lower half of the upward slope below us. The cars sped up the bridge, two abreast. No cars followed the posse. They must have blocked access to the bridge back in St. Pete in anticipation of some grand standoff. I was sure that I'd disappoint many of them.

"They'll be here soon," said Bender.

My tormentor seemed content to hang out and not harass me, which was fine because I wasn't in the mood to try and will him away. I was too tired. "No shit," I said.

Within a minute, the first pair of cars screeched to a halt about thirty feet from my cab. Detective Kendyll Hall exited the passenger side of the first cruiser with her gun in her hand. I hoped that she would shoot, but I knew she wouldn't. We had to finish the last act.

"Well, well, well, look who's here." I said to Bender.

"Did you expect someone else?"

I didn't answer him, but it occurred to me that somewhere I had moved to a state of acceptance of Bender and my situation. Hall turned to her colleagues and commanded by hand to let her take the lead. They held back as she approached. When she was close enough to speak without being overheard she said, "Go ahead and jump."

"You'd like that wouldn't you?" I asked.

"For the record? No. In truth, yes."

"You're not much of a negotiator."

Bender started to laugh very loud on my left. I guessed I cracked him up. I smiled. I thought I was pretty funny too.

"I'll do my job, but I don't like you."

"You really are an asshole, Hall."

"You'll never change, Mason."

Considering the current situation, I didn't think I had to be nice to her anymore. I really did think she was evil. She hadn't caused any of this, but she sure had made it harder on me. I was ready to unload on her, when the thought occurred to me that I really didn't want those kind of actions to be my legacy. I didn't want to be remembered as a bad man.

"Seriously, Kendyll. I never meant to hurt you. I was never very good at letting anyone know how I felt. Instead of talking and facing things like a man, I ran."

"Oh, brother."

"I'm serious."

"Well, even if you are serious. That doesn't change the situation we find ourselves in, now does it?"

"She has a point," Bender said.

I turned to the tormentor and said, "Mind your own business."

Hall turned to see who I was speaking to. Seeing no one, she turned back to me. "You really have gone over the edge haven't you?"

I saw no reason to lie, "Yes."

"You killed those women, didn't you?"

"Yes."

"Whoa, man. Now you've gone and done it." Bender rolled his eyes and said, "They'll throw us in jail for sure."

"Shut up."

Hall started to object, opening her mouth to speak.

"Not you, Hall." I pointed to where Bender sat. "Him."

"We can get you help, Mason."

Bender shook his finger at me and laughed. I felt a chasm in my mind open wide. All the anger bottled up inside of me poured out in a torrent. I cringed, trying to make the storm subside. When it finally did, I felt at peace. Not that I was at peace with what I'd done, but that I was willing to accept the consequences of my actions.

"No offense, Kendyll. I don't want your help."

"Okay, but the important thing is that we make it safe for you and protect the women around you."

"You are right. For the first time since that night long ago, we actually agree on something."

The young blond boy raced across the road, determined to reach the lake before his father. He liked to race with his daddy. It made him feel older and stronger, but it frightened the daddy.

"Mason, wait for us."

He grabbed the mommy by the hand. Together they chased the boy across the road, catching up with him near the shore. Daddy grabbed him under the arms and lifted him high above his head. The boy squealed with delight as daddy spun him around several times before setting him back down on his feet.

"I'm hungry."

"We'll eat in a minute," Mommy said. "Help me spread the blanket."

The boy was glad to oblige. He liked to help. He loved his parents and their life together. He always wanted it to be that way. They spread the blanket and kicked off their shoes, they placed a shoe at each corner to hold it down in the wind.

Mommy tousled the boy's blond hair. "Here," she handed him the picnic basket. "Take everything out and set the blanket."

"You mean set the table." He laughed at his mother's joke.

"Mason," Daddy called. "Come here."

The boy dropped everything, much to the chagrin of his mother and raced to his father's side on the bank of the lake.

"Look." Daddy held up the turtle. "It's a snapping turtle."

"Snapping?" The boy watched the turtle sideways, from a safe distance.

"It's okay, but don't put your fingers near his mouth."

Daddy always kept him safe.

I had traveled well past ever being safe again. The word no longer had meaning for me, but I could damn well make sure that Annie stayed safe. She had to know that she was in my thoughts at the very end. She had to know that I loved her, and that I didn't mean to hurt her.

"I know you don't owe me anything, Hall."

"You have that right."

"But I need a favor. For old time's sake."

"I won't promise anything, but go ahead and ask. This is a

negotiation."

"Please tell Annie at the Coconut Hut that I really loved her and give her this note." I had written a short good-bye before I left the cab. I crumpled the paper and tossed it to Hall.

"You're such a sucker." Bender could not keep his mouth shut for long. I would never be able to live with him.

"I don't like the sounds of that. Do it yourself later." She picked up the paper and took a step forward, trying to give it back to me.

"Don't."

"We can get you some help."

"Please, Hall. Just do this one thing for me."

"Okay, but don't do anything stupid."

"That's an impossible task for him." Bender said and laughed.

"You're not lying to me, Hall?"

"No, Mason. I'll take care of it for you. I promise."

Her acceptance of my request was the only thing left in my life that mattered. I thought back to the tears streaming from Annie's eyes, from Arthur's eyes. I thought back to the looks from DeCarlo that made me feel like scum. I thought back to Nancy keeping dear little Jenny girl from her evil uncle. I thought back to my brother Poco and his acceptance that his little brother might hurt his family. I would prove to them that I was not pure evil. I was only a man caught in a nightmare he didn't understand.

Detective Hall's mouth kept moving. I knew she was speaking, but I couldn't hear a word. The world seemed to have suddenly gone silent. No wind, no traffic sounds from the opposite lanes, only silence. I could still see the light on Egmont Key warning sailors of the dangers.

"You might as well give it up," Bender said. "There is no escape."

I wanted to choke the smirk from his face, but I didn't want his image to be the last thing I saw on this earth. I turned back to the light and watched it flash, once, twice. In the light, I saw the smile of Annie during the good times. At least this way I could be sure that she would have many more good times. I hoped that she would think kindly of me one day.

I let go of the rail. The bay rushed up to welcome me.

ABOUT THE AUTHOR

Chet Stevens is an author, teacher, web developer, and biker. He lives on the Fox River in Aurora, IL, but spent many years on the west coast of Florida. Family and humor are the staples of life, and spending time with the wife, daughters, grand children and three dogs serves both purposes quite well. Website: chetstevens.com

Made in the USA
Lexington, KY
12 May 2017